Pra...
A Love Through Time

"A very special book, and a time travel with a twist. Fans of Scottish adventures will revel in *A Love Through Time*."

—Christina Skye, author of *Christmas Knight*

"Ms. Brisbin . . . shows her talent for writing a beautiful and poignant story of splendid dimensions."

—*Bell, Book & Candle*

"Ms. Brisbin's debut novel is a tantalizing blend of history, fantasy, and romance. This emotionally beautiful time travel will capture your attention and your heart as the story of two destined lovers—a courageous heroine, and a sexy, protective hero—unfolds and they experience *A Love Through Time*."

—*BookBug*

"*A Love Through Time* is a light and enjoyable night's read that will sweep readers away to the moors and glens of Scotland."

—*Romantic Times*

"There is only one word for *A Love Through Time*: Delicious! This book is a decadent treat from beginning to end. You'll want to savor every word, but just like chocolate, you'll soon find you've gobbled the whole sweet. This book is a must-have! Full of surprises. Terri Brisbin is a rising star. Can't wait to see what she comes up with next."

—*Writer's Club*

continued on next page . . .

A Matter
OF *Time*

Terri Brisbin

JOVE BOOKS, NEW YORK

TIME PASSAGES is a registered trademark of Penguin Putnam Inc.

A MATTER OF TIME

A Jove Book / published by arrangement with
the author

PRINTING HISTORY
Jove edition / November 1999

The Penguin Putnam Inc. World Wide Web site address is
http://www.penguinputnam.com

ISBN: 0-515-12683-7

A JOVE BOOK®
Jove Books are published by The Berkley Publishing Group,
a division of Penguin Putnam Inc.,
375 Hudson Street, New York, New York 10014.
JOVE and the "J" design
are trademarks belonging to Penguin Putnam Inc.

PRINTED IN THE UNITED STATES OF AMERICA

10 9 8 7 6 5 4 3 2 1

*My thanks to George Seto of Nova Scotia, Canada,
for his help with the Gaelic translations in both this book
and in* A Love Through Time. *George answered a
plea from me on the Gaelic language listserv
and I appreciate his time and efforts.*

*Thanks also to Kay Swanson and Jody Allen for
their help in researching parts of this book.*

*And, once more, a special thank-you to my unofficial
critique group, Paul and Rochelle Adler,
Helen Levin, and Colleen Admirand.*

Prologue

An rud a bhitheas an dàn, bitheadh e do-sheachanta.
One cannot bypass one's fate. 'Tis as 'twas meant to be.

THE HEAT! DEAR God, the heat!

He tried to move away but it surrounded him, entrapped him. He forced his eyes open and still his body would not obey his commands.

Flames! Taller and wider than he. Waves of heat washed over him, stealing his breath, overpowering and terrorizing him. His mouth and throat were parched, but sweat gathered and ran down his face, his chest. He knew he couldn't survive much longer—he felt his strength draining away. He could fight no longer.

Then she was there. Her presence called to him, urged him on in his struggle. He stared at her, amazed that someone could brave the fire's heat. In an instant, she stood before him—her head barely reached his chin. With her head bowed, he could not see her features, only the porcelain translucence of her skin and the flowing black hair.

Look at me, *he thought, unable to speak the words.*

Her head lifted, revealing to him long lashes matching the black strands of hair and a full, red mouth.

Open your eyes, *he pleaded soundlessly.* Look at me.

Her glowing green eyes startled him. She raised her

hands and reached out to touch his face. Their gazes locked as he waited for her touch. A blessed coolness spread through him from her hands, through his head, chest, stomach, limbs. He saw the flames and knew their heat had not lessened. But he felt only her hands. He allowed her comfort to strengthen him, to remove his pain, to bring forgetfulness.

Then the glow left her eyes and she stepped away. His stomach clenched in fear of the heat and the pain he faced without her intervention. He tried to reach for her but his body would still not respond. He saw regret in her eyes as she backed away and moved through the flames.

She was gone.

No! his mind screamed.

Stay. . . .

Please . . . help me. . . .

"Help me!"

The loudness of his own cry woke him from the troubled sleep. Douglas lurched up in his bed, entangled in the damp sheets, covered in sweat. Panting, still in the clutches of the fear and pain of the dream, he pushed his hair out of his eyes and pushed the sheets down and off his legs.

He balanced unevenly on those still-shaky legs, dragged his fingers through his sweaty hair and swallowed long and deep trying to clear his clogged throat. Then he made his way to the bathroom, not bothering to turn on a light. He knew from experience that the terror would pass quickly and he would be left with . . .

He would be left with a vision of a woman who either saved him or tempted him every night in his sleep. He'd never met her, didn't know her, other than in his dreams.

But, his soul told him that she would alter his life when they met . . . and they would meet. In turning away from other women, real women in his life, he knew it was just a matter of time before he found the lady with green eyes.

Just a matter of time. . . .

Chapter 1

"So, HAVE YE come to seek out yer destiny?"

Douglas MacKendimen turned around slowly at the familiar voice. Mairi, fortune-teller extraordinaire, stood before him awaiting his response.

"No, Mairi, I know my destiny." Douglas laughed as the old woman's face tightened with stubbornness. They'd played this game before.

" 'Tis coming yer way soon, boy, and ye willna be able to stop it." Mairi wagged a bony finger close to his nose. She clutched her woolen shawl around her stooped body and whispered something he couldn't quite make out.

"What did you say?" Douglas moved closer and bent down nearer to her. "I couldn't make out your last words."

"I said that ye be as stubborn as yer father and mother. Ye tempt the Fates wi' yer cockiness just as they did, so long ago."

"Mairi, please don't start with those tales you told me as a child. They are just stories you made up to keep me interested in coming back here."

Douglas stuck his hands into the pockets of his warm leather jacket. What ever made him come out to the ruins in this weather, at this time of night? He hadn't even stopped at the manor house other than to drop off his bags. The pull was always at its strongest when he arrived. For reasons he'd never been able to discern or understand, his first stop on every trip back here to Dunnedin was this ancient stone arch. And, as always, Mairi knew he was here. His breath curled around him in the cool air.

"Is that what ye believe? Only stories for restless bairns? Och, there will be a reckoning for ye, lad, and it comes to ye soon." Mairi paced now, in front of him, in front of the old stone arch.

Doug ran his fingers through his overlong hair. This trip to Scotland for the family reunion had been a last-minute thing for him. He was tired, jet lagged and exhausted from double shifts at the hospital . . . and from sleepless nights caused by the strength of the dreams. Maybe now that he was here he would get some rest.

So, he thought as he readjusted the collar of his jacket, he really needed to sleep and not be standing here arguing with this distant relative . . . especially one who should be in her own warm cottage and not exposed to the harsh weather surrounding them.

"Mairi," he started, placing his hands on her frail shoulders and drew her into an embrace. "I will visit you tomorrow and you can tell me those stories again . . . when I'm awake enough to pay attention." Douglas stepped back and smiled. "Can I walk you back home?"

"I amna ready to go back." Mairi's voice trembled as she answered. Was she cold or frightened? he wondered. He knew she was stubborn—if she said she wasn't ready, she wouldn't go home yet. "But ye should come to me in the morn, afore the noon meal. I have something to tell ye, lad."

Douglas kissed the waxen cheek she offered and nodded at her in farewell. He'd taken a few steps when he turned

back to ask if there were any messages for his parents—
something Mairi always gave him to carry to the "new"
castle.

The arch stood alone, moonlight reflecting off the sharper
edges and cascading over its curve to the barren rocky
ground around it. Smaller boulders lay on the ground some
distance away but the arch dominated the landscape.

And there was no sign of Mairi.

Douglas blinked a few times and squinted into the moon-
lit night, looking for some sign of the old woman. But there
was none. She'd disappeared into the mist-filled night without a trace . . . again.

One day, maybe even during their chat tomorrow, he
would gather up his nerve to ask how she did that. For
now, the heat and comfort of the clan's manor house called
undeniably to him.

"Dr. MacKendimen, it's good to see you, sir." The butler
closed the thick oak door behind Douglas and reached out
to take Doug's jacket as he removed it. "I'm afraid the
family has retired for the night."

"That's fine, Mr. Parker, I'll see them in the morning.
Do you have me in my regular room, then?" Parker was
the epitome of an efficient butler, managing the entire
MacKendimen household and making it look easy. In all
his years of visiting the ancestral home of the Mac-
Kendimens nothing . . . no one . . . ever frazzled Parker.

"Just Parker, sir. And yes, the corner room in the back
on the second floor," Parker nodded in the direction of that
room as he hung Douglas's jacket in the hall closet. "Breakfast will be informal and begin at seven, sir."

"Good night then, Mr. Parker."

"And a good night to you, too, Dr. MacKendimen."
Douglas noticed the small wink as the older man turned
and left the hallway.

With each step on the creaking wooden stairs leading up
to the second floor, the weight of his exhaustion grew. By

the time he reached the assigned room, Douglas knew he would be asleep before his head hit the pillow.

"No, please, help me. . . ."

He forced the words out of his constricting throat, the pain of the scream waking him.

Gasping for air, Douglas sat up and threw off the covers. The coolness of the room made his sweat even more uncomfortable. The quiet knock at the door gave him something to focus on until the terror seeped away.

"Douglas? Are you okay?" His mother's whisper seemed to echo across the stillness of the room as he tried to calm his ragged breathing.

"Yes, Mom, I'm fine." Knowing she would not leave until she assured herself by seeing his condition, Douglas grabbed his robe from the foot of the bed and threw it on. Moving quickly to the door, he turned the knob and eased it open a crack.

"I heard you as I went by," she said, pushing the door open and entering the room. "Do the dreams still come?"

By the time Douglas turned to face her, his mother Maggie MacKendimen had taken a seat on his bed. "I'm just overtired, Mom. I'll see you in the morning." He opened the door and gestured for her to leave.

"You may as well close the door, Doug. I'm not leaving." She sat staring at him from across the room and he knew he'd lost the battle. She was already in mother mode and wouldn't leave until . . . well, until she was satisfied with his answers. He really didn't need this.

"Tell me about them. Are they as frequent as last year?"

"They come and go, Mom, as you should know." He looked pointedly at the door but it did no good. He didn't want to talk about the dreams, or how frequent and strong they'd really become. "Now, I'd like to go to bed, if you don't mind?"

"If you'd answer my questions, rather than try to evade them, we could both go back to bed." Her cut-to-the-chase attitude shouldn't surprise him; his mother always preferred the short, concise version to the long, flowery one.

He dragged his hand over his face and through his hair. Could he tell her? What would her reaction be to the power and clarity of the dreams? Maybe his workload at the hospital was the cause—too many all-nighters and too many weekends could do this to a person. Right?

She must have sensed his reluctance to reveal details, for she rose and approached him where he stood at the door. Stepping closer and rising up, she took his head in her hands, pulled his face to hers and kissed his forehead. If only that were all it took to banish the dreams and the sense of disorientation they brought with them and left behind.

"I try to remember that you're an adult and a 'doctor,' but the sounds I heard from the hall scared me, Doug. I'll wait until you're ready to tell me. Good night."

He turned the knob and pulled the heavy wooden door open. Without another glance, his mother walked out. Her acquiescence didn't fool him—she would have the truth from him and on her own schedule.

Chapter 2

"'WARE THE WOODS at night, Caitlin."

"I think 'tis you I should fear at night, Craig Mac-Kendimen, and no' the woods." Caitlin MacInnis shrugged off her cousin's heavy hands and stepped away. The moon shown full and bright on this brisk, autumn eve. She was losing precious time standing here fending off Craig's tentative advances. She had but one more night to collect the lifesaving herbs from their sheltered growing place.

"I could come with ye, protect ye from harm." Craig's bright blue eyes gleamed in the shaft of moonlight that covered him. "What do ye say, Caitlin?"

"I have an important task to complete for my mam and you and your big feet will trample the very plants I need. Nay, Craig, I dinna need your help this night."

Confusion showed clear on his face. The heir to the laird and clan was not used to being thwarted, not in battle and not in his dealings with women. Caitlin looked over his features yet again and wondered why they did not inspire

her to the same devotion . . . the same silliness that affected
the other women in the clan MacKendimen. He stood tall
next to her, she could stand a step above him when they
were on the stairs leading to the great room in the keep and
still not meet his gaze eye-to-eye. His face was ruggedly
handsome, angled with a strong chin and brow. He wore
his lion-mane hair loose and flowing, the very picture of
clan manhood at its best. But none of this made her feel
the "tingling" that others claimed when his gaze fell their
way.

She sighed and pushed her hair back over her shoulders.
They were cousins, mayhap that explained her lack of attraction to his charm? But nay, she was cousin to most in
the village and he, too, and that didn't stop the others from
looking at him with cow eyes.

Mayhap 'twas the stranger she dreamed of. . . .

Craig jumped back when the door of her cottage opened
and her father stepped out in the moonlight. Caitlin laughed
out loud when Craig showed the same reaction that all the
boys and young men in the clan had to her da. Even years
of working the fire and iron for the clan had not lessened
his height or bearing. Pol, the blacksmith, still managed to
intimidate anyone who thought themselves her suitor. And
his timing was impeccable, as ever.

"I thought ye were doing yer ma's errands, Caitlin. 'Tis
not like ye to dawdle when she awaits yer return."

"I am on my way there now, Da. Craig was just now
leaving." She nodded at him and he looked at her father.
There had to be a way to discourage his attentions without
humiliating him . . . again.

"Craig, tell Robert that I will speak to him on the morrow
about our stores and weapons." Pol stood his ground and
Caitlin watched Craig's confusion clear. He knew he had
no choice but to leave without her now.

"Aye, Pol, I will take yer message to him now. Caitlin,
have a care in the woods." He turned and stalked away

without looking back. She watched him disappear into the shadowed path of the village.

"He fancies himself in love with ye, lass." Her father spoke little but saw much.

"Aye, Da, he does . . . this week. But his affections will move next week onto someone more accepting." They'd been through this every year for the last three, ever since Craig's betrothed had died of fever. Persistence was a trait he'd perfected.

"Robert asked me if there was a chance for the two of ye. Is there?" 'Twas difficult to read more into his question because he had that frustrating ability to keep his tone low and constant even when upset. Her da had been around her mam too long.

"The laird asked? I would think he and Anice would want Craig to look elsewhere for a new wife."

"Ye didna answer my question, lass. Is there a chance for ye and Craig?"

Caitlin tried to think of a way out of this. Her parents had looked on with a disinterested air while Craig made his intentions quite clear to everyone in the clan. Obviously, she had missed their true feelings about this possible match.

"Would it make ye happy if I accepted Craig's offer of marriage, Da?"

"Have I told ye aboot yer uncanny ability to steer the conversation away from things ye dinna want to discuss?" Her father laughed.

"What has Mam to say aboot this? What has she seen?" Caitlin's mother was renowned for her *an-da-shealladh*, her gift of second sight.

Pol laughed again, louder this time. Caitlin did avoid things she didn't want to talk about.

"Weel, I really should go now, Da. I don't want to waste the light of the moon." She wrapped her cloak tighter around her shoulders and bent over to pick up the basket she'd prepared.

"Yer mam hasna told me of any visions, lass. Ye are the

only one she shares her wisdom with when it comes to her. But, yer hesitation tells me more than any sight could tell me. I will share this news wi' Robert on the morrow."

Caitlin sighed deeply with relief. Robert could direct Craig's interest elsewhere. She was safe . . . for now.

"Caitlin, have a care in the woods." She caught her father's wink before he turned and went back inside.

"I will, Da. I dinna fear the woods at night."

Mayhap she did fear the woods this night? Caitlin followed the small stream to its split and looked for the pathway off over the hill. She didn't see it.

She stopped and looked back at her approach to this place and it did not look familiar at all to her. She knew that the moonlight made all appear as shafts of shadow and light but she should recognize something . . . *something*.

Her breath escaped in puffy clouds of steam in the autumn night's chilly air. Caitlin tucked the loose strands of hair behind her ears and adjusted the heavy woolen cape another time. The moon's progress through the night sky was more than it should be—she'd been walking only a short time . . . hadn't she?

An owl's sudden shriek made her turn too quickly and she caught her foot on a gnarled root of a huge tree. Her cry of pain and alarm as she fell echoed down the paths and through the valleys.

Caitlin untangled her hands from the cloak and the basket and straightened her legs in front of her. Pulling her skirt down over her knees, she felt gingerly down her left shin and pressed on her ankle. The immediate pain and wave of nausea told her what she wanted to know—her ankle was most definitely injured, mayhap sprained and mayhap broken.

She groaned loudly in frustration and anger. This night was not turning out to be the familiar search for herbs she'd hoped for. First Craig and his attempts to woo her and now this. After a few moments of self-pity, Caitlin's bottom let her know that she could not remain on the damp, cold ground for much longer. The dampness seeped through the layers of skirt and chemise underneath it.

Struggling to turn over and get to her knees, Caitlin noticed the quiet of the forest. She'd disturbed the peace of the night here with her squawking and groaning. Pushing herself up onto her uninjured foot, she gently tested the other on the ground.

Damn! She could put no more than a bit of her weight on it. How was she to walk back to her home? She leaned back against the tree whose traitorous root had done this and looked around. Mayhap Craig would disregard her pleas not to follow? Nay, he would face her father's displeasure if he did and no man in the village did that without strong reasons—stronger than a stolen kiss.

Caitlin crouched down and searched the foliage at the tree's base for something she could use to support her foot. No long branches or sticks were there.

There was one thing she could try before giving in to her fear and anger. It had never worked on her before but mayhap this time it would? Sliding down to sit, Caitlin took a deep breath in and blew it out forcefully. She repeated this again and twice more before she began to feel her control grow. When her breathing was deep and regular, she slid her hands down and laid them on the now-swollen ankle. Concentrating on her breathing, she waited for the heat to build in her hands.

It did not come.

Her healing gift was for others and not for herself, and never to be called upon lightly. She choked back a cry and pushed back to her feet. She would have to rely on her "normal" abilities to get herself home, or wait for morning and rescue by one of her clan.

Hours later, well, it seemed to her that hours had to have passed, she'd managed only to make it back to the stream. Her basket remained where she'd fallen and she'd dropped her cloak along the way, too. Sweat beaded and slid down her chest and back and legs even in the coolness of the night, making her shift and skirt stick to her wherever they touched. Her efforts were quickly sapping her strength.

'Twas then that she heard him.

A man's raucous laughter shattered the stillness of the night. Then another voice joined in and another. Their voices carried on the air, making their location difficult to determine. She almost called out to them . . .

Then she heard a name . . . MacArthur. A chill tore through her body and mind. Good God, her clan's enemies were on their land? Reports had come in over the last weeks about raids made by the MacArthurs and all included tales of beatings and worse for any MacKendimen caught in their grasp.

Without thought, she took one step, and then another. And ended up facedown in the dirt. A cry escaped her and floated through the glen. Oh, God, too late, too late. She had to hide, she had to hide.

Struggling anew, she got to her feet and cocked her head to one side, searching the woods for more sounds. None came. This was not good, not good at all. Tears made her vision watery and unclear. She rubbed briskly at her eyes with the back of her hand. She had to move off the path, and get out of sight before they found her.

. Realizing that her best way might be to crawl, Caitlin dropped to her knees and dragged her bad foot along. She'd gone no more than a few yards when the voice came to her through the darkness at the side of the trail.

"Look, Angus, the wee lass must have heard aboot ye, she's trying to get away."

Sheer terror forced her to move faster . . . and her haste caused her to misjudge the men's location. Rolling off the beaten track into the brush, she landed on a man's booted foot. She looked up. The twisted grins of three men greeted her.

And each of them armed to the teeth with swords and daggers and ready to use them.

The one across the way called Angus stepped toward her and drew a dangerous, long dagger that reflected the moonlight into her eyes. As he took long strides toward her, she struggled to get up. The man closest to her trapped her by stepping on her long, loosened hair. She could not move.

The one called Angus lowered the knife as he approached, the blade appeared to grow larger and larger as he got closer. When the point of it reached her neck and lowered to the valley between her breasts, she could hardly breathe.

The sharp edge sliced through the ties of her bodice. The cut laces were the last thing she saw as she lost consciousness.

Chapter 3

"FOR A WOMAN who claims to be of such an advanced age, you do get around." Douglas approached the archway straight on. He'd been chasing her all day, from manor house to cottage to every sort of place the village had to offer. He thought he'd caught up with her at suppertime only to have her slip away.

"A lack of respect will get ye nowhere, lad. I had important things to accomplish today."

She stood at the side of the stone structure and gazed skyward. He looked in the same direction and saw the full moon overhead, lighting the landscape to almost the brightness of day. Suddenly a shooting star blazed a path across the edge of the moon and exploded in the sky, showering splinters of light and color above them.

Douglas could not move—his lungs refused to take in air and his heart thundered in his chest. Suddenly the woman in his dreams came into his thoughts. Like the dream returning, the heat rose in him until sweat poured down his limbs. He finally managed to force out a word, a plea.

"Mairi?"

" 'Tis a sign, lad, a powerful sign." He watched, unable to move as she neared him. "Ye must not fear, lad. 'Tis as 'twas meant to be."

She placed her hand on his arm and feeling began to return, painful prickles of sensation reminding him how complete and mystifying the numbness had been.

"What was meant to be?" Douglas was free of the paralysis but felt drained, exhausted by the brief experience. "What do you mean?"

She took her time in answering him. She gathered her cloak tighter around her shoulders and then she finally gifted him with her reply.

"Ye were conceived in the past, Douglas, and born in the present. Ye are time's child and are being called home."

"Mairi, have you lost your mind?" He realized her age must be catching up to her. She'd always seemed so clear-minded but apparently even a physician could miss symptoms of loss of mental acuity.

"Nay, I am certain that what I say will surprise ye in some ways and yet, part of ye must ken how true my words are. Ye are not of this time. Ye were created from yer parents' love on their own journey through the time. The dreams are the call. One awaits ye, needs ye to survive and ye will need her to survive as weel. Ye have ignored the Fates for longer than I thought possible even by one with yer father's stubbornness and yer mother's spirit."

If he didn't know better, he'd swear her eyes glowed as she spoke. Must be the reflection of the moonlight. What was she talking about? Oh, sure, he'd heard his parents' stories and he'd believed not one word of them. Traveling back to the past? Not possible, end of story. No matter what this dear old family soothsayer said.

"Mairi, let me get you to your cottage. This damp autumn air can't be good for your arthritis." He put his arm around her frail shoulders and began to guide her away from the site. A few steps was as far as he got before she stopped and became as immovable as stone.

"My basket, Douglas. I have left it on the rocks near the arch. Can ye get it for me?"

Pleased that she hadn't started on him again, Douglas nodded. As he walked toward the basket, he heard her speak.

"Whether ye believe or no' isna of importance, Douglas. 'Tis the past where ye belong and 'tis the past that seeks ye now."

Leaning over to pick up the basket, he sighed. There'd be no way to get her off this train of thought now. Once she focused on her stories of the past, she was locked onto them like the jaws of a hunter's hound on his quarry. He straightened back up and turned, ready to put up with the nonsense about time travel and his family's past. She was gone.

Gone? How could that be? A woman of her age and problems with arthritis did not rush anywhere. But she was gone. He looked around the open fields and toward the forest. She could not have taken more than a few steps in the time it took him to reach over to get the basket. And yet, the landscape was clear, only he and the archway stood in the moonlight.

That's when he noticed it. At first he couldn't identify it because bees didn't swarm at night. It was a buzzing sound, growing and waning, as if thousands of insects were coming and going around him. He cocked his head, trying to ascertain the sound's direction. Near the arch—was it coming from near the arch?

He took a few steps and listened again. Definitely near the arch. Douglas could see nothing out of the ordinary in the night, but he began to feel heat emanating from the arch. The arch hot? Not very likely after so many cold and damp Highland nights. But it was the source of the heat. He lifted his hand and placed it on one of the boulders in the arch.

Ouch, damn it! His hand throbbed after its sudden exposure to such a powerful surge of heat and power. He was shaking off the stinging burn when the cry came through the darkness.

It was a young woman screaming in terror, begging for help. In Gaelic? Most of the inhabitants spoke English around here. He'd learned it during his childhood visits but only the Old Ones of the clan still clung to the Gaelic.

It came again, a piercing, shrill cry of fear and pain that gripped his heart and made his mouth and throat go dry.

Where was she? He scanned the area around him, the cry was so loud that she had to be close. But, nothing, no one was nearby. He trotted in the direction of the cry when it came a third time. A dreadful certainty told him it would not come again. He must find her—now.

Without realizing it, he picked up speed and headed toward the plea for help. It led him straight into the archway . . . and a black void.

Darkness enwrapped him—the completeness of it stole his breath and the ability to move or speak. He wanted to fight against the bonds it created, but his body refused his mind's commands. Douglas tried to calm his thoughts—he handled emergencies every day of his life; this should not be new to him.

But it was. He tried to recall his last steps before the blackness overtook him. He'd heard that scream and then ran to find her. He was alone now . . . or maybe he wasn't. No sounds or movements or perceptions invaded his cocoon of senselessness. Nothing. . . .

As quickly as it had begun, the darkness was gone. Sharp points poked into his arms and legs, a freezing dampness spread through his clothes, forcing him to move. He scrambled to his feet and searched the area for anything, anyone. His fingers tightened around Mairi's basket. He couldn't believe that he still carried it.

He was in a forest—tall, thick vegetation blocked his path and his view. In the quiet of the night, the movement of water over rocks traveled to his ears. Where was he? There was no spring or river near the arch.

Then, it came once more to him through the darkness. A girl's desperate scream followed by the husky laughter of men. He finally, finally got a fix on where the sound came from and spotted in that direction. Douglas slowed to a walk as the sounds became louder. The flicker of flames in a clearing ahead brought him to a halt. Bile rose in his throat at the sight before him.

A girl no more than a teenager being pawed by three . . . actors? The men were wearing old-style hunting plaids and leather jackets. With filthy beards and hair matted to their heads, these men looked far more fierce and realistic than any of those he'd worked with in medieval reenactments.

And actors or not, they were bent on terrorizing this girl. Being held captive by two men and facing another with a drawn dagger probably would have been enough to scare her into submission, but one was tracing lines with the point of his knife down her throat and onto her chest. Even from his position, he could see thin rivulets of blood from the pricks of the blade, each one getting closer and closer to the edges of the girl's open and dangling blouse. Her long, dark hair hung from partly loosened braids and covered most of her face. He could see her eyes and they were wild with fear. She let out another moan as the biggest of the three approached her again, his knife already stained with her blood and at the ready once more.

Distracting them was the only chance he had to save her. Douglas drew back the basket and prepared to throw it as he ran toward them. The muffled clanging of metal drew his attention. Pulling back the cloth in the basket, he found his own two daggers. Why would Mairi be carrying his weapons? A thought of her true intent began to swirl in his mind but he stopped it instantly. Mairi could not have known he would need them, *she could not*. Well, at least he would not jump into the fray unarmed.

Taking a deep breath, he dropped the basket and grasped the knives in his hands as he'd done many times before in practice and play, and cleared his mind. With a roar that came from the bottom of his being, he crashed through the trees and threw one of the daggers as he ran. The anguished cry told him his aim for the shorter of the men was true. Now if he could be lucky with the other two. He focused on the one with the dagger drawn and plowed into him, both falling to the ground. Taking advantage of the surprise of his attack, Douglas jumped to this feet and struck again.

With a swift kick aimed high in the chest, he pushed the man back to the ground. His opponent lost consciousness when his head hit a rock on the ground, freeing him to face the last one. He turned and repositioned his knife, angling the blade downward for more control and power.

"Lad, I dinna ken ye but ye could hae joined us in our fun wi' the lass. She's got enough for all of us to share."

He'd said the words in Gaelic which threw Douglas for a moment. Gaelic in this day and age? He shook his head and translated the words to himself. Douglas took a step closer, distributing his weight evenly on the balls of both feet for better balance.

The man's hands were blackened shadows against the girl's pale skin and white blouse. He held her in place in front of him by her hair, grabbed and pulled back from her face now to expose the whiteness of her throat. His knife aimed directly at the major artery, he smiled showing a near-toothless grin. If he severed that vessel, the girl would have little or no chance at survival even with his own advanced skills. He stepped back.

"Who are you?" he demanded. At the questioning frown, Douglas repeated his words in Gaelic and added, "Let the girl go and I'll let you leave."

Laughing, the man shifted his captive, tightening his hold until she gasped. Douglas avoided looking directly at the girl. He knew her fear would distract him and give his opponent an advantage.

"Since I hae her, ye'll be the one to leave. I amna giving her up now that ye've taken twa men from me. She's my payment for your actions." He began to back up toward the trees, dragging his hostage with him. Twisting around, his actions placed the girl's face directly in the moonlight and Douglas saw her for the first time.

"You," he bellowed, shocked to his core with recognition. She was the woman in his dreams, now flesh and blood before him. "Who are you?" he screamed out again following the pair's movements into the forest. He wasn't sure who he was asking now, his mind reeling at the sight of his dream savior.

She must have recognized him, too, for her eyes widened and she slumped into a faint. Her weight, though slight, caused her captor to pause and turn, giving Douglas an opportunity for a clear throw.

The dagger left his hand, directed at the back of his adversary. At the moment of impact, Douglas savored a moment of satisfaction.

An excruciating blow on the back of his skull sent him to his knees, clutching at his head as he fell. A nauseating wave of pain pulsed through him and then the darkness pulled him down, again into nothing.

Chapter 4

"How does he fare this morn, daughter?"

Exhausted from another night of caring for the stranger, Caitlin shifted in the chair next to the pallet and touched the man's brow yet again. Shaking her head, she looked at her mother. "He still haes the fever."

Caitlin slid down to the dirt floor and picked up the basin of water. Gathering up all the used rags, she rose and limped to the doorway, favoring the injured foot. "I will freshen the water and begin again."

"Nay, lass, I can see to him now. Now that ye can put yer weight on yer foot, ye need to clean yerself up. And get some rest."

"But, Mam . . ." she began to argue.

" 'Twill be no arguing wi' me, lass. Ye are nigh to fainting wi' exhaustion and havna even washed since we brought ye both here. Go. I put a jar of ointment and some fresh bandages to wrap yer foot in on the table for ye. Wash at the cave and use it."

Caitlin started to tell her mother that she was fine but one look at the older woman's face told her not to bother. "I'll bring the fresh water to ye first."

At her mother's nod, Caitlin ducked through the low opening and fetched cold water from the outside well. After taking one last look at the unconscious man, she gathered a drying sheet, clean clothing, a small container of soap and the healing salve made by her mother.

Following a path around the perimeter of the village crofts, she soon reached the loch. Looking for signs of anyone close by and finding none, she followed a rough trail off to one side of the loch and soon came to the cave. Pushing back the brush that grew wild at the opening, Caitlin stepped inside.

Allowing herself to adjust to the darkness, she stood and listened to the quiet. Gradually, the bubbling, gurgling water sounds came to her in the dim cavern. Since she was a common visitor to the hot spring that flowed through the cave and out into the loch, she could find it with or without light. With a hand on the wall to steady her steps, Caitlin made her way into the steamy room.

Stepping carefully along the wet floor, she put her things down on a dry rock. She unlaced the bodice and skirt and dropped them into the heated pool at her feet. Her chemise followed next. Upon her return, her mother had cleaned up the cuts as best she could. Now, Caitlin untied the end of the braid and shook her head until her hair hung loose and long down her back. 'Twould feel good to remove all traces of the touch of those villains.

Bending down and sliding into the hot water, Caitlin submerged herself for as long as she could. The pool's water came to her waist when she stood so she sat on the bottom, letting the heat and motion of the water bubble over her, removing the first layers of blood and grime.

When she stood, she twisted her hair behind her head and let it hang with its edges in the water. She reclaimed her clothes and with quick efficiency scrubbed some soap in the blood and dirt stains and dunked them to rinse. Repeating the motions with each garment, she twisted them and piled them next to the pool. Then she turned the soap on herself, lathering up and scrubbing every inch of her skin where the filthy men had touched.

Suddenly, the waves of panic poured over her again, the terror filled her mind as it had when she'd first realized what her fate was to be at the hands of these outlaws. Her throat tightened until air would not enter and fill her chest. Tremors moved through her limbs, making standing in the slippery pool difficult. She leaned back against the side wall and let her head fall back on the edge. Gradually the heat soothed her quaking and her terror subsided.

Tears filled her eyes and Caitlin let them fall in the water as she remembered when she'd finally realized the danger she was in. She'd been manhandled before by boys in the clan but their gropings were filled with a misguided need for attention and a desire for her. The other night had been something different, something evil. Not misguided attempts to fondle or caress. A prelude to danger and pain *and death.*

Even as she allowed the words in her mind, she rebelled against them. She wanted to return to the sense of security being under the protection of the Clan MacKendimen offered her. She could go where she wanted or needed, she went about her mother's errands and never thought about danger. Until now. Now she realized that her world had shifted and fear had entered.

And, so had a stranger.

Caitlin sunk down deeper into the heated water. Her breathing was almost back to normal. The scratchy tightness left her throat.

Finally she would admit it to herself, he was not really a stranger. She'd seen him before . . . in her dreams.

The fire dream came often in the last weeks. He stood surrounded by flames as tall and taller than he. She stood outside the circle of fire and could hear his moans for help. Her hands pulsed and throbbed in her dream until she touched the flames around him. Her hands pushed through the fire without injury and soon she stood before him.

Look at me, he would beg without saying the words. *Open your eyes and look at me.* She would raise her head and eyes to him and he would gasp. Then she would raise her hands to his cheeks and draw the heat from him.

But before she could finish she would be pulled from him, taking her healing touch away. His final words haunted her dreams and her waking hours—*Please stay . . . help me.*

Caitlin shivered at the power of the dreams even now. She could not even believe that the same man was here now, in her home, *in her life.* She hadn't recognized him at first. When he'd burst through the trees yelling the MacKendimen battle cry, he sounded so much like her cousin Craig that she thought he'd followed her into the woods after all.

But this man was not Craig, although he carried a strong resemblance to the clan's men. His coloring was similar to that of her cousin as well.

She'd not gotten a thorough look at his face until he faced her in the moonlight, just as the outlaw MacArthur turned her to drag her deeper into the forest. The moonbeams revealed the face she'd come to know in her dreams. Overwhelmed, she'd fainted and awoke in Craig's arms, being carried back to her parents' cottage.

How could that be? How could she know him already when they'd not yet met? How could he look every inch a MacKendimen and yet be a stranger to her?

She shook her head at her own questions. Scooping more soap from the small jar, she rubbed it into her hair and spread the lather through the long, wet curls. Dipping once and then again into the spring-heated water, Caitlin rinsed the soap and then stayed low in the water. The warmth seeped into her body and soothed her frayed nerves. More tired than she realized, Caitlin felt herself drifting off to sleep.

●　　●　　●

She opened her eyes and he stood before her at the side of the pool, a torch's light flickering over his manly form. Without saying a word, he loosened and dropped his plaid and stepped down into the heated water. Caitlin sat up straighter but stayed below the waterline. She'd seen him naked but he would not see her that way.

He walked toward her in the water steadily, his gaze never straying from hers as he came closer. He was but a step away from her when he reached out and placed his hands on her waist. Lifting her from the water, he pulled her to him and wrapped his arms around her. Flesh to heated flesh, he held her and then lowered his mouth to hers.

The kiss was unlike any she'd had before. Her mouth opened to his probing tongue and waves of heat and pleasure swept through her as his tongue moved into her mouth. She moaned at the sweetness and the strength of the feelings pulsing through her body. His hand slid down her back and under her buttocks, lifting her even closer to him. She could feel his hardness—his muscles rippled beneath her touch. And, at the place where all of the sensations coursing through her body seemed to meld, she felt his hardness and his heat.

The kiss went on and on; his tongue teased hers and drew hers into his mouth. He tasted of some unknown spice. She swirled her tongue and met his again and again, tasting . . . teasing . . . licking.

He lifted her more now and she wrapped her legs around his waist. She gasped in his mouth as she felt his maleness move between her legs, against her, making her crave the motion he'd begun, the hardness, the heat.

The heat!

The heat built around him, from him until she could no longer stay near him. She pushed at his shoulders and he released her; he backed away, his eyes filled with pain and fear. Flames encircled him and his screams echoed through the steamy cave.

"Help me, please, help me."

• • •

Caitlin awoke at the sound of his plea. Blinking, she looked around and knew no one else was with her in the cave. She still sat low in the water and yet she knew he had called to her. Her body tingled, pinpricks covered her skin and she rubbed her arms and shoulders trying to rid herself of the sensation. She had to return home. Now.

Dipping once more, she rinsed her hair and then twisted it into a knot. Caitlin lifted herself from the water and then stood next to the pool, balancing herself carefully until her foot could take the weight. The ankle had lost its stiffness and soreness.

After wrapping it tightly as her mother had directed, she slipped a loose leather shoe over the bandages to keep them dry. Using the large cloth, she dried her body, surprised at how heavy her breasts felt. The tips of them hardened to points as she moved the cloth over them. And Caitlin was startled at the moisture that seeped from the place where the stranger had touched with his hardness in the dream.

She knew that this was the place where men sought their pleasure and where bairns came into the world, but this throbbing wetness was something new to her. Her mother could explain it to her. Pulling her clothes on and braiding her hair quickly, Caitlin gathered up her supplies and left the cave.

"He drifts away from us, daughter, farther and deeper away."

Her mother's whispered words struck fear in her heart. Would he die without ever speaking to her of his identity and of the dreams? Nay, she could not let that happen.

"I heard his cry for help and came as quickly as I could." Caitlin dropped the bathing supplies she carried and approached the still form on the pallet.

"Ye heard him?" Moira turned to face her. " 'Tis true then . . . ye and he are connected in ways not seen."

"In the dreams, Mam, he speaks to me in the dreams."

Caitlin leaned down to test his forehead for the remnants of the fever. His brow was hot to the touch. Even in this deep unhealthy sleep, the stranger responded to her touch by turning his face into her palm.

" 'Tis time, lass. We canna wait any longer or he will sink too deeply for even your touch. Are ye ready?"

Caitlin thought of the ritual ahead. Was she ready to call him back from death's door? It would take all of her physical strength and her faith in her gift for it to work. No distractions could be permitted once she began.

"But, I dinna ken his name, Mam. What should I call him?"

"Douglas MacKendimen is his name, lass. Now, call him back to you afore 'tis too late."

"Douglas MacKendimen? He's of the clan?" Caitlin looked at her mother, waiting for an explanation of this knowledge.

"Aye, he's of the clan but of a distant branch, I think. He has mumbled his name several times in his sleep. Now, Caitlin, call to him now."

Caitlin knelt beside the pallet as her mother moved aside. Moira went to the hearth and added a few more chunks of peat to the fire. Then she lit a tall candle and brought it nearer to Caitlin.

Taking his hand in hers, Caitlin closed her eyes and took three deep breaths, pacing herself to a slow count. Then three more and three again. Clearing her thoughts, she brought the image of the man on the pallet to her mind.

"Douglas MacKendimen, can ye hear me?" she whispered. "Douglas," she called out a bit louder. Leaning closer, she whispered her words into his ear. "Douglas, come to me now."

She let his hand drop to his side and placed one of her hands palm down on his head wound. The lump had decreased in size but was still too prominent to her. The bleeding had ceased after stitching the wound but the swelling still frightened her. Then the fever had taken hold of him. . . .

Touching his cheek with her other hand, Caitlin took three more deep breaths and sighed his name again.Feeling a pulse of heat moving through her hands into him, she entered that black emptiness in her being where the healing happened. Caitlin could see nothing—not the man beside her or the room around her. This was the way . . . the touch . . . the healing.

Then, he was there. Standing before her surrounded by flames as in the dream. She parted the flames with her hands and walked to him. His moans grew lower and lower and she could see that he neared the end of his strength. In her thoughts, she came nearer and reached up for his face, placing her palms on his cheeks.

The heat, Holy Mother, the heat! It surrounded her when she touched him. How could he stand it? How did he yet survive with it sapping away his strength, his life?

She began to feel the pulsing in her hands as she drew the fever's heat from his body. In the vision, his face soon felt cool to her touch and he stirred. Looking into his eyes, she recognized his fear and his uncertainty.

"Come to me, Douglas. Come back to me now," she coaxed.

The flames that had once danced tall and wide around them began to lower and thin until they were gone completely. Caitlin released Douglas and backed away from him calling out, "Come with me now."

Caitlin once more was in the black emptiness. She felt the heat in her hands recede and the pulsing eased in its intensity. Then her vision cleared and she could see the dimly lit cottage and the man on the pallet. His brow felt cool beneath her hand and the lump on his head was gone. Her gift worked once more.

Suddenly her vision clouded over and she began to sway, unable to steady herself. After a moment, she could feel her mother's strong arms slip under her own, pulling her back, lifting her. Then her father picked her up like a bairn and carried her to her own pallet. This was the price of the gift—her own strength in payment for the one she healed.

Her head felt as though someone had hit her from behind and the heat spread through her own body until she could hardly draw a breath without pain. A moan escaped and she slid into the darkness.

Chapter 5

THROUGH THE DARKNESS that voice came again, urging him to follow. He tried, he really did, but his legs would not carry him far enough or fast enough. The pain in his head grew and intensified until he could only moan. He couldn't fight much more.

Then she was there, just as before, but this time she called him by name. *Douglas,* she said in a whispery soft voice that floated through him, around him. Despite the hushed tones, he heard the power in it, calling to him, commanding him to follow.

He moved his head toward the sound and the pain roared again, the weakness invading his limbs and head. Then he opened his eyes and she was there.

Walking through the flames, she called to him again. *Come to me, Douglas. Come to me now.* Then she was near enough to touch, and her glowing green eyes looked into him. Her gaze never left his as she reached up to touch his face.

Her hands were cool, blessedly cool, and he felt the heat draining from his body. He shivered in relief, the absence of the pain suddenly making him dizzy and light-headed.

She kept her hands in place and steadied him a bit longer.

Then she backed away and disappeared from his view. But her voice beckoned from the darkness . . .

Come with me now, Douglas.

Douglas fought to open his eyes. And even when he did he couldn't see anything. He turned his head to look around and waited for that crushing pain to return. But, it didn't. Peering into the darkness of wherever he was, Douglas saw nothing.

Then, slowly, images began to raise themselves before him. He could make out a small fireplace against one wall and a doorway in another. He inhaled and the full earthy odor of peat burning in the nearby fireplace entered his lungs. He stifled a cough that threatened, still afraid of aggravating the pain in his head; the pain that had apparently disappeared.

Shifting his body and trying unsuccessfully to sit up, the rough sheet and scratchy straw mattress rubbed his naked back. Naked? Where the hell were his clothes? And where the hell was he? He slumped back and tried to remember what had happened to him.

Douglas ran his hand through his hair. He remembered trying to find Mairi all day and finally catching up with her at sunset at the archway in the fields. Then, Mairi had disappeared and the screams started.

The screams! And the terror that called to him in that young girl's voice. He remembered the sounds of it.

Then he'd followed the cry through the arch and into the forest and found her. It was her—the woman who'd appeared in his dreams for years now. He couldn't believe it—the green-eyed and black-haired dream woman, and in the clutches of three of the toughest-looking men he'd ever seen.

Wait a minute, this was crazy. How did he get from an open field with nothing but the old stone archway to a dense forest and weapon-wielding warriors? He shook his head and tried to sit up again but the weakness in his body betrayed him.

Searching through his memories, he saw the scene unfold: him charging through the trees, drawing his daggers and throwing one at the closest man near the girl. Then knocking another one down with a kick. And then approaching the leader who'd been enjoying the girl's terror, the pain he'd given and the blood he'd drawn with the thin slicing action of his dirk against her milky-white neck.

The leader tried to leave, dragging the girl with him, and that's when he saw her face. She'd fainted at the sight of him, her slight weight pulling and giving him the opening he needed to hit the mark. But one of the others must have regained consciousness and hit him from behind.

Douglas rubbed his head to find the injury but could find none—no area of tenderness or swelling. That was damned odd since the blow that knocked him out would've left a lump the size of an egg, and it would take well over a week to shrink.

He heard someone approaching through the doorway and waited to see if he knew them. Maybe he'd been left in the woods and someone had brought him . . . here? . . . and gone for help?

"Ah, lad, I thought I heard ye stirring in here."

The woman's voice came to him through the darkness but it sounded familiar. He'd harbored a small hope that it would be the woman from the dreams, but it wasn't. This voice was older, and *familiar*. Without more light in the room, he couldn't see her face. He struggled to rise but couldn't do that, either.

"Here now, lad. Yer still weak from the blow to yer head. Drink this, 'twill help ye regain yer strength."

A hand behind his head lifted him up and a cool metal cup touched his lips. He hesitated to drink—God only knew what was in this cup. The woman felt his pause and tilted the cup more, forcing the liquid against his lips and into his mouth. In a reflexive action, he swallowed and grimaced at the bitter taste.

"No better than yer mam, lad. She fought my brews, too."

"Mairi, is that you?" The identity of the woman finally became clear—it was old Mairi! She must have seen the fight and had someone help him here to her cottage. But what was she giving him and why? He was the doctor, he should be the one in charge of dispensing medication, not the old woman who claimed to have been a clan healer in her younger days! "What in the hell did you just give me?"

"Nay, lad, no' Mairi but Moira. Moira 'tis my name." She stood up and moved toward the door.

"Wait. I know your voice. Mairi, why are trying to confuse me? What was in that cup?"

Suddenly a torch thrust through the doorway revealed the layout of the small room to him. He could see the fireplace—well, a crude hearth built into the wall was a better description. He lay on a mattress of straw in one corner of the room with a low table and bench next to it. His rough bed laid directly on the dirt floor of the cottage. Wait, this couldn't be Mairi's home—hers was about the same size but had all the comforts of a modern home, including a real floor.

Then he caught sight of the man holding the torch. Douglas knew that both he and his father Alex were tall and in good physical condition, but this man put them both to shame with his height and powerful body. He had to be over six and a half feet tall with the muscles of a bodybuilder. He ducked to enter the room and came to stand next to the woman.

The light from the torch gave lie to his words—this was not Mairi. This was a much younger woman with long, brown hair that she wore pulled back into a loose braid. Her eyes were like Mairi's but this couldn't be the same person. Maybe this was Mairi's daughter?

Then he realized his foolishness; these two were dressed

in clothes from a different time. The man had a very worn plaid held by a belt around his waist, knee-high boots and nothing else. The woman wore a long skirt and blouse and a kind of jacket over it—what did they call it in the reenactment? Oh, a bodice with sleeves. This did not make any sense at all. Obviously the blow to his head had scrambled his thoughts.

"What did you say your name was?" He looked at one, then the other.

"I am Moira and this is my husband Pol." She spoke very slowly, as though to a small child.

"Where am I? How did I get here?" He felt very much out of control and he didn't like it. In his years of training and practice, he'd prided himself on his ability to stay cool under the pressure of any situation. And, doing a residency in one of Chicago's larger urban hospitals, he had seen it all. At least he'd thought so until now.

"Ye were injured trying to help our daughter in the forest. Those damned MacArthur villains were on our lands again. She'd be dead now if 'tweren't for ye." The woman Moira dabbed at her eyes with her apron corner.

"Something's not right here," Douglas began, "what do you mean by our land? Where am I?" He rubbed his temples and shut his eyes. "None of this makes sense to me."

"Only a bit makes sense to me, lad. Ye are Maggie's son, are ye no'?"

"Yes, I'm Douglas MacKendimen, Alex and Maggie's son. You know my parents?" As he looked on, they looked at each other and a multitude of unspoken messages passed between them. Finally after a few moments, Moira faced him and spoke.

"Aye, lad, we ken yer parents. They visited here many years ago."

"And where is here?" Douglas was glad to be getting somewhere in trying to find out what had happened to him and where he was.

"Ye are in the village of Dunnedin, seat of Robert, chief-

tain to the MacKendimen clan. And ye are here on the days
just past the equinox of autumn in the year of our Lord one
thousand, three hundred and seventy."

His thoughts froze, his mind refused to process the information she'd just given him. Dunnedin? Robert wasn't
the laird of the MacKendimens; that title had fallen to Uncle Calum's son William, his own first cousin on his father's side. And the date, the equinox of autumn? That was
the day he arrived in Scotland—September twenty-first,
2000, and . . .

She'd said something drastically different . . . it sounded
like . . . 1370? Couldn't be, of course, that would be in
the—

"Aye, 'tis in the past, your past and our present, Douglas.
'Tis hard to believe, but if ye give yerself a bit of time,
ye'll understand it as yer parents did all those years ago."

"Couldn't be . . . it isn't possible." Douglas's mind rebelled at the thought that his parents' stories had been true,
that they had traveled back through time to his ancestors'
land and clan. Absolutely impossible, no question about it.
He must be dealing with some very irrational people here.

Suddenly, his head began to swim, his thoughts began
to swirl around in his mind and he could feel the overpowering dizziness take over. A moan escaped, though he
tried to control it. It would not do to let these people think
he wasn't in control of his faculties.

"Dinna fight it, lad, 'tis the brew I made for ye. 'Twill
help the fever and the weakness and help ye to rest weel."

"Oh, dear God, you've drugged me?"

"Ye will wake up feeling refreshed and ready to roar at
the world, Douglas. Let it help ye now."

He really couldn't do anything else but let it take effect.
His head and limbs felt so heavy, it was difficult to keep
his eyes open to watch this Moira and Pol. If he closed his
eyes for a moment, he could fight it better. Just for a moment. . . .

Chapter 6

"COME, LAD, TAKE my hand."

Douglas opened his eyes at hearing the voice. His vision was clear; he felt no pain or weakness. The man, Pol, stood over him, reaching out a large hand to him. Warily and without any other choice, he took hold of it and was pulled briskly to his feet. He waited for the pain or dizziness but neither happened.

"Here ye'll need these," Pol said as he handed Douglas a length of plaid and a wide leather belt. Trying to be as *nonchalant* as possible about his own nudity in front of this stranger, Douglas took the plaid and wrapped it old-style around his waist, securing it with the belt. He looked around the room to find his own clothes but his belongings were nowhere to be seen.

"Come, I'll show ye the well where ye can wash and then Moira and I want to speak to ye outside."

The giant left, leading the way, and Douglas followed, stooping down under the short doorway, through the main room of the house and out in the yard. As Douglas stepped into the early morning sunlight, he knew something was altered. The sun's light was somehow brighter and the smells of forest and plants and *everything* were clear in the air around him. Fresh and strong and intense. He turned left and right, scanning the area for anything familiar but nothing was. Apparently this Moira's house was in a separate location from the rest of the village. Other than a large garden, the well and a low stone wall around the perimeter, he saw no other buildings closeby.

"Here is the pail and some soap. Ye can relieve yerself over there," Pol pointed at the dense forest next to the stone fence. "Moira and I will be waiting."

As he watched, Pol turned around and walked back toward the cottage where Moira waited near the door. Dipping his head to her, he kissed her on the lips. Douglas turned away and focused his attention on cleaning himself up. His head and hair was the worst by far; his hair was filthier than he'd ever allowed it to be. He lowered the pail into the well, pulled up a bucketful of water and leaning over, he poured it over his head. The coldness of the water immediately sent shivers racing through his body, shocking him even more awake than he thought he was. Since he wasn't offered hot water, he'd assume there was none. Highland hospitality was well-known and if his hosts had it, had anything, they would offer it. So this must be one of the few remaining undeveloped areas in Scotland if they didn't have indoor plumbing with hot water.

Scooping out some of the soft soap in the stone bowl, he rubbed it into his scalp, loosening the grime and God only knew what else with his actions. It was then that his fingers encountered the raised ridge along the back of his head. He probed again, finding the three-inch-long path of evenly placed stitches and not remembering how they were placed there.

He rinsed his head and repeated the cleaning two more times to rid himself of the dirt encrusted in his hair. Each time his fingers found the raised area, increasing his puzzlement over the how and when of them. Somehow he knew that the answers lay with Moira and Pol and their mysterious daughter. He wondered what her name was . . . neither of her parents had mentioned it.

Well, the longer he took here, the longer it would take to get the answers he wanted. He loosened the belt and the plaid, freed from its holder, swirled to the ground. Refusing to look over to see if they were watching him, Douglas stepped closer to the well and continued with the soap, washing until his body was clean. Filling and pouring another bucket of water, he was done with his ablutions. Seeing no other towel, he did as he'd done on his many times with the medieval reenactors—he dried himself off with one end of the long piece of tartan before wrapping it back around his waist, the damp section thrown over his shoulder to dry.

They met him halfway and guided him away from the cottage to a place at the far end of the gardens. He waited, assessing the situation in his analytical way. He would be patient until they spoke first. And they did.

"Ye get that trait from yer da," Moira began. "His well-ordered life taught him to wait and watch afore speaking. Ye get yer spirit and yer zest for life from yer mam."

"So you knew my parents?"

"Aye, they visited this village about a score of years ago. 'Twas my duty to help them at that time and 'tis my duty to help their son."

"Twenty years ago? But Mairi said I was conceived in the past, so how can that be? At least be consistent if you're trying to convince me of the impossible."

Moira took a step closer to him. "Who is this Mairi you speak of? Ye thought I was her when you awoke yesterday."

Douglas looked at her, still amazed at some of the resemblance between the Mairi he knew and this woman. The eyes were chillingly the same but nothing else matched, really.

"Mairi is one of my distant MacKendimen relatives. She lives in Dunnedin and I've known her for as long as I've lived. I must have been confused when I woke up—you do sound alike but you don't look alike. Well, your eyes are the same."

"She lives in Dunnedin, ye say? Weel, no' in this time, she doesna." Moira looked at Pol and then continued, "Och, lad, ye mean in yer time she lives in the village? So the clan and village still prosper then?"

What could he be thinking of? Standing here discussing time travel as though it were possible? And these people looked so very serious about it! He needed to find out a few more bits of information and then he needed to check out the area himself. He would get to the bottom of this.

"Do ye live in Dunnedin as weel as this Mairi? Do yer parents fare weel?" Pol asked.

"I live in the United States," he paused as they exchanged a puzzled glance between them. He'd play along for now. "Across the water to the west, it will begin as a territory to England and Spain. I visit Dunnedin each year for the clan festival."

"And that's what brought ye here?" Moira looked at her husband again and he nodded. "Yer parents were at a clan festival when they traveled here as weel."

"Look, I've heard the stories, about the way my parents met. I don't believe any of them. They sound like something my mom made up to entertain her students and her children."

"Children? She had more than one bairn, then?" Moira questioned.

"Yes. My parents had three children—myself, and my younger sister and brother."

"Weel, praise be, lad. Did ye hear that, Pol? They have other bairns." A wide smile graced the woman's face and she patted him on the shoulder. " 'Tis good to hear."

Douglas ran his hand through his hair and shook his head. This was becoming more and more strange. He was getting nowhere fast. Maybe it would be better if he just left and explored on his own. These people didn't seem to be holding him prisoner, he could leave if he wanted to. He glanced to the edge of the gardens and saw a well-worn path that had to lead somewhere.

"Nay, lad, give us but a few moments afore ye leave. We hiv much to explain to ye." That was the second time she'd seemed to read his mind. Just like Mairi. . . . "Here now, sit a spell and hear us out."

Moira and Pol sat on the short wall and waited for him. He was too tied up in knots to sit now so he paced back and forth. He only stopped when met with Moira's laughter.

"Ye see, Pol, he is his faither's son after all." At his mystified look, she went on, "I hiv seen yer faither pace a bit when he's puzzled." Douglas sat next to them on the wall; he didn't want to think about the source of her knowledge right now.

"First, we maun thank ye for saving our Caitlin from harm," Pol started. "Our daughter was never in danger in those forests afore the MacArthurs started their raids. I should hiv gone wi' her that night."

"Caitlin." He tried out the name. "Caitlin is her name?" At their nod, he let the name sink into his mind. He now had a name for this mystery woman who had haunted his dreams for years. Caitlin, of the glowing green eyes and flowing black hair . . . black as coal, which she's obviously inherited from her father. Her very big father. He cleared his throat.

"I didn't know her name."

"But, ye hiv seen her afore?" Moira leaned closer to hear his answer.

"In my dreams. . . ." Shrugging, he watched to see their reactions—that made him shrug again.

"Aye, lad, and she haes seen ye afore as weel. Dinna worry, we ken the power and truth in the dreams sent to us." Pol nodded his head in agreement with his wife's statement.

"How did I get here?" That was the real question he wanted answered. "How?"

"Weel, lad, one of the MacKendimens carried ye here from the forest, after the MacArthur's man hit ye on yer head. Pol, was it Gordy or Iain?"

" 'Twas Iain," Pol answered.

"No, I mean how did I get to this time from my own?" However ludicrous this situation seemed, he would not let it deteriorate into an Abbott and Costello routine. He stood back up and faced them both. "Explain it to me."

" 'Tis the archway, of course. It brought ye back to us wi' its power. Or should I say that the Fates used the arch to bring ye back."

"The archway? Are you talking about the stone arch out in the fields near Dunnedin?" This made no sense to him at all. The arch contained some power?

"In this time, the archway still exists within a section of the keep wall. But I too hiv seen in the wisdom the arch as ye describe it."

"Okay, even if I believe you about the arch, and I don't, tell me why? Why would I be yanked out of my own time and brought here?"

Moira stood, walked to him and took his hand in hers. Stroking it lightly, she gazed at him. Her eyes became brighter, clearer, *glowing.* . . .

"Mayhap the journey is to find out why? The Fates obviously hiv their own plan for ye." Moira's voice became lower and lower as her fingers glided over his skin, raising goose bumps with each stroke. "But, are ye willing to listen when they speak, follow where they lead, learn the lesson they teach?"

He was completely entranced by her voice, he could feel the power of her words as she spoke. He couldn't tear his gaze from hers, they glowed even brighter as she continued.

"Ye and Caitlin are linked, in yer dreams and in life, just as ye saved her life, she haes saved yer own."

"Saved my life? How?" Douglas pulled his hand from her grasp.

"When they brought ye from the forest, ye haid a head

wound, a bad one. The rock haid cut long and deep to the bone, laying ye to ground."

"So Caitlin is the one who gave me these stitches? Nice work," Douglas asked as his fingers found the raised row on his scalp again.

"Nay," Moira shook her head at him, "those are my work. Caitlin healed ye from the fever and called ye back to the world of the living when ye drifted away from us."

"What do you mean, 'she healed me'?" Douglas asked.

"Just as I said, lad, she healed ye." Moira looked at him squarely, challenging him in some way that he didn't quite understand.

"Look, I'm a doctor, I see patients every day. I know about medicines and surgery and how to treat injuries and diseases. So, how did she *heal* me?" He crossed his arms and waited for an answer.

He was tired of being dragged around and not having any idea of what was happening to him. He didn't for a minute believe this incredible story of traveling to the past. This had the looks of an elaborate prank. After all, hadn't Mairi promised as much when they'd last talked? What did she call it? Oh, yes, a *reckoning*. So this must be part of what she and others had planned! Were his parents involved?

His parents? No, they couldn't have a part in this. But they'd been warning him to change his life, too. Hounding him about too much work and about his lack of time for anything but work. No. They wouldn't have planned anything that would have had him injured—that would be too dangerous.

"Douglas, I ken that yer no' ready to listen but our Caitlin has a special gift." Moira lowered her voice and took a step toward him. "She can heal with her touch."

Douglas looked at the older woman and man before him and was struck with their complete belief in Moira's words and their sincerity. But, did she say the girl healed with her touch? Ha! He only believed in those treatment modalities he could verify through use and research. Psychic healing?

"She heals with her touch? And, you're saying she used this magic touch on me?" He heard the sarcasm and couldn't stop it. Enough was enough.

Moira shivered and exchanged a worried look with Pol. This was not going at all the way it should. Douglas was much more cynical than she expected for the son of Alex and Maggie, and for a healer in his own right. It was apparent to her that Alex's Scottish blood may have passed down, but his mother's celtic spirit had not.

"We dinna call it magic, Douglas—we call it a gift."

"Well, you're asking me to believe in magic, aren't you? Traveling through time, an arch with magical powers, and now a girl who heals by touching?"

Moira caught his glance as he threw out his disdainful comments. For a brief moment, she read a bit of fear and confusion in his MacKendimen blue eyes. Ah, so he hid his fear behind the sarcasm. Well, then he was not a complete loss.

"I am telling ye that Caitlin can lay her hands on an injury or a sick person and make them weel again. 'Tis as simple as that."

His laugh, loud and raucous, filled the garden. This was not going well at all. He had to believe, he had to or—

As quick as it had begun, the laughter stopped and Douglas was frozen before her. She turned to see what he saw.

Chapter 7

CAITLIN, STILL PALE and weak, stood clutching the framework of the door. Her hair was loose and wild like a collar of storm clouds around her face and neck. Her green eyes were still fever-bright, the lingering effects of the healing touch.

Douglas stepped toward the cottage but Moira blocked his way. When he tried to go around her, she grabbed his wrist. Pol came to her side to stop the younger man's escape.

"Ye maun keep yer knowledge to yerself, Douglas. No one, no' even Caitlin, can ken aboot ye, and where ye come to us from. No one. Do ye understaun me?"

Standing where she was, Moira could feel the pull between them, a force not yet at its full strength. Douglas's gaze never left her daughter.

"Ye dinna remember where yer from, the blow to yer head haes confused yer thoughts and memories."

He once more tried to evade her, shaking his hand to free him from her grasp, but this was more than just her and her family involved. The Fates were in this and would not be ignored.

"Dinna mistake my words, Douglas MacKendimen. There will be a reckoning if ye ignore my advice."

He shuddered at her words and finally gave her his attention.

"Did you say a reckoning?" His eyes, those MacKendimen blue eyes, darkened to almost midnight as he focused on her.

"Aye, I did, lad. We will finish our talk later but in the meantime, say nothing to Caitlin or anyone else who happens along. We will put together a tale to satisfy all questions."

He nodded briskly and she dropped his hand. Pol stepped back and she turned to look at Caitlin. The lass looked near to fainting. Moira hurried to her side and felt Douglas move with her step by step. Pol was but a step or two behind both of them as they reached her daughter. She was faster than either of the men.

"Come, lass, ye need a bit of tea." Taking hold of her under the arm to give support, Moira guided Caitlin back into the kitchen area of their cottage. Pol pulled a bench closer to the long table and they placed Caitlin on it. She was not quite herself yet; this healing had taken much from her. Each was different but each the same in that she paid a price for the gift bestowed on her.

Since Pol now stood behind Caitlin, Moira went to her worktable and chose the herbs she needed from her jars and jugs. Mixing them in a small earthen cup, she walked to the hearth and took water from a boiling pot over the low fire. She offered a prayer under her breath as she mixed the powders and the water. She watched the swirling liquid until all was dissolved and then offered it to her daughter. The herbs would help restore her strength. Caitlin took the cup and sipped it slowly. No one uttered a word until Caitlin finished the drink.

"Do ye feel better now, lass?" Moira watched Douglas out of the corner of her eye, he'd seemed completely overwhelmed since the moment Caitlin appeared in the doorway. He'd never taken his eyes from her. He'd started toward Caitlin more than once and then stopped. Now he approached the table where Caitlin sat, this time making it to her side.

As she watched, he raised his hand to Caitlin's face, gently touching her cheek, then sliding his fingers up to her forehead, testing the same way she would for the heat of the fever or the clamminess of illness. His eyes revealed surprise when he put his flesh to her daughter's.

Good.

After a moment or two, he lifted her hand into his and encircled her wrist with his fingers. Caitlin didn't seem to fight or question his actions. Her face was still pale and empty. This healing took much from her and she would need more time to recover from it.

Douglas raised his arm and gazed at his own wrist and then shook his head. The area where he glanced was paler than the skin around it—that's where he wore that strange piece of jewelry. She'd taken everything he wore from his body while he slept. No one else in the clan could be allowed to see those things. Too many questions. His shaking head told her he realized that it was missing. What did it have to do with her daughter's wrist?

"Her heartbeat is slow, too slow," he said, looking right at her. Heartbeat? In her wrist? She could feel the beating of the heart in the chest or sometimes in the neck, but she'd never found it elsewhere. There would be much to learn from this one.

More importantly, she heard the tremor in his voice. Linked, oh, aye they were linked, this one and her daughter. Even better. . . .

"The tea I made for her will help that. It will bring back her strength," she explained.

"What is in it? Is it the same that you made for me?" She winced at the tartness in his question.

"Nay, lad, the brew I gave to ye was to make ye sleep.

The one for Caitlin will restore her strength—she haes already slept enough."

"Tell me what you put in it."

Even Pol heard the challenge and anger in Douglas's voice, for he straightened to his full height behind their daughter with his fists and jaw clenched. Douglas acted as one whose orders were never questioned, a man of authority. *Mayhap physicians in his time all acted this way? Nay, he had the same attitude and stuffiness that his father had carried as well. He would learn, the Fates would teach him their lesson.*

"Some herbs that strengthen the heart, others that clear the head. Nothing that would harm my daughter, ye can be sure." She let the tone of her voice carry her displeasure at his.

He faltered. His words tripped over one another and she could see him realize his place and the situation around him.

"I'm sorry, I didn't, I mean . . ." He stepped away from the table, looking from Pol to Caitlin and then to her. Douglas let go of Caitlin's hand and backed away until he bumped into her worktable.

"Mam, Douglas has been through much in these last few days. Leave him be."

Her voice cut through every bit of confusion in his mind and soul and spoke to him. He'd heard this voice countless times before—like a siren's call in the night. He'd know it anywhere. He leaned against the workbench for support. It was real, *she was real.*

Of course she couldn't be. A rational part of his mind rebelled at every piece of information, every bit of explanation that Moira and Pol had provided him with. Maybe he lay somewhere in a coma from the head wound and this was his brain's unconscious wanderings? He shook his head against that thought.

If this was a dream or some dreamlike state, it was as real as, well, real life. Icy rivulets of water ran down his back from his still-wet hair. The wool plaid rubbed against his naked skin. His bare feet felt the cold dirt floor and goose bumps rose on his legs and chest from the chilly breeze that swept through the cottage's open door.

Too real to be anything else.

Suddenly, the world around him began to spin. His lungs tightened, drawing in no air to clear his head. He had to get away from this. Away. He looked at Moira, then Caitlin, then Pol. Everything, everyone felt so real to him. An awareness of this truth swirled around him until he was overpowered by it.

Get away, his brain screamed. *Get away!*

And, having never before experienced a panic like this, Douglas obeyed, running through the open door and out into the yard. Looking left then right, he spied a pathway leading away and he followed it. A few moments later, Douglas left the forest behind and entered a clearing. The sight before him brought him to a dead stop.

The path split into three more and each one went in a different direction, but any of them would have taken him into the village that lay before him. The smells of animals and their droppings assaulted him. Geese clucking, pigs snorting and sheep making that irritating baa sound surrounded him. He saw too many cottages to count; most of them were smaller than Moira's but of similar design.

And, on the other side of the village, away in the distance but close enough to give him a glimpse of its true size, stood a castle. Not the one he knew from Dunnedin, but one he'd seen portraits of in the old family histories. It looked just like the original one, built long before Wallace and Bruce had entered into Scotland's politics. And, of course, his reason and common sense told him it was not possible.

His eyes and soul told him a different story.

It was then that the mutterings of people nearby pierced through his confusion and disbelief. They stood with dumbfounded looks on their faces, staring at him. Douglas almost laughed out loud at the situation. He didn't know who was more bewildered—him or those around him.

They'd ceased their labors where they stood, gaping openly at him. He touched the plaid around his waist to make sure he wasn't again naked. His mishaps with fastening the plaid securely were known throughout the clan. But, no, the belt and length of wool were still in place and snug around him.

Then, he really began to look at the villagers. Men, women and children all appeared healthy and well fed in spite of their rough and rugged faces. Even in the brisk autumn air, most were barefooted and without outer cloaks. Goose bumps raised on his own bare skin as he felt a cold breeze pass him by. He'd left Moira's in such a rush, he was barefoot and without a shirt.

A few men nodded greetings to him and he returned the gesture. Several children crept a bit closer then ran away to find a hiding place behind the skirts of some women watching him. A smile threatened as he watched their antics. The women wore expressions that ranged from fear to suspicion to open appraisal of him. Some were so straightforward in their staring, he was tempted to blush!

Someone clearing their throat behind him grabbed his attention and he turned around quickly, coming face-to-face with Pol. Well, almost face-to-face. Pol still had at least five or six inches on him.

"Come, lad, Moira says not to overtax yerself yet." Pol encircled his upper arm with one hand and pulled Douglas back toward the healer's cottage. Douglas tried to pull away but the man never faltered in his hold.

"Is all weel, Pol?" one of the men called out.

"Oh, aye, 'tis weel. The lad is no' yet recovered from the blow to his head," Pol called out in answer, waving his free hand at the man who'd asked. Douglas noticed much more sympathy in their glances at him. Moira warned him not to answer any questions and to play up his injury and confusion. Pol had obviously been sent on her orders to bring him back.

"Come, lad, let me help ye back to Moira." Pol's voice was raised artificially high so that all around them could hear clearly. Douglas realized he had no chance . . . yet.

"I'll come with you," he whispered so that only Pol heard.

"Wi'oot a fight?"

"Yes," he muttered.

Apparently pleased with his response, the older man released Douglas's arm and stood aside for him to pass. Douglas took the first step back along the path into the forest.

"Don't you have anything better to do than follow me?" A few seconds more and he could've . . . could've what?

"Aye, lad, I do. But Moira begged me to bring ye back to her."

"Begged you? I can't believe that woman has ever begged in her life." In all truth, he couldn't. Moira had a certain strength of personality that wouldn't allow her to beg for anything. He knew that about her in just the few minutes they'd spent talking.

Pol's laughter filled the air around them and echoed back at him from the forest. "I see ye ken my Moira already."

Douglas stilled. He realized that he'd actually been thinking about *Mairi* but the similarity between the two women struck him yet again. He shook his head to clear his thoughts.

"Dinna fight me, lad. Moira needs to talk wi' ye afore ye go into the village and keep."

"I'm not fighting you. Now, let me walk by myself." He shook his arm free of Pol's grasp and strode down the path under his own power.

"If ye will go on yer own, I will tend to my other duties." Pol tilted his head and raised an eyebrow, asking for Douglas's cooperation.

"Fine. Go do whatever you need to do," Douglas agreed,

waving the other man off. It was only a few more paces until Moira's cottage would come into view anyway. Pol watched him take another step or two and then trotted off back toward the village. Douglas returned, as he'd agreed, to Moira . . . and to Caitlin.

Chapter 8

HE WALKED WITH a swagger her clansmen would be proud of. His muscular arms were held close to his side as his long legs covered the ground between the path and her mother's garden in a few paces. Soon he stood before her and she sat back on her heels to look at him.

Like Craig, but not. His hair and beard, although much the same color as Craig's, were cropped closer than Craig's were. The beard was just a few days' growth. She remembered his clean-shaven face when he stepped into the beams of moonlight that first time. His eyes, she could now see, were MacKendimen blue.

So, he was of the clan? Mam had said a distant cousin, a physician by training. She shivered at that thought. He would no doubt be very suspicious of her and her gift. Those who studied medicine and surgery in the universities of the great cities of Scotland and on the continent did not look kindly on those who had other gifts or skills. Especially not peasant girls from small villages in the Highlands. Cousin or not, she would know him better before she spoke of her healing touch.

They stared at one another. Their glances locked and her

breathing was shallow, her chest tight with anticipation and
a bit of fear. He didn't move but she could see from the
corner of her eye that his fists clenched and unclenched.
Then he said exactly what she was thinking.

"I thought you were only a dream." His voice was rough
and husky, filled with many emotions.

"And, I you. But Mam told me ye were real enough,"
she answered.

"Then you had an advantage over me. How long have
you had the dreams?" He reached down and held out his
hand to her. She placed hers in his and stood, gathering her
apron together to hold onto the harvested plants. He guided
her to her feet, but his hand kept hers.

She was aware of every inch of her skin that touched
his, even in this innocent gesture. Her hand tingled with
feelings, pulses that moved through her hand, into her arm
and then into her body. 'Twas not unpleasant this sensation,
just like the heat from a fire as it warned every part of her.
Caitlin glanced over at him to see if he was affected by
their touch. His answering look said it all clearly; words
were not necessary.

"The dreams hiv come for nigh to three years. And ye?"

"For about the same." Douglas ran his other hand
through his hair and shook his head. "I still cannot believe
that I am talking to you. Do you have the same two dreams?
The one with the fire?"

She nodded, unable to speak.

"And the one in the cave?" he asked, his voice husky
and deep once more.

Caitlin felt the fire enter her cheeks. *The cave.* He knew
of that one, too? She closed her eyes, remembering the sight
of him, wet and naked in the steaming pool. And she remembered his touch, his hands on her waist and her breasts,
and . . . everywhere. Another shiver raced through her, pulling her from her memories of the dreams.

"Damn, Caitlin, you've been ill and I'm standing here in
the cold air with you. Come," he tugged her hand, the one

he still held in his grasp, "let me take you inside."

"Nay, I amna cold, Douglas. And I amna ill. This happens after . . ." Holy Mother! Already she had done exactly what she'd decided not to do—to reveal her healing abilities to him. No matter the strength of her feelings or their shared dreams. This man was a stranger. She pulled her hand from his and turned from him. She swallowed deeply waiting for his reaction. Would he damn her as many of his worldly profession would?

"Well, I am cold even if you aren't so come inside and help me find something warmer than this." He pointed at the single layer of plaid thrown over his shoulder.

She could only nod. She knew her voice would have shaken and she didn't want to appear weak in front of him again. Caitlin gathered the folds of cloth more securely around her bundle and followed him through her mother's door.

Her mother stood with her back to them at her worktable. Caitlin carried her precious bundle over and opened her apron. Moira gently lifted the various herbs and placed them on the surface before her. Douglas still followed and stood close enough that she could feel the heat from his body on her back. He was not chilled as he'd said. She'd been maneuvered by someone with the skill and practice of her mother.

"And what are these? More strange ingredients to feed to some other unsuspecting victim?" His voice came from so near her own ear that it tickled as it passed. Another shiver pulsed through her body.

"These, lad? These are but simple cooking herbs for use in the castle's kitchens." Moira carefully wrapped the dried and fresh herbs she'd been working on in small bundles and placed them in a sack.

Douglas grasped Caitlin's shoulders and moved her to the nearby bench. "Here, you should be sitting. I don't think you've recovered yet from . . ."

"The healing?" Moira offered, glancing one to the other with those wise eyes.

Caitlin gasped. Her own mother who urged caution at every step had revealed her dangerous secret to some stranger. "M-mam . . . ," she stuttered, "I didna think ye would—"

" 'Tis weel, lass. He kens." Her mother nodded in that infuriating way she had and turned her attention to the herbs yet again.

"She's recovering from this healing touch or whatever you call it. It's obvious she's been ill and shouldn't be outside on her hands and knees digging in that damp garden." His eyes grew darker. He was angry!

She didn't know whether to be flattered or insulted. In one breath he'd defended, nay, even protected her, and in that same breath insulted her gift with his disbelief.

"Caitlin kens her limits. Getting back to work often clears her head and gets her body back to what it should be after the—"

"The healing?" Both Moira and Douglas said the word at the same time. But *his* voice echoed with mockery.

"If ye twa are done talking aboot me as though I didna stand before ye, I'll go see to our meal." The two culprits turned to her as one—both had been too involved in their war of wills and words. She rubbed her hands together, ridding them of the last of the garden's dirt, and walked to the door.

"You should rest, Caitlin. You still look pale." His voice was softer this time and more difficult to ignore.

She pulled her kerchief from her apron's pocket and wrapped and tied it around her head. "I go to see to our meal." Douglas looked as if he would object again but said nothing. A faint smile touched her mother's lips. Oh, aye. She was up to some plotting or another.

"Please give greetings to the lady Anice and tell her I will visit her on the morrow."

Caitlin nodded and left without another word. Walking

the paths she knew so well that she could walk them with eyes shut, she thought about her mam's actions . . . and *his*.

She remembered his touch and experienced those feelings again. The heat had surprised her; 'twas only his hand to her hand after all. Not like in the dreams when he touched her breasts and other places. But the sensations and the heat that passed through her body were the same. The dreams were not their only connection or else she wouldn't have this strong reaction to him.

He felt it, too, she knew. She'd seen him startle when they clasped hands. It had happened when he touched her face for those few moments when she was still rousing from the effects of the healing. Her thoughts were in a fog but his weren't. She'd seen his hand shake when he touched her cheek.

Her feet followed the next path that branched off from the main one and she headed for the castle. Although her thoughts were elsewhere, she greeted anyone she passed. Soon she entered the gate to the main courtyard. Walking through the dust and around the castle's people and creatures, Caitlin approached the kitchen entrance.

"Caitlin, do ye hiv something for me from yer maither?" The oversized cook left the hearth area and came to greet her as soon as she entered. "I've been out of the herbs I need for the rabbit stew."

"I hiv them here as promised, Calum." She passed the sack over to him and watched the older man chortle as he opened the various bundles and smell the contents.

"There are rabbits for Moira"—Calum pointed at a brace of skinned rabbits hung over one of the tables—"and take some of the bread, too, lass." And then he was gone, off to try out the new seasonings on his latest creation.

He'd not given her a chance to ask about Anice. She looked around as she headed into the great hall. Spying a familiar face at work on the tables, she called out.

"Hello, Siusan. Can ye tell me where to find the lady Anice?"

"Oh, aye, Caitlin," her friend answered. "In her solar." Siusan pointed off in the direction of the room and went back to her scrubbing. Caitlin nodded and made her way quickly down the length of the main room and off into a hallway. The door to the solar was closed so she knocked lightly before entering.

She opened the door when she heard Anice call out her permission. As usual, the lady Anice sat at her loom, weaving threads into a fine cloth at a fast pace. Her two younger daughters imitated her movements but without the same success as their mother. A maidservant stood nearby working with the girls, correcting their mistakes and praising their accomplishments.

"They look more like ye every day, my lady." Caitlin walked closer to see the design on the tapestry the girls were embroidering. Nessa, being ten years old, had more skill than her six-year-old sister Bonnie, but the younger lass made up for her lack by trying harder. Both girls did indeed look like miniature Lady Anices—they matched her coloring with their fiery red hair and flashing green eyes. None could mistake with their looks or temperament who their mother was.

"Aye, they do, Caitlin, as you look more like your mother." Anice's hands never paused in their work as she turned slightly to face Caitlin. After a thorough look, Anice asked, "How do you fare this day?"

"I am weel, my lady. My maither says to bring her greetings to ye and tell ye that she'll visit ye on the morrow."

"Good, I look forward to seeing her." Anice ceased her work and stood up next to the loom, stretching her arms and shoulders. The lady approached and drew Caitlin away from the others in the room.

"How fares the stranger? Has he awakened?" Anice's voice was pitched lower as well.

"He is awake but confused. The blow to his head was very bad." Even she heard the trembling in her voice.

"And Moira? What has she to say about him?" Anice leaned closer.

"Mam believes he's a MacKendimen, but a distant cousin at that. He haes the look of the clan." Caitlin remembered how she thought it was Craig coming to her rescue. Aye, Douglas had the look of the MacKendimens.

Anice gasped, then peered around to see if anyone had noticed her reaction. The lady looked very nervous all of the sudden.

"My lady, what ails ye?" Caitlin took a step toward Anice, reaching out to steady her.

" 'Tis of no account, Caitlin." Anice straightened and rubbed her palms down her work dress. "I'll see your mother on the morrow, then?" At Caitlin's nod, Anice turned back to her loom. "Come, lassies, let's finish our work and then see what your father is doing in the practice yards with that new horse of his."

Caitlin smiled at the girls' reactions. If she had more time, she would have gone to watch the Laird work a new horse. 'Twas a sight to behold. But she had to bring the food back to the cottage to prepare the meal. And to see how Douglas fared under her mother's scrutiny.

Chapter 9

Damn THE WOMAN'S arrogance! During the time he'd spent with her, Moira had not given any more information than he had when they'd entered the cottage. He let out his breath in an exasperated huff that got her attention. And once more she gifted him with that enigmatic smile she had. He could really see Mairi in that look.

Well, this was getting him nowhere. His short attempt to visit the village had been quashed by Pol and his continued probings into anything Moira knew were met with a wall . . . and that damned smile.

She kept saying they'd talk about everything when the time was right. God only knew when that would happen. The only concession he'd won was that she showed him where she'd stored his belongings. His clothes, wristwatch, pager and wallet were all in one of her trunks in the room she and Pol shared.

Caitlin's return to the cottage didn't ease the tension in the room at all. As a matter of fact, it increased it measurably. He found himself holding back and he didn't know why. Well, certainly her mother standing guard was one reason.

From his seat opposite of Moira at the worktable, he watched as Caitlin put two sacks on the other table and opened one. She pulled out the carcasses of some animals and placed them on the table. She worked quietly and efficiently, collecting the necessary tools and preparing the meat. As if she'd felt his stare, she turned her eyes to his.

The electricity was still there! A jolt of it connected them whenever their gazes met. What was this? How could he ever speak to her calmly with these feelings raging through him? He would have to control this. He swallowed deeply, trying to regain his equilibrium. She blinked and returned to her tasks.

He didn't want to watch. In spite of his fascination with her, he had no desire to see this food prepared. The last time he'd watched game prepared it was in a spotless kitchen, with the cook's hands washed before and after butchering the hunter's bounty. This was too much for his surgeon's sensibilities. His thoughts must have shown on his face.

"Hiv I offended ye in same way?" Her brow was wrinkled with concern. She really didn't understand.

"No, Caitlin. My thoughts were elsewhere." What else could he say? She wasn't ready to hear about salmonella and disease transmission and he certainly didn't want to try to explain it to her. If this was the past, he had to be careful not to influence those around him in ways that might change his time.

That sudden realization was like a bucket of icy water. It startled him—that he was beginning to accept this bizarre situation. Could he possibly have passed through time? A part of him believed it already but another part fought not to. It really was too strange to be happening. There was no proof, nothing in his experience or knowledge that said time travel could occur. Never been proven, never been done!

He turned his attention back to the older woman. Moira sat sorting and trimming plants and leaves. Again his confusion must have shown or these women were too damn perceptive for his own good.

"Ye will come to understaun what haes happened to ye, Douglas, and the why of it as weel." She paused and that smile returned. "Mayhap ye can teach us some of yer healing ways?"

"Would that be a good idea, Moira? When I return"—he saw Caitlin's head snap up at his words—"home, you may not wish that things had been changed by me."

"I amna worried aboot that. Ye hiv learning that could be of good for the clan," Moira explained. "And I am interested in anything that will help the Clan MacKendimen."

"But medicine and healing is not the same in my . . ." Again, Caitlin's head came up and her gaze focused on him. And this time he knew it without even looking at her. "In my training, that is. It's not the same as what you do with these." Gesturing with his hand, he pointed to the herbs she worked with and those in her pots and jars.

"I am willing to show ye my ways while ye are here."

"How will we explain it? I don't remember much about before I woke up in your cottage." Douglas was trying to get his story straight. Moira had forbidden him to discuss the truth of it with Caitlin. He would leave that for another time and abide by the woman's rules for now.

"But, ye do remember some of the healing ways?" At his nod, she continued, "Then ye should accompany me, and Caitlin, as we visit the sick and injured of the clan. We will tell the laird and the lady Anice of it on the morrow when we visit them."

"Mam, yer certain of this?" Caitlin finished putting the meat into the large pot and walked over to the larger table, rubbing her hands on her apron. "Is Douglas truly a healer?"

"I am a doctor and surgeon, by training and experience, Caitlin. Truly." He waited for her reaction; he wanted to hear the respect in her voice.

"Then why no' just say so to the clan? Why must he keep it a secret?"

"We willna keep it a secret. We will tell the laird and the lady Anice of his skills but since he kens little of his own past, 'tis best to keep the whole story quiet. Let the laird decide when and who to tell."

"I see yer point, Mam. The MacKendimens dinna react well to strangers, do they?" The two women shared a laugh and then looked at him.

"So tomorrow you'll take me to the laird?" Since he believed he would learn much in that encounter, he looked forward to the meeting. And it would get him out of these close quarters. Having the woman of his dreams this close was beginning to wear on his nerves. Especially since every time he looked at her, he saw her as she'd looked in the cave dream—naked and welcoming. Water glistening in the light of the torch and sliding down into the most interesting places on her body. He'd always had the urge to dip his head and trace the path of those drops with his tongue. Touching, following, tasting. Down, past her creamy neck and over her smooth shoulders and then even further.

Moira cleared her throat bringing him back to the present. He was certain now that she could read his mind. And those thoughts were certainly not ones that a mother should read. He couldn't meet her gaze.

"Mayhap, ye could bring in more wood for the fire?"

"Of course. Where is it?" He stood, but not quickly. Thank God for the loose kilt. His body had responded to his thoughts more speedily then he'd believed and at least the plaid hanging as it was would hide the erection.

"On the side of the yard," Moira motioned with her hand and Douglas followed her instructions. She kept him busy with chores the rest of the day.

Like a moonstruck boy, he watched her from outside the doorway where she couldn't see him. He would have to lure her away to some moment of privacy so they could talk more. Having parents so close the whole day didn't give him a chance to speak coherently to her. Oh, they'd talked—spoken of the clan and relatives and day-to-day things of importance. But there was so much more he wanted to learn from her, about her.

The night was coming and the darkness spread around him. The temperature dropped rapidly and his idea of a quick wash before dinner quickly lost its appeal. Pulling the end of the plaid around his shoulders, he stood in the quiet and watched her chatter with her mother as they finished preparations for the meal. She moved with the same grace and ease that he'd seen in the dreams. Her smile was generously given and her laugh sent ripples through his soul.

It was difficult to believe she was only eighteen to his thirty years. Everyone here seemed much older than he would have thought. Moira was not even forty, yet she appeared so much older than that. Obviously he was in a different place and time—one that was not so kind to those who lived and survived here.

Her hair was loose now and lay like midnight waves over her shoulders and down her back, reaching her waist with no trouble. He bet that if it were straightened, it would nearly reach the floor. A man could get lost in that hair. His hands clenched with the thoughts of her hair wrapped around them, trapping their faces and bodies close together.

And those eyes! Green, so green that they almost glowed. And when he looked into their depths, he saw flames of emerald and turquoise and sea green. There was a magic there even though she denied being magical.

"Another bucket of water over yer head may help ye."

Douglas wheeled around to face Pol as he entered the yard. Just great—he stood here in lust for Caitlin and her father saw it all.

"Ye are no' the first lad to look at her that way, ye ken."

"I shouldn't be looking at her that way. Very cold water may help after all." Pol was obviously a practical man, or he would have used his fists first to answer the insult Douglas had offered, intentionally or not, to his daughter.

"She be a fetching lass, Douglas. I may be her faither but I hiv eyes that see. Many in the clan hiv wanted and still want her to wife."

He frowned. Why hadn't she married? If they were being truthful, she would have been married with babies by now. Pol had given him the opening; he would use it.

"And she is not married?" Pol shook his head. "And not engaged either?" Again a negative shake. "Why not?"

Pol laughed heartily. "Ye hiv met maither and daughter. Do ye think any man would stand a chance if they both decided no'?"

Douglas thought about it for all of a second and joined Pol in his laugh. "No, I guess not."

"I'll wash and we can go in for supper. We men should band together when we can." Pol dropped the sack he was carrying and walked to the well.

After drawing and pouring several buckets of water over his head, they were ready for food. How difficult could dinner be?

Chapter 10

S HE WOULD HAVE seen him but she was too busy staring at Douglas. She got caught up in his smiles and never saw Craig's approach. And never realized until it was too late that he'd seen her mooning at the handsome stranger at the table.

"So, he lives?" Craig's booming voice announced him to all present. She knew from years of friendship that he felt threatened, in danger, on the defensive. But why?

"Aye, Craig, he fares weel. Come in, lad. Hiv ye eaten yer fill yet?" Moira opened the door the rest of the way and waved him into the room.

Craig stood staring at Douglas from across the room. Men could be such fools sometimes! His glance moved from one onto the next and onto the next, finally coming back to her mother.

"I thank ye, Moira. I hiv eaten already."

"Then sit wi' us a bit and meet Douglas." Moira pulled a chair over next to the bench where she and Caitlin sat and invited Craig to sit. His face was nigh to rigid. He nodded and without saying a word sat down in it.

Douglas stood and offered his hand in greeting but Craig

only nodded again. Looking confused Douglas sat down in his seat. Then the two imbeciles started glaring silently at each other in spite of her mother's best efforts to talk to them! She decided to take this into her own hands.

"Craig, hiv ye something to say?" She fixed her gaze on him and tried out her mother's intimidating stare. It worked, for he began to stammer out something.

"Does he ken?" Craig shifted in his seat yet again and Caitlin realized he was waiting for Douglas's response to his part in her rescue. Oh, dear. Brave, fearless Craig looked as if ready to fight. His hand kept sliding down near his *sgian-dubh*, ready to draw it.

"Nay, Craig, he doesna." Pol stood as he answered and moved closer to the two younger men. Her da was just as ready. To draw a weapon on a guest in her home was an insult to the guest and to her father. Men!

"Since you both know something I don't, why don't you tell me?" Douglas also shifted but stayed in his seat with his hands on the table. Stranger or not, he understood this situation.

"Douglas. The blow to yer head . . . ," Moira interjected. "Craig was the one to deliver it."

Anice watched as both men heard the words. She'd known, she'd seen it coming. Craig creeping quietly out of the forest, approaching Douglas from behind. Of course, at that time she had no idea who Douglas was. Only after gaining a glimpse of his face in the moonlight did she realize it. She almost felt herself slipping into another faint as she recalled Craig in those last moments as he came at Douglas from behind, cudgel raised to strike. She shivered remembering Craig's strong arm arched up in the moon's light.

"I didna ken ye were helping Caitlin," Craig began, his hand still at the ready. "I thought ye were one of the MacArthurs, trespassing on our land and trying to harm her." Craig met her gaze now and she saw the fullness of his feelings toward her. Oh, if she could only return them in kind to him.

"Then we were there for the same purpose?" Douglas's voice deepened with his response. Craig nodded in answer. "Then you need not fear reprisal from me for your attack."

Her mouth dropped open, gaping at Douglas's easy acceptance of a near-death blow. Who could explain how their minds worked? Any other man in her family would never have accepted it with such open candor. But this was Douglas, the man in her dreams. The man *of* her dreams?

"Why are you surprised, Caitlin? You had passed out. I stood with weapon drawn. I'm sure Craig couldn't tell who was the villain and who was the rescuer in the dark and in the heat of the moment." Douglas's assessment of this was flawless but still troublesome. He wasn't behaving as most men she knew would. Not at all.

"Aye, that's exactly as it happened." Craig began to relax in his chair and Pol stepped away as well. The dangerous moment seemed to have passed. "When I finally tracked ye down, Caitlin, that damned MacArthur was dragging ye backwards through the trees. I saw his"—he nodded his head in Douglas's direction—"knife aimed for ye and hit him as soon as I reached him. 'Twasn't until ye woke from yer faint that I kenned he was no' an enemy like the others."

"And when Pol brought the torch closer, I could see yer resemblance to our clan. Even some of the villagers saw it this morn when ye walked there. Is it true then? Are ye of the MacKendimens?" Craig was staring at Douglas's face, looking for the similarity that anyone could see.

The coloring, the nose, the cheekbones were all the same. The villagers were already talking? News traveled quickly within the clan. The laird and lady must have heard it as well.

"Oh, aye, Craig. He is a distant cousin from the south but a MacKendimen by blood and by name. That much we ken." Moira's words were strong to stop any challenge or question. "The laird and lady will hear of it first. Attend them in the morn if ye wish to hear it for yerself."

Her mother stood, ending the conversation. Pol reached out to Craig, shaking his hand and leading him to the door. Douglas remained at the table, looking very shaken. Caitlin leaned closer to him and touched his arm.

"What is it, Douglas? Are ye no' weel?" She reached out to feel his forehead. 'Twas a bit clammy but not hot. For a moment she thought the fever had returned.

"Those men . . . I had not thought of them till just now. I'm a healer—a physician—and I killed three men." His face was ashen, his words stuttered. A groan escaped from him and he held his head in his hands. And he looked ill, truly ill.

"Nay, Douglas, ease yer worries. Ye wounded them and one gravely so. But ye didna kill any of them, though they did deserve to die."

"I attacked without thought, without hesitation. I knew this was not a reenactment and I threw those knives trying to kill them for real."

"Re-en-act-ment?" She let the strange word roll off her tongue.

"Playing a role, fake fighting . . ."

"Oh, like in training?"

"Yes, but made to look real." His voice was gravelly now, she could feel his despair.

"Douglas, if ye hadna, we would both be dead, or worse." She tried to soothe him. It was obviously his first battle. She guessed that his training in the university didn't allow much time for fighting. But she saw his familiarity with the weapons and with fighting strategies. He was just not ready to face killing.

"Caitlin, take Douglas out for some fresh air. The coolness of the night should help clear his head."

He stood at his seat and let her lead him out of the cottage and into the yard. A quarter-moon barely lit the sky and a chilled breeze whispered through the trees. She kept his hand in hers, experiencing that feeling again but not as strong this time. She brought him to the garden wall and guided him to sit.

"Breathe now, Douglas. Let the night's air refresh yer spirit and relieve yer worries." She sat next to him. Taking his hand in hers, she savored the pulsing that ran through from him to her. "Dinna fash yerself over something like this. Ye acted the warrior first, which saved our lives."

"I still cannot believe it. I acted without thought."

Men could be such . . . bairns about some things. Most men in her clan would be out boasting about their strength and their ability with the *sgian-dubh*. Not Douglas, though. No, he was berating himself for trying to save their lives.

She looked back at their clasped hands. Without thought, she lifted them to her cheek and touched his hand to her. The heat flowed into her cheek and she smiled. There was more here than met the eye. That's when she saw him staring at her.

" 'Tis something wondrous, ye think?" she asked him. She had no explanation for it.

"I feel it, too, Caitlin. It's like a pulsing whenever we touch that races through my body and mind. It's not as strong as the first time but I think that's because we already expect it."

He now lifted their hands toward him and as she held her breath, he placed his lips on her hand. She waited to see what he'd do next and he didn't disappoint. One by one, he placed a light kiss on each of her fingers and then he turned their hands and kissed the inside of her wrist.

Never had she felt anything to compare with this. Her hand, her wrist, her body ached for more. When she finally took in a breath, she found herself panting. He pulled her closer and brought her lips to his. First just a gentle touch, almost too light to feel, then he pressed a bit more and she lost the ability to think.

His tongue crept out to lick her lips and after a few strokes of his, she met it with her own. She pulled back a bit, startled by this unusual kiss, but he followed and soon their lips were touching again. He pressed against hers, rubbing them and licking, angling his face to get even closer to her mouth. She closed her eyes and remained completely still, not yet daring to breathe.

Then he stilled and slowly pulled away from her, releasing his hold on her hand. She waited, hoping she'd not done something wrong to stop him. She shivered, in anticipation of something she didn't understand, in the loss of his heat and in being deprived of the wondrous feelings his touched caused in her.

"Caitlin, I should not have kissed you. You offered me comfort and I took advantage of it. I am sorry."

He'd said the words so quietly, so sincerely, she found herself ready to cry. Another part of her wanted to take his face in her hands and drag him back into the kiss he interrupted.

"Come," he stood and again offered her his hand. She took it and felt the connection between them reestablished. "Your parents will be waiting for you."

They walked in silence to the doorway. He'd opened the door for her and she was about to enter when he paused.

"Good evening to you, Craig," he called out.

The rustle and crunch of leaves and the loud frustrated moan told her he'd been correct—Craig had been watching them. He must have seen them together and watched them kiss.

Caitlin knew that this would not go unremarked by either her parents or by Craig. She wondered as they entered the cottage which would be the easier to endure.

Chapter 11

"MIND YER STEPS, lad."

Douglas stumbled once more on the uneven surface beneath his feet. If he would keep his eyes in the same direction his body was heading, he'd probably not trip again. But the sights and sounds surrounding him were too fantastic to ignore.

A castle! This was a real working medieval castle, complete with a huge outer bailey, keep wall and a multi-storied keep. There were warriors on the battlements keeping watch from on high. When they entered through the gates, he could hear the yells and bellows of the men in the training yards. Smoke rose from the top of the back of the keep, from a building somewhat separate in one corner. The kitchens from the smell of it.

He'd tried to follow Moira and Caitlin without drawing attention to himself but he failed. His own gaping was met with the same from the countless villagers who were within the castle compound. Douglas again tugged on the waist and belt of the plaid he wore to make sure he still wore it. Activities around him ceased as he passed.

Douglas nodded politely if he made eye contact with

anyone. Again and again he heard "MacKendimen" whispered as he passed. His father's looks clearly marked him as one of them.

"We are here, Douglas." Caitlin's voice cut through his musings. Moira knocked on the door and opened it when told to enter. Douglas followed both women into the room.

The solar. As in the descriptions, large windows sat high in the walls, allowing the day's brightest sunlight to flood in. Large and small looms sat to one side of the room, where the sunbeams were the strongest. A few wooden chairs and tables were scattered throughout with a particularly attention-grabbing arrangement in one corner. The intricately decorated and carved chairs were larger than life and fit for a . . . king?

The man seated in the larger of the two held himself as though he were royalty. His proud bearing was matched by the woman seated to his left. Their appearance and coloring was as different as night and day. He was tall, Douglas could tell, even though he was seated and his blue eyes were all that linked him to the Clan MacKendimen. She was smaller, barely reaching his shoulders as she sat, with hair that showed little tendency to gray from its brilliant auburn and red shades. Green eyes followed his progress across the room.

Robert Mathieson and Anice MacNab, the laird and lady MacKendimen, earl and countess of Dunnedin.

Caitlin had been trying to tell him their story as they walked to the keep but he'd been so caught up in scenery around him he'd not listened as closely as he should have. There was clearly more to know about how the laird and chieftain of the clan bore another man's name. It certainly wasn't the normal way of inheritance as he knew it.

"Robert. Anice. Good day to ye both. May ye ken Douglas MacKendimen, a clansman visiting us for a bit," Moira began and he looked from one to the other, meeting their curious gazes. Anice's face suddenly drained of all color. Robert, obviously paying attention to his wife's every move, turned at the sound of distress she uttered.

"Sandy? How can it be ye?" Anice's pained whisper was
the only warning before she fainted.

Douglas stepped forward to help but Moira and Caitlin
and Robert were there before he could move. Robert's
quick action saved Anice from landing facedown in the
rushes. Her faint was brief and soon her eyelashes were
fluttering open.

"Here, now," he said as he walked around the others to
her side. "Put your head down near your knees," he put his
hand on the back of her head and guided it down toward
her lap. "This will make you feel less faint." She didn't
fight his hold. "Breathe slowly now, in and out slowly." He
repeated it over and over until he could hear her breathing
reach a normal pace. Douglas released her head and stepped
back in front of them.

"Anice, ye did that on the day of our first meeting and
my good looks werena the cause of yer faint that day, either." Robert smiled at his wife and she tried to return it
but the terror in her eyes prevented it. "Ye resemble my
wife's first husband, my half brother, Alesander Mac-
Kendimen, God rest his blackened soul. Are ye his bastard?"

Douglas choked on his answer. Insult was not meant by
Robert's question. Bastards were common in medieval
times.

"He does resemble his faither but 'twas no' Sandy. His
parents are Alex and Maggie MacKendimen." Moira's
voice took on that mesmerizing tone, the one you could not
ignore.

Anice looked once more as though she would faint. But
she didn't. " 'Tis true? You are Alex's son?" At Douglas's
nod, she called out, "Everyone leave, please. The laird and
I would like privacy to greet our kinsman. Jean, see that
no one comes in until I give you leave to open the door."

Anice's women and maidservants picked up their sewing
and embroidery and, taking as much time as they could,

made their way out of the room. In a few minutes only
Douglas, Moira and Caitlin remained with the laird and
lady.

"So," Anice demanded, color and spunk returned, "you
are the son of Alex MacKendimen and Maggie Hobbs?"

"I am. Did you know my parents?" So this was a fake.
How could she know his parents and be from long-ago
Scotland? He ignored the little nagging voice in his mind
that said there was a way.

"Aye, I did. They were here in Dunnedin for some
months in about twenty years ago."

"Anice, they were the visitors of whom ye spoke? The
ones . . . ?" Robert's words trailed off as he turned to face
Douglas.

"The visitors who came through the arch. Aye, Robert,
they were. And they returned to their own time through the
arch as weel." Moira explained as though traveling through
time was the same as walking down a road.

"Mam? Can this be?" Caitlin now looked as pale as Anice. Douglas stepped to her side and grasped her arm, brac-
ing her with his. She looked at him, her eyes wild with
confusion and . . . He thought for a moment he saw disappointment, too.

"This must stay between only those in this room. Robert,
for the good of the clan we maun never tell this to outsid-
ers." Moira looked one to the next, at the laird's nod, each
one in the room also agreed. "Douglas has come back to
us the same way his parents did—through the archway by
the power of the Fates."

"But why, Mam?"

"I hiv never questioned the Fates's reasons and neither
should ye, lass. He is here and will stay as long as the Fates
allow."

"But, I thought . . . he was . . . ," Caitlin's voice came to
a choking halt. Douglas's own throat tightened at her obvious distress. He tried to speak, but it took a few tries
before the words would come out.

"Do you know why I'm here, Moira? For how long?"

"Nay, lad, I dinna ken. But while yer here, I may call on yer healing skills to aid the clan. With yer permission, of course, Robert."

"Ye are a healer, then?" Robert directed the question to him, the man's piercing gaze from those unusual catlike eyes was on him, assessing his every movement.

"Yes, I'm trained as a physician and surgeon," Douglas answered.

"Then the Clan MacKendimen would welcome yer services for as long as ye are here."

Douglas nodded at Robert in acceptance. Caitlin turned and pulled from his grasp. Her face was white and her eyes looked huge in her pale face.

"As long as yer here?" She shook her head in denial and part of him understood. He'd believed from the dreams and then when he first saw her that they were meant to be together. But Moira's words implied this was a temporary stay. He apparently had a chance to return home, to his time and to all that was familiar to him.

He watched as she took one step and then halted and looked at Moira again.

"Mam?"

" 'Tis as 'twas meant to be, lass. Ye ken?"

And with a cry, Caitlin ran from the room. Douglas felt as though a rock sat at the pit of his stomach. He should follow her, but what could he say? I didn't know if I could go back or not and I'm happy to find I can return to my time? Whatever we thought was between was our imagination? I didn't feel the pull between us and the power every time we touched? Somehow he knew that a part of each one of those excuses was a lie.

Three years of those dreams, and for what? To make him long for this woman with every part of his being and then not be able to be together? To make him shun every woman he'd met since medical school and for what? Well, Moira might have faith in the Fates as she called this higher power but he wasn't so sure about his own belief in their scheme.

"I should follow her, Moira, she's very upset."

"Nay, Douglas, give her time. She will understaun more with each passing day."

"And will I understand, too?" He then took notice of the rapt attention being paid by the laird and his lady. They missed not a word of what was said.

"Moira, stay and talk with me," Anice began, rising from her seat. "I have more questions and I am sure that Robert does as well." Robert simply nodded.

Douglas turned away and strode toward the door. It opened with a crash as he reached for it.

"What the hell hiv ye done to her?" Craig roared out in anger. Without a moment of warning, he grabbed Douglas by the throat and pushed him up against the wall. "No one harms Caitlin wi'oot answering to me for it." The younger man tightened his grasp and shook him for effect.

Douglas struck from below with both fists to loosen Craig's stranglehold. He then applied his knee with some force to Craig's groin for an added bit of satisfaction. He was left gasping for air, but Craig lay groaning on the floor.

"Are ye two done with yer show?" Now it was Robert's voice that shook the rafters. "Get on yer feet, both of ye, and bring yerselves over here."

Douglas stood upright and took a few more deep breaths before answering Robert's call. He got there before Craig did and at least he could move without much pain. A smile found its way to his face. He'd been dying to strike out at Craig since he'd discovered that Craig's blow laid him out in the forest that night.

He had a feeling that Craig had watched for longer than he'd admitted to Caitlin or her parents. Douglas was sure that Craig had known he was no danger to Caitlin. He was also certain that it was Caitlin's recognition of him that sealed his fate. Craig wanted no competition for Caitlin's hand.

"Craig, what were ye thinking? Ye attack a guest in our home wi'oot cause?" Robert began.

"But, Caitlin . . . ," Craig stuttered. "He . . ." He pointed at Douglas and tried to speak.

"Caitlin haes a faither to stand guard over her, Craig. She is no' yers, ye hiv no claim to her." Robert walked over to the younger man and put his arm around his shoulders. "Let it be, Craig. She haes made her wishes known to me and yer maither, and to ye."

Craig looked around at the others in the room and slowly nodded his acceptance. Robert dropped his hold and Craig turned to Douglas.

"Ye hiv a care for her or ye will answer to me regardless of my lack of claim on her."

"I understand, Craig." Douglas answered and held out his hand. Craig looked from him to Robert and then to Anice and then he turned his glance away and walked out of the room without accepting Douglas's offer.

"He is young," Anice offered with a shrug of her shoulders.

"No' so young that he kens no better than to attack a guest in front of me. His temper gets the best of him even now." Robert turned to face him. "I offer ye my hand, Douglas, in welcome to our home and our clan. Ye are welcome to stay here in the keep wi' the other men while yer here. Moira, what say ye?"

" 'Tis a good arrangement since we hiv no room for him in the cottage. We can let it be known that he has a great interest in the healing arts and that he will visit the sick and injured with me if ye give yer leave for it."

"Douglas, since only a monk or holy brother would devote all of his time to healing others, ye may want to take some training with my men as weel? Do ye think this will be to yer satisfaction?"

What could he say? No, I don't want to sleep here in this filthy, cold, drafty castle when I could be in the same house with Caitlin? That he didn't need to train or work out since he wasn't staying here? That was what he wanted to say but common sense won out.

"Yes, laird, that's fine with me."

"Come later this day and I'll find you some quarters in the men's barracks. Now, Anice, attend me, for I hiv many questions to put to ye aboot things ye hiv left unsaid." Robert held out his arm and Anice placed hers on top without a moment's hesitation. Douglas stood aside to watch them pass. They were a fitting pair, and so deeply in love that anyone with eyes could see it.

"Come, lad, I will gather some supplies I need and we will be on our way now." Moira gathered her cloak around her shoulders and moved to the doorway.

"And Caitlin?" He couldn't just leave knowing how distraught she was and not knowing where to find her.

"She will be fine. There is still much we dinna ken and she will hiv to find her place in this as weel as ye. Now, come. There are many to be seen this morn."

He followed her into the main room of the castle and found a crowd in front of the door, all jostling for a better view of the goings-on in the solar. When found out, they all turned as one and tried to look busy. Unsuccessfully.

It was as they made their way out of the great hall and toward the stairs that he realized his newest problem—how could he treat or even diagnose patients without the tools of his trade? Without the technology he relied on to provide him with valuable information, how could he tell one affliction from another?

The Fates must surely be laughing at him now.

Chapter 12

THE FATES MUST surely be laughing at her now.

How could she ever forget she was the daughter of a blacksmith and a clan healer? Not someone that a trained physician from a big city would be interested in claiming. And now she finds out he isn't only a visitor to the clan, but a visitor to this time? Her mother had spoken of the arch's powers and of the other visitors before, but she'd not paid much heed to those stories. Travelers from her clan's future held no interest for her.

Other than Douglas, that is.

Caitlin dipped her cloth into the bucket and wrung out the excess water. Wiping her eyes and face, she tried to remove the evidence of how much she was interested in him. Somehow, the strength and frequency of the dreams had led her to believe that they were meant to be together. Just like the laird and Anice. They would overcome their differences and learn to trust and care for each other and the clan.

Together.

For the rest of their lives.

She sighed and laid the cloth over the edge of the well.

'Twas not meant to be, after all. Her mother had said as
much to Robert and Anice . . . and Douglas. And how his
eyes had lit when she said he was there for as long as the
Fates permitted. Caitlin wondered if he knew how much he
wanted to return to his home. It was clear in his eyes when
she looked at him and that's what caused her to lose control.

He didn't look disappointed that he would leave her
someday. No matter how she felt when he touched her,
when he kissed her, even when he spoke her name. The
ties between them must be in her own thoughts and not in
his.

Well, now that she knew how things would go, she
would learn as much as she could from his skills as a surgeon while he was with them.

Caitlin went inside and gathered up the sacks and jars of
herbs and medicaments that she and her mother had prepared for their visits today. She would find solace in her
work, as she had before Douglas arrived—and as she would
after he left.

She walked down the path toward the village. Her first
stop would be to look in on Iain's wife and new bairn. The
birthing had been a difficult one and Mildread had not yet
recovered her strength after the long labor and heavy bleeding. A new concoction promised to aid in her recovery and
Caitlin carried it now in her bags.

This was what she was meant to do, and Caitlin forgot
her worries about Douglas or questions about when and
where he came from in the face of her duties to the clan.

Much later that morning, Caitlin had finished visiting those
who needed her mother's healing herbs and potions and
went back to their cottage to prepare the noon meal. Instead
of her mother, she found Douglas rummaging through one
of her parents' trunks.

"Can I help ye find something in there?"

Douglas jumped at her voice and turned to face her, shoving that "something" behind his back.

"Oh, Caitlin, it's you. You startled me," he laughed nervously. "Your mother put my clothes in here and I was looking for them."

She moved closer and saw the pile he held in his hands. Those strange breeches in that fabric she'd never seen before. They were a dark blue heavy material and they had the most outrageous fastener at the waist. She'd caught but a glimpse before her mother folded them and put them aside. And his jacket—leather this color she'd seen, but again not made in the same way. No laces or buttons on it to hold it closed, just that strange row of tiny metal fastenings. There were other objects, but none was familiar to her.

"I wanted to check my watch to see if it worked," he began, holding out a metal bracelet before her. "It's stopped." He shook his head and stared at the strange object.

"What is a watch?" she asked, looking at the brightly colored bracelet. It had tiny numbers etched into its surface. She knew her numbers and letters and could read and write them, so she recognized them immediately. But what startled her was the flashing coming from the *watch*. In the dim light of her parents' room, it seemed to glow in front of her eyes.

"This is a timepiece, Caitlin. A clock I can wear on my wrist to tell time. It works in the light"—he turned his wrist toward the door of the chamber so she could see the etchings change—"or in the dark." Facing the wall, the etchings were again visible in the dark.

"You were wearing this when you . . . ?" Her voice betrayed her discomfort, shaking when she'd rather it be firm and smooth.

"Yes, I was wearing this when I found you in the forest," he purposely misinterpreted her words.

"So, you dinna hiv a clear understauning of this, either?"

She could feel her throat tighten and tears threatened in her eyes.

"No, I don't, Caitlin. As a matter of fact, I still find it very hard to believe at all." He put the pile down in the trunk, closed it and turned back to her. His face was so serious and she could see he wrestled with his own disbelief and uncertainty. It made her feel a bit better.

"Douglas, about this morn . . ." She was determined to take control over her own emotions. He was here and would stay for some amount of time. She could not walk around on the verge of crying the whole time. "I think the last days hiv worn heavily on me. I thought the dreams meant some-thing . . . something different from what it appears they meant. I'd accustomed myself to certain plans, certain feel-ings, and now I dinna ken what they mean."

He reached out and took her hand in his, entwining their fingers. That feeling was still there, fainter but still there.

"Before I passed under the archway, a wise woman in my time told me that you would save my life and I would save yours. Maybe the dreams were just to ensure that we would be there to do that?"

" 'Twould seem so." But the feelings went deeper than that, she was sure of it. If their task was finished, Douglas would be gone and this pull she felt with his every touch would cease.

"Caitlin, about this morning . . ." Now it was his turn to hesitate. "I did feel some relief, a great deal of relief ac-tually, with your mother's words. I live a different life in my time, a very different life from how I will or can live here. I found out very quickly in trailing your mother today that my skills as a physician depend more on the technol-ogy of my time than on my healing skills."

"*Tek-knoll-o-gee*? 'Tisn't the Gaelic?" She felt so stupid when he spoke in words she couldn't understand. Another demonstration of how different they were. She was a peas-ant in a village in the Highlands and he was a physician who knew wonderful things from another time, when they had objects such as watches to tell them what hour it was, in the light or dark.

"No, it isn't the Gaelic." He laughed, his deep voice came out in a rumble that she felt inside of her heart. "I didn't realize how much of what I do in treating my patients relies on the . . . gadgets or machines, some like this watch, and not on my ability to heal."

"Physicians in your time use these *gadgets* to heal?" Caitlin didn't understand this, either. You didn't heal people, they healed themselves. Healers helped by making the body stronger or by repairing damage whenever possible.

He sat down on the trunk, pulling her down next to him. She noticed that their fingers were still entwined and did nothing to loosen them. With her free hand, she pushed her long braid over her shoulder. His gaze followed her every movement.

"Physicians in my time rely on others to give them the signs and symptoms of disease and injury and spend little time with the person who is ill or ailing. We come, we treat, we leave."

"And who cares for them afore and after ye?" She was appalled at this. She and her mam would sometimes spend days when needed with one person. They watched for signs of improvement or worsening and changed their treatments accordingly. No one else told them how to care, or when not to care.

"Nurses and assistants. We reserve our skills for the procedures that only we perform." She saw a look cross his face, as though he suddenly recognized how pompous he sounded. Then a flash of pain before he controlled his expressions better. Pain? Regret? She wasn't certain which she saw in his eyes.

"What is it, Douglas? What pains ye so?" She couldn't stop the words from leaving her mouth. He shuddered and then looked into her eyes.

"I always wanted to be a doctor to take care of people and help them heal. I only just realized that I haven't done that." He hung his head and brought her hand to his mouth. Breathless and waiting to see if he would repeat his caress of her fingers with his lips and tongue, she waited and watched . . . and hoped.

"Caitlin? Douglas? Ye be here?"

Her mother's voice startled them. Douglas jumped up from his seat and dropped Caitlin's hand. She ran her hands through her hair, pushing the loosened tendrils back behind her ears.

"Aye, Mam, we are," she answered, walking toward the door of the chamber. "Douglas was looking for his clothing and belongings."

" 'Twould be a better idea to leave them here, Douglas. Ye will hiv no privacy at the keep."

"The keep?" she looked from her mother to Douglas. "Ye go to the keep?"

"After you left this morning, Robert suggested that I stay there in the men's barracks. It will draw less suspicion than if I stay here." Douglas turned to her mother. "I think you may be correct, Moira. I'll leave my things here with you."

"Robert has let it be known that Douglas is a distant cousin who is visiting and who haes an interest in the healing arts. He wants Douglas to train as weel with the men at the keep."

" 'Twould seem a good plan." So, he would be here but not? Other than passing in the village or at the keep, she would not see him?

"I hiv asked Douglas to teach us some of his healing ways while he is wi' us, Caitlin. Surely the clan can benefit from his knowledge."

"I was just telling Caitlin that I think you have more to show me than I you. But I will share what I can with you." Douglas nodded and smiled at her. So they would have time together after all.

"So, we will work together then, for the good of the clan?" she asked. Something felt very right and good about this plan. 'Twould work.

"Aye, daughter, as always, for the good of the clan."

Chapter 13

THE MAN AND horse were magnificent. Watching them work together as one, Douglas could detect none of the signals used. There! A slight press of the knee and the stallion reared on the hind legs and kicked out his front ones. Robert never moved in the saddle.

Douglas walked around to the other side of the yard to get a better view. Now two warriors charged from either side, bellowing out their war cries. The man and horse repeated the move to perfection. That horse would save a warrior's life in battle.

Robert shouted his satisfaction to the crowd and dismounted, talking to the horse, rubbing it, rewarding it for its performance. He called to one of the younger men to take it to the stables. Spying Douglas watching him, he motioned him closer.

"What do ye think of him?"

"He's as fine a piece of horseflesh as I've seen," Douglas admitted candidly. None he'd seen at the reenactments and fairs and shows came close to the form and size and lines on this one.

"That he is." Robert beamed like a proud papa. Douglas

smiled in return, understanding how much time and work went into the teamwork he'd just witnessed. "Douglas, hiv ye much training in fighting and weapons?"

"Some in both." He didn't want to overplay his expertise at either; some information was better held close.

"I would like ye to fight Brodie to give me some inkling of where and with whom to place ye while yer wi' us. Brodie!" He shouted and waved, bringing the attentions of a large, older warrior with red hair and beard. A wave of nervousness passed through him as the big man came nearer—maybe this wasn't a good idea after all. "Brodie, try him out on sword and quarter staff. I want to see his skills. Here now, Connor, bring Douglas that sword and staff." Robert gestured to a red-haired boy about twelve years old and with the gangly arms and legs that went with that age.

Connor ran to do his laird's bidding and Douglas climbed into the yard. The cool air rushing over his skin and under the kilt reminded him of how much he'd rather have a good pair of exercise pants on for this than the plaid he wore. He approached Brodie and was again struck by the size of him.

"Alex and Maggie's boy, ye say? Ye hiv their looks but do ye hiv yer faither's skill?" Brodie asked quietly so that only Douglas could hear. "Weel, then, let's give the staff a try first." Connor handed one of the weapons to each of them and Douglas watched his opponent's movements. " 'Twas a favorite of yer faither's, as I recall," he whispered.

Douglas was still thinking about the reference to his parents and didn't see the first blow coming. A second later he was looking up from the very hard ground, listening to the laughter and calls of the spectators. Standing up and dusting himself off, he laughed, too. He would not underestimate Brodie's quickness again.

The next blow caught him on the back and he stumbled forward, catching himself before landing facedown. He took a deep breath and regained his balance and allowed the years of practice to take over. He felt the energy flow through his body and his movements became strong and smooth. He blocked Brodie's blows and thrusts and delivered some of his own. A few minutes later, Robert called a halt to their mock battle.

He leaned over and rested his hands on his knees, trying to catch his breath. Standing up straight, Douglas pushed the hair out of his face and looked at Brodie. Damn, the man wasn't even winded! He stood quietly exchanging words with the laird. At Robert's wave, Connor approached again with swords.

Douglas took hold of the one he was given and shifted it in his hand, testing the weight and balance of the blade. Turning away from Brodie, he closed his eyes and practiced with it for a few moments. He allowed his strength to flow through his arm and into the sword. It was an excellent weapon, well-made and well-balanced.

"Are ye ready?" Brodie asked. Without waiting for his answer the warrior charged him, sword at the ready. Already on the defensive, Douglas deflected one blow after another. Brodie barely gave him time to react before he thrust again and again.

This didn't feel like practice. Brodie attacked with the fervor of a warrior in battle. Douglas's skills were nothing when faced with the ferocity of this experienced fighter. A few minutes and he found himself once more on the ground, this time with the sharpened point of a sword on this throat.

"Do ye yield?" Brodie stood above him, not even breathing heavily.

He could only nod in answer. Brodie lifted the sword away and extended his hand to Douglas. When he regained his feet, Douglas handed the sword off to young Connor who stood waiting.

"Ye handle the staff aboot the same as yer faither but yer sword fighting is much better than I remember his to be." Brodie pounded him on the back, driving what air there was in his lungs right back out. "Robert, I think he would do weel with Aindreas and his men. He needs work on the sword."

Robert nodded in agreement and motioned to one man standing off in the distance. As the man approached, Brodie said under his breath, "I hope to speak to ye privately aboot yer parents. Come to see me one night soon." And, after one more "pat" to Douglas's back, Brodie walked off with Robert.

The man called Aindreas shook his hand and told Douglas to meet with him and his company of MacKendimen soldiers after a short break. Aindreas appeared to be younger than Brodie but almost the same size with huge arms and a broad muscular chest. He knew he was in for a strenuous workout—probably more than his body had ever endured. But, he'd be here for just a short time . . . he could withstand it for that long. A quiet sound of distress distracted him from his fighting duties.

Caitlin.

How would she stand it? She knew not for how long he'd be with them but it would a torturous experience for her. When Caitlin saw him enter the yard with Brodie, her breath caught in her chest and she forgot to breathe. He was skilled; she remembered him bursting through the trees and throwing his daggers without hesitation. And he hit his target with ease even in the dark shadows and under the strain of the moment. Aye, skilled he was.

But, against a warrior of Brodie's brawn and experience? She thought not and his first stumbling made her wince for him. Then she watched him grasp and move the wooden staff. His hands became part of the rod; it became an extension of his body as he moved with it. He was concentrating so much she didn't think he'd seen Brodie's smile but she had. He'd ended that match on his feet.

The sword was different. She knew Brodie would not try to hurt him, this was only Robert's way to test his skills. However, she also knew that opponents could be injured very easily in these little exercises—she'd patched up the wounds more than once. Caitlin fought the urge to close her eyes until this match was over.

The murmured comments and then muted cheers around her forced her attention to the two men who now circled each other a few yards away from her. Caitlin stepped back into the group of people around her, fearing that her presence would distract Douglas. Most of the men were admiring his ability to keep Brodie on the move and most of the women were admiring his . . . legs!

She blushed as her gaze caught a glimpse or two of more of his legs than she thought to. Most of the men of her clan wore breeches or trews when they practiced, except for the old ones who always wore the plaid. There were, of course, benefits to watching men fight in both. She laughed as a woman said nearly the same thing right behind her.

She'd seen all of him when she and her mother were taking care of him but alive and fighting like this was definitely more attractive and more . . . stirring. Little tremors of jealousy pricked her as well as she listened to the women around her.

Would he take his pleasure with one of them while he was here? Many of them would enjoy a tumble with him and attach no more importance to it than scratching an itch. Now that he was to stay here in the keep at night, would his nights be filled doing what the other bachelors of the clan did?

She forced her eyes back to the field and to the two doing battle. The jealous feelings didn't feel very good. It was becoming obvious that she and Douglas weren't meant to be together—but could she watch him with other women?

Jealousy was soon pushed aside when Brodie shoved Douglas from one side and then stood over him with his sword poised at Douglas's neck. The sight of that long weapon against his skin brought forward too many memories of a night not long past—the MacArthurs and their damned long daggers on her own skin.

She shivered as the daylight disappeared and she was in the moonlight once more. The three of them had dragged her to their campsite while she was still unconscious and she'd woken to their filthy hands on her. The leader had kept his blade at her neck so that any movement caused another gash and more pain . . . and moaning. It was the moans that seemed to feed their desires and increase the pace of their assault. She fought to keep the sounds inside, she fought against the fear but she lost and the three continued to touch where they may.

Unable to move yet shivering vigorously, Caitlin moaned yet again in spite of her best efforts to contain it. She felt the hands around her wrists, and fought with all her might to loosen their grasp this time. Then she heard his voice.

"Caitlin? Caitlin, it's me, Douglas. Can you hear me?"

She blinked and felt the tears pour down her cheeks. She blinked rapidly and Douglas's face began to appear in front of her. Her body still shook with the terror of the memories.

He smoothed her hair from her face and using the edge of his plaid, he dried her tears. She could hear his voice but not the words, only the soothing sounds he made. When she could move her hands, she fumbled for her neck, certain that the cuts were bleeding again.

"No, Caitlin, you'll scratch yourself," he said as he managed to stop her from pulling her chemise loose. "Your neck is fine."

"The dagger . . . the point . . . it hurts. . . ."

"Shhhh, shhhh, Caitlin. It's over, love, they're gone. They cannot hurt you anymore."

She only knew that she was in his arms. He held her close and rocked her like a bairn as she cried. The warmth seeped into her and she tucked her head onto his chest accepting his comfort. When all the tears seemed spent, she raised her head to look at him.

His eyes were filled with concern and caring, watching her every move. She rubbed her eyes and then wiped her cheeks on his plaid. He loosened his hold enough to smooth her hair back from her face again.

"Ye maun think I'm a bairn wi' all this crying today."

"I think I know what just happened to you but I can't

figure out what caused it. You were remembering what happened in the woods, weren't you?" At her nod, he asked, "Do you remember what you saw before the feelings came back to you?"

"I was watching ye and Brodie and saw his sword at yer throat, nay, on yer skin." Another shiver ran its course through her body. "Then, I just remembered."

He wrapped her in his arms and vigorously rubbed her arms and back until the shuddering stopped.

"Come, I'll take you back to your home. I'm sure Moira has a potion to calm you a bit?" He stepped away and released his hold on her.

"Dinna ye hiv to follow Aindreas?" Caitlin looked around and found that most of the crowd had left. But, they had been there, they had seen her in Douglas's arms. Another deed would surely be brought to Craig's attention.

"I have some time to take you home first. Come on," he reached for her hand. "Let's go."

They walked in silence out past the keep and through the castle's gate. He never said a word until they'd almost reached the center of the village.

"I can explain what you experienced, Caitlin. I've seen it many times in my medical practice back home." His voice was quiet and serious, at odds with the wild look he carried after fighting with Brodie. His face was covered with dirt and sweat and his hair was clinging to his neck and face.

"I would prefer no' to speak of it right at this moment, Douglas. I am so embarrassed by what happened, and that 'twas in front of most of the clan."

"What happened to you is very common in people who have suffered a great trauma, Caitlin. This will happen again unless you talk about it."

"No' here, Douglas and no' now. Please?" She pulled her hand free of his. "The clan will already make more of this than is true."

And Craig would hear every word . . . the woman he desired for a wife sought comfort from a distant relative. No matter that her parents and Craig's knew the truth. Words would be spoken and tempers would flair and it promised to make this whole situation even worse.

"Make more of what? I am trained to comfort people when they are in need, Caitlin. That is not strange for a healer in this time, is it?"

A healer? He thought he was a healer? Right now he was being a pompous ass! So, the compassion and caring he'd shown was in the line of his duties? And nothing more? She looked him straight in the eye and his gaze never wavered. Caitlin was certain that she'd be able to tell he was lying but he gave no sign of meaning anything but what his words had said.

Finally feeling her spine strengthen, she turned to him. "Ye can go back to yer duties now, Douglas. I need to see my faither afore I return home. We are nearly there." She'd been so busy mooning and longing for him that she'd lost her backbone, her ability to survive alone. Well, 'twas returning at last and she had his words to thank for it.

He planned on returning to his time and home and apparently had no problems leaving her behind. He was already holding himself separate, apart from her. Well, she could do the same and then at least she'd have her heart intact when he did leave. Mayhap, it was not a bad plan after all?

Douglas looked as if he wanted to argue but recognized that her decision was final in this. "Fine, Caitlin. I'll return to the yard for practice. I will see you in the morning?"

"Why?" The word was out before she could stop it.

"Your mother has asked me to go with you tomorrow to visit the people you are tending. She said to come an hour past dawn." She nodded at him and watched as he trotted back up the path they'd walked.

So, if this plan to hold herself separate as he did was such a good one, why did she feel so sad?

Chapter 14

WOULD THIS DAY from hell never end?

Douglas turned once more on the lumpy, scratchy pile they'd called a mattress and repositioned his head on his arm. The day had started out on the wrong foot and he'd never regained his balance. His first mistake was in thinking that with his background and training he would fit in comfortably while he was here. That mind-set had sabotaged him every step of the way.

His introduction to the laird and lady went smoothly enough until Moira offered her opinion that he'd be there only for a short time. His experience, other than finally meeting Caitlin in the flesh, had not been a particularly good one up to that point. So naturally he was overjoyed to hear that he wouldn't be stuck here. Who wouldn't be?

The look on Caitlin's face would stay in his memory forever. For just a moment he could see her soul and he glimpsed despair, anger, and longing, and he sensed such a feeling of loss that he wanted to take back his words. And, stay. . . .

Then, when he sat next to her in her parents' chamber, he fought the urge to pull her into his arms and kiss that mouth that enchanted him so much. If he were leaving soon, it wouldn't be fair to take advantage of her in that way, in spite of the anticipation that the dreams had created in him. And, it appeared, in her as well.

The morning with Moira had also been a rude awakening, and a powerful blow to his ego. He watched in amazement as the uneducated healer ran circles around his abilities to diagnose and treat her people. Countless times he reached for a nonexistent blood pressure cuff or stethoscope or the pulse oximeter. And he lost count of the times he wanted to ask the attending nurse about vital signs or symptoms or blood counts.

Instead, Moira touched and prodded and questioned. She felt and listened and smelled to gain her information. He didn't know much about the herbs she used, but her explanations of what needed to be done for each person made a lot of sense to him. Her understanding of infection and fever and bodily functions amazed him. Oh, she called them by different terms, but she knew how to help a patient return to health.

And she said that Caitlin was both more knowledgeable about healing and about the herbal medicines that they used. Not a word was said about her supposed ability to heal with her touch. His skeptical side was glad not to have to argue about that.

Douglas turned again on the thin narrow pallet he called his own and tucked the length of plaid around him. The barracks room he shared with twenty other men was cold and damp. It didn't seem to bother any of the others—the chamber resonated with snores of different paces, volumes and tone levels. The others were quite content in their places of rest.

Just when it seemed that his ego would end the day as the only part of him bruised, Robert had asked him to meet Brodie on the field. His skills with the staff and sword were well-known in the MacKendimen clan—he'd won every contest and challenge he'd faced once he'd beaten his father. Alex had held the title of champion at the clan's festivals until ten years before when Douglas had wrested that honor from him.

All of that meant less than nothing when he was face-to-face, toe-to-toe with the red-haired warrior who intended to beat him into the ground. He didn't know how he held his ground for as long as he had, especially with the sword. And afterwards, he heard from some of the men that he'd far outlasted Brodie's previous challenger, and so he felt some measure of pride in his abilities.

That pride was wiped away in facing Caitlin again. It was obvious to him that she was experiencing post-traumatic shock syndrome. When he'd reached her next to the practice yard, she'd been hyperventilating and losing control. Her eyes moved wildly, watching a scene that no one else could see. She clawed at her neck, pulling at her blouse in sheer panic and terror. The cuts from the attack were not quite healed and he grabbed her by the wrists to stop her before she could injure herself.

He called to her and after a few tense moments, she recovered. Douglas offered to walk her home. He sensed that more had happened to her in the woods that night than she had revealed to anyone. Yet when he had tried to talk to her, she'd shut him out. He tried to recall his words, the ones he'd said just before she'd taken off in anger.

He'd been telling her that he was escorting her home because it was something he should do, as a physician and healer. He'd done it on purpose. She couldn't know how much she affected him. If he were to leave, he would not trifle with her feelings. It was best to keep himself a bit apart. In his mind he knew this was the best course. But his heart whispered something else.

And now his back and arms and legs were giving another message. Every muscle ached from head to toe. He'd put on a good show but he needed to sleep. Douglas barely made it through dinner and to dark before he fell onto this heap of grass in a sack. His overwhelming exhaustion was not enough to rid his mind of thoughts of her. He felt himself slipping away and she was the last thing on his mind. How could he ever go back to his own time after meeting her?

The sun rose at an ungodly hour here, he was sure of it. And he was just as sure that his eyes had never closed during the night. Except . . . Douglas did remember waking up and feeling very warm. Caitlin had come to him in the cave dream again and he woke from it hot and hard. It added to his level of discomfort and kept him tossing and turning even more than before.

Douglas rose from his bed, shook out the plaid he'd laid in all night and wrapped it around his body. He'd left the big shirt on overnight as some protection from the cold. After his boots were in place, he followed the other men outside to the place where they relieved themselves. A nearby well provided buckets of very cold water to wash, although he was the only one to do so.

He really needed a shower—a shower in water so hot that his skin would redden from the heat. And a good deodorant soap to use in it. And, his electric shaver. And, his water bed heated to just the right temperature and adjusted to just the right amount of support. And clean sheets, and . . .

The men were on the move again, this time toward the castle's great hall through a side entrance near the barracks. He followed along, exchanging brief comments with some of the men he'd worked with yesterday. On entering the large room, the smell of bread greeted him. His stomach rumbled in anticipation and he remembered being so tired the night before that he'd not eaten more than a few chunks of bread and cheese.

They lined up before one of the hearths in the room and were handed a stale piece of bread scooped out in the shape of a bowl. As they passed by the huge cauldron hanging in the hearth, one of the kitchen maids ladled steaming porridge into the bowl he carried. Sitting down with Aindreas's men, he found carved wooden spoons, wheels of some dark yellow cheese and loaves of bread on his table. After pouring water into a metal cup, he focused on replenishing his body's fuel. He knew he would need the fortification to spend the morning with Caitlin.

Douglas couldn't tell if she knew he was there. Caitlin stood in the center of the cottage, talking to herself. He heard names and then what sounded like the names of old herbs. She gathered each named item together in the center of the large table. Some were in jars or small clay pots, some in leather flasks and some hung in bunches over her head from the large drying rack above the table.

"Do you always talk to yourself?"

She whirled around at his words, startled out of her concentration. A look of confusion was replaced by one of recognition. "Oh, Douglas, 'tis ye." He nodded a greeting to her from his place by the door.

"Your mother said I should join you this morning. She said you could teach me more about the herbs you use than she can." He walked into the room and approached her by the table.

"Did ye believe her?" Caitlin's eyes sparkled this morning and he drank in the sight of them. And of her. Morning absolutely suited her. She looked alive and full of energy. Her hair was still free and hung down her back, moving in waves with every step or turn she took.

"Of course I did. She wouldn't lie to me, would she?"

"Mayhap it was her way of getting free of ye today?" She laughed and turned back to the table, gathering some small bowls close to her. " 'Tis sorry I am for saying that, Douglas. Mam had to visit some of the elder women of the village who wouldna take kindly to a stranger or a man tending to them. So, she left ye wi' me for this morning."

Her good mood was catchy and he sensed that she was teasing him in part, too. "So, in other words, your mother was so appalled by my lack of skill yesterday that she went on her own today?" He raised his eyebrows at her, daring her to lie about it.

"I think ye ken the way of it, Douglas. Mam said she'd never seen a man so helpless before. She said that my da has spoiled her all these years." She brushed some loose hair over her shoulders and laughed in his face. He knew he was frowning. He didn't think he'd been *that* bad.

"That bad?" he mumbled, now truly insulted. Well, today was another day and he had a chance now to work with Caitlin. Maybe he could work better with her than with her mother.

"Weel, come and tend me as I prepare the things I need for this morn. I'll show ye how I work, and 'tis different than Mam's way." She gestured him closer and he then noticed the pieces of parchment on the table near her collection of ingredients.

"What are those?" he asked, pointing to the pile of papers.

"I write down my recipes so I can change them as need be. My mam is much better at remembering wi'oot help but I canna keep in my mind the adjustments I make for each person as one of my brews works or doesna. So"—she lifted a piece toward him—"I mark all the ingredients and how much I use and if it helps."

He looked at her through new eyes now. She was a scientist but didn't know it. It was remarkable that a peasant girl in this time would have been taught to write at all and here she was keeping lists of her concoctions by ingredients and strength. A medieval pharmacist hidden away here in the little village of Dunnedin.

"Is something the matter? Ye are looking at me strangely."

"This is incredible, Caitlin. When your mother told me you knew your letters and numbers, I had no idea that you used that knowledge for something like this." He smiled at her, so very proud of her accomplishment. "Now, can you tell me about the herbs you'll use today?"

The next hour passed quickly as she described to him each of the mixtures she'd use and their actions when administered. He was appalled by his lack of knowledge about medicinal uses for herbs. And, in concentrating so much on what she knew, he forgot his resolve not to get involved with her.

Chapter 15

ALL OF THE crying the day before must have lightened her spirit, for she woke from a deep sleep feeling refreshed and ready for a new day. Or her mam had done what Douglas had suggested—given her something to calm her down after her two outbursts. Valerian root added to her tea would have been her first choice as it was probably her mother's.

Well, no matter, she felt much more herself this morn and she was honest enough to admit that she looked forward to spending time with Douglas. Her mother had told her of his behavior while visiting the ill yesterday. She wouldn't have thought that the self-assured man would hesitate in any situation.

And now he was here with her, listening intently as she spoke with Mildread about the woman's condition.

"And the bleeding, Mildread, has it slowed yet?" she asked as she slipped her hands under the covers and pressed against Mildread's stomach, feeling for her womb. Good, it was nice and firm and even smaller than the day afore. The healing was progressing well.

The young woman stammered and looked at Douglas and then at Caitlin. "Aye, Caitlin, 'tis lessened."

Caitlin placed her palm on Mildread's face, feeling her cheeks or forehead for signs of fever. None were present. This was good. Mildread appeared to be gaining strength with each passing day, and her babe, too.

"Yer color is much better and the fever is gone." At Mildread's hopeful look, Caitlin continued, "I still want ye to have Iain's sister here during the day. Ye are no' ready to take care of the other children and yerself. Give it another day or two?"

"Aye, Caitlin, I will do as ye say."

Caitlin stood and tucked the heavy plaid around the woman on the pallet. "Hiv Iain speak to me if he haes any problems about this."

" 'Tisn't Iain," Mildread whispered, " 'tis his maither making trouble. She said she never spent a day abed after birthing her ten bairns and that I am just being lazy." Tears filled her eyes and Caitlin watched as she struggled to control them.

"Now, now, Mildread. Dinna greet. Let me tell ye some things I've learned aboot giving birth."

"But, Caitlin, ye've never given birth!"

"That doesna mean I can't see wi' my own two eyes, does it, now? Some women, like yer mother by marriage, are like broodmares—they carry and birth wi'oot ever stopping to take notice." Caitlin laughed with Mildread. "Some women must struggle their way through the carrying and must fight to give birth to healthy bairns—like you, Mildread."

Caitlin leaned closer and smoothed the younger woman's hair back from her face. "Now, ye hiv a big healthy lad to bring ye and Iain much joy after losing the last three too soon. Take a day or two more and let me be assured that ye hiv healed." She stood now and gathered her supplies into her satchel. She turned and saw that Douglas still stood near the door, in the same spot since they'd entered.

She reached the door and almost shouted to Mildread. "Another day on yer pallet and then another in a chair by the fire. And do nothing more than feed little Colin. Ye hear?"

Mildread smiled in return. Iain's sister was listening to every word from the other part of the room.

"And," Caitlin whispered, "if Iain's maither haes questions, I'll send my da to answer them for her."

Then, she guided Douglas out of the cottage and onto the main path through this side of the village before she burst out in laughter. She thought she'd better explain to Douglas since he was looking at her as if she had grown another head.

"The only man in the village who Iain's mother fears is my faither," she explained. "They had a run-in aboot my maither some years ago and Da won. She does everything in her power to avoid him now. I kenned I could just use his name to put some of that fear back into her now."

"Mildread has lost three babies?" Douglas looked sad as he asked. "How?"

"How? Weel, the first time 'twas too early in her carrying to tell what happened. The second time, she started bleeding some months before the bairn was due and then the birthing started. That little one wasna ready to live." Caitlin remembered the poor wee babe in her mother's hands, not even able to draw a breath. "The third made it to the birthing but never took a breath. And then we nearly lost Mildread from the bleeding."

"So, this time seems to have worked? How did you do it?"

Caitlin smiled, enjoying a moment of satisfaction at this birth. The clan had suffered when the plague had moved through, killing many, leaving no family untouched. Every birth was important, Robert had said, in directing her and her mother to help in any way they could. He sent Moira to the monastery north of Dunnedin to trade with the monks for the healing herbs that she needed. His constant support had even forced some of the more rigid in the clan to accept some changes in how things were done.

"What did I use to treat her?" At his nod, she smiled.
"Weel, first I made sure as her time approached that she
dinna overwork herself. Since the birth, I've been brewing
her a tea with daisy for the fever, and lady's-mantle and
shepherd's bag to control the bleeding."

"And it's worked?" His face was full of confusion.

"Aye, 'twould seem so. I still want to watch her a bit
more since she haes shown this tendency to bleeding."

"That sounds reasonable."

"I thought ye would hiv examined her wi' me." She had
expected him to but he stayed away and watched from the
door.

"Mildread seemed too nervous for me to come any
closer."

She took him by the arm and pulled him down another
path. "Come, Douglas, I hiv someone who willna seem so
nervous to ye. I would value yer opinion of how to treat
him."

The rest of the morning went by quickly and it was soon
time for the noon meal. Caitlin and Douglas walked back
to her cottage silently. Caitlin thought about how the morning had gone after their visit to Mildread.

It had been a normal day, most of those she treated were
for minor injuries and wounds, a few with fevers, some
with digestion problems and coughs. She'd dispensed her
herbs and ointments as she always had, but this was different. Douglas was a quiet observer. Only once or twice
had he approached the one she was examining and asked
questions or felt for himself.

She could feel some tension growing within him. He
asked fewer questions as the morning moved on and now
simply walked at her side. Caitlin tried to imagine how he
must feel—being pulled from his world where he was important and knew so much and coming here. He was unknown here, and without any of the tools of his trade to

help him do his work. She could only imagine how confusing it must be for him.

"Douglas, ye are so quiet. Are ye unweel?"

"No, Caitlin, I'm fine. I am just so overwhelmed by what I've seen. You've not had any medical training at all?" He frowned at her as he asked.

"Nay, Douglas. Only men are invited to the universities or monasteries to study. All that I know I've learned from my maither and from my own studying of what we do."

"I don't think you have any idea of how incredible that is to me, Caitlin," he took her hand in his as he spoke. "You showed me more about taking care of people today than I've seen in my last five years at a major hospital. And without a bit of the training or schooling that I've had."

"Och, Douglas, ye will find yer way here. Ye just need to watch a bit longer and then ye will be able to do as we do. Ye are a physician after all. Ye probably ken more than I ever will, ye hiv probably saved more lives than will ever be entrusted to my care. Dinna demean yer own skills and talents in yer confusion."

He raised their hands and brought them close to his mouth. Gripping hers more tightly, he pressed his lips to it. "Thank you, Caitlin, for your kind words."

She waited for more—his eyes said there was more to say—but the words never passed by his lips. He released her hand and stepped away from her side.

"I must meet with Robert before working out with Aindreas and the men this afternoon. Excuse me?"

"Aye then, Douglas, I willna keep ye any longer."

She watched as he turned away and almost ran up the path to the castle. But, before he could leave, she'd caught a glimpse of something unexpected in his eyes. Regret. What did he have to feel regretful for, she wondered.

The mornings were growing colder as the month came near its end; the trees had shed their leaves and prepared for the coming winter. Caitlin and her mother had finally finished drying and grinding the rest of the late bloomers from the last of their garden patches. The ground would lay fallow until the spring brought it back to life once more.

Their days began to follow the same pattern and one week turned into two and then into three. Douglas worked with her in the morning and then left for the castle to train and eat and sleep. Although she'd heard a few comments from the single women in the village about his time in the keep, she never saw him once he left at the noon meal. After that first day, Robert had granted him his own small chamber as befitted a visitor so he no longer slept in the men's barracks.

He observed her, asked questions and even wrote down a few notes on some parchment about the recipes she used. Somehow, though, she sensed that a large part of his drive and passion was missing. He'd decided that he wasn't staying, so why get involved? She could see the struggle in his eyes whenever they approached someone in need. A wall was brought down and he stood on the other side—politely watching and politely asking questions but not caring.

She knew something would happen to shake his resolve and let the real Douglas MacKendimen come through, the one she saw from time to time when he didn't know she watched him. And, in that last week of October, a young girl started his wall crumbling.

She and Douglas were talking about one of his training exercises when they heard the screams. Douglas froze for a moment and then pulled his *sgian-dubh* and ran in the direction of the cries. Caitlin followed right behind him. Instead of an attack, they found a crowd of villagers surrounding a lone woman and child.

The mother clutched the girl close to her, leaned her head back and wailed her pain into the air. The sound of it brought chills to her but Caitlin ran to the woman and peeled the child from her arms. She could see no sign of injury, no wounds to explain what had occurred.

"Tell me, Bonnie, what haes happened here? What is the

matter with Rose?" Caitlin continued to look but could see no breath in the little girl's body and could feel no heartbeat in the places that Douglas had shown her. "Now, Bonnie, afore 'tis too late."

" 'Tis too late. Och, God haes taken the puir wee lass! Oh, Caitlin," Bonnie screamed again and fainted. Caitlin was about to help carry the body into their home when Douglas took the child from her.

"You there—tell me what happened?" His tone said he would brook no delays.

"She was eating and fell backwards. She fought for a bit and then stopped," one of the women offered.

Douglas opened the girl's mouth and peered inside. Shaking his head and muttering to himself he then wrapped his fingers around the child's upper arm and counted. After a few moments, he shouted again. "When? When did this happen?" He crawled to one side of the girl and turned her head to one side.

"A short time ago. Ye were but at the edge of the lane when it happened." The same woman answered again but others nodded in agreement with her answer.

"Caitlin, turn her head to one side and hold her." She moved to do his bidding and gently cradled the girl's head in her hands. Then she sat back and watched as Douglas finally used his physician's skills.

He started by placing one hand on the girl's stomach and pressing in and up with each stroke. He repeated it but apparently didn't get the result he wanted for he then turned the lass over and pounded on her back. Unsuccessful, he looked in her mouth again, then laid her back down and tried with the pushes on her belly once more.

To Caitlin's surprise, a wad of half-chewed food came shooting out of the child's mouth. Douglas didn't hesitate; he moved once more to her side and placed his ear near Rose's mouth and nose. He shook his head and she heard him whisper, "No breathing, no pulse."

He tilted the girl's head back and breathed into her! She

met the shocked stares of those around her but could not say a word. After two puffs of air, he placed his large hand on her chest and pushed again, but this time the movements were straight downward and rhythmic. Douglas went back and forth between breathing into the girl and pushing on her chest for a few moments.

Caitlin looked around and saw that Bonnie had been revived and was watching everything Douglas did. Suddenly Rose choked and sputtered and drew in a breath on her own. Bonnie screamed again and tried to get closer but Caitlin waved her off. Two others held her back while Douglas finished checking the little one over again. Then he stepped back and let the terrified mother hold her now-screaming child.

"She will be very sore where I placed my hands, Bonnie. Caitlin can give you something for any bruises and her pain."

She looked at Douglas and felt the tears pouring down her own face and onto the ground. He had breathed life back into that child! Her gift paled in comparison to this—regardless that her gift was becoming stronger, she had never been able to restore life as he had. She covered her face and sobbed at the wonder of this.

He pulled her from the ground and wrapped his arms around her as she wept. This must be one of the ways he knew from his own time and place. Did all physicians do this? Or was his skill better than others in his time?

"Douglas, ye gave life back to her. 'Tis more wondrous than my gift." She rubbed her eyes to clear away the tears.

"No, Caitlin, you don't understand. It's something anyone can do . . . ," he started to explain, and then looked around to see if they were alone. "Anyone can do that in my time. We even train schoolchildren to do it."

"But she was dead and you gave her life." She stared at him as he tried to deny the astonishing act he'd performed. He was shaking his head at her again.

"She was not dead, Caitlin. Her heart had just stopped and I helped it beat again."

She was confused. When the heart did not beat, you died. What kind of place and time did he live in that children were taught to make the heart beat again? After weeks of feeling his respect she now felt very humbled again before him.

"Come, I'll take you home and try to explain it to you. When you're calm you will understand."

She walked with him through the village and back to her mother's cottage. She could not think clearly because of what she had seen. Then she remembered the first time her parents had witnessed her using her gift to heal someone. She was sure she now wore the same expression and felt the same turmoil inside.

She could heal with her touch but he had the power of life and death in his hands. Something very important had happened and she didn't know yet what the impact would be on both of their lives.

Chapter 16

DOUGLAS LAY ON his back, squinting up at the sun. The sun didn't come out much here in the fall, but of course it would decide to burst through the thick clouds at the very moment his back hit the ground. Between the sweat and dirt and now the sun's light in his eyes, he really couldn't tell who stood over him and whether or not a weapon was drawn. Now spots appeared before his eyes and he tried to draw a breath into his bruised chest.

Pushing his hair back from his face, Douglas attempted to lift his head without much success. Aindreas would surely strike the death blow now. He closed his eyes and waited.

" 'Tis no' the time for a nap now, Douglas. Only bairns and the eldren hiv the time for sleeping."

It was Aindreas.

The man had turned into a monster today in the training yard, demanding more than he thought he had to give. Normally, Douglas would spar with a few of the younger soldiers, have a round or two against Aindreas and his second-in-command with his sword or quarterstaff and be done. Not so today.

As soon as he had warmed up with the sword, Aindreas was on the attack. Blow after blow rained down on him, forcing him to defend himself vigorously. He blocked and blocked until his arms felt like huge anchors. Finally, as he stepped backwards to fend off another well-aimed and powerful strike, he tripped and went down hard onto the unforgiving ground.

"Ye insult me and my men wi' yer lack of effort." Aindreas reached down and offered a hand to him. He took it and was on his feet a second later.

"My lack of effort? I have been here every day working with you." Using his arm and the back of his hand, Douglas wiped the sweat from his forehead.

"Ye call this working? Ye parry and thrust like a man on a stage. Ye play at this and I will no' accept that from any MacKendimen, no' even a *visitor*."

Douglas heard the insult in the man's voice, in the way he said *visitor* as though he wanted to clear his mouth and spit it out. He picked up the dropped sword and swung it once more, never breaking eye contact with the warrior standing before him.

Aindreas was correct. He had been playing at this, at everything he did here. He was simply biding his time until he could return home. The problem was, of course, when that would happen. Other than that one cryptic comment, Moira never again mentioned it. Oh, he'd asked her countless times but she would give him that damned smile and say she knew nothing until the wisdom was shared with her—whatever the hell that meant.

He'd heard her speak of "the wisdom" with Caitlin. Others in the clan had also spoken of her way of "kenning the future," but he dismissed that the same way he'd dismissed Caitlin's claim of healing with her touch. These simple people just didn't understand how things truly worked, so they chose to believe in supernatural ways of knowing and doing things.

But until Aindreas spoke today, Douglas had not thought

about the repercussions of holding back. He did a disservice to the whole clan, himself included. The truth hurt and Douglas reeled at its sting, both to his pride and to his beliefs. He would have to think about this more. Maybe his approach was wrong.

"Go, now, Douglas," Aindreas said without anger. "Return to this field only when ye are truly ready to give yer all. The clan deserves nothing less."

Unable to answer the challenge, Douglas turned and handed his sword off to one of the boys who were there to assist with the weapons. At Aindreas's nod, Douglas walked off the field and headed for the castle's gate. Some time alone would be the best thing for him right now.

He found the archway completely by accident. After spending some hours by the lake, he came back toward the castle on a path that was different from the one he usually used. He noticed it when the sun's setting rays exposed it. The path was overgrown near the lake but opened a bit farther up. Now he approached the castle wall and it didn't look familiar.

But the feeling he experienced felt very familiar. A wave of anxiety raced through him and he heard the buzzing of insects around him. It was then that he saw her—Moira ducking through the bushes toward the wall near him. He waited for her to pass and then followed her silently.

For a moment when he found her in front of the arch, he was completely confused. Even though he knew it was Moira, he felt just as certain that Mairi now stood before him. He shook his head and it was clearly Moira once more.

She stood close enough to touch the arch but her hand never rested on the stones. With her head bowed, she reached out toward the opening of the arch and he heard only some mumbled words.

Then the unbelievable happened, right in front of him. Smoke began to pour through the arch. But there was no fire or torch to cause it. And, it came out and not through!

Moira raised her head and stared into the arch. Her head moved as though she was watching something in the arch. All he could see was the smoke and every few seconds a burst of light would escape from the stone gateway.

Douglas began to shake, severe tremors passed through him, but he could not look away. His mind refused to accept what his eyes saw. Recognizing panic for what it was, Douglas forced his breathing to slow down. He concentrated on inhaling and exhaling, counting to himself while his mind still reeled. Soon he was almost back in control. When he looked at the arch, it was dark and quiet once more, no smoke or lights visible at all.

"There will be but one more to pass through the archway, Douglas." Her voice cut through the darkness to him. She'd known he was there all along. "And nothing can happen until the day when the night reigns over the earth, when the sun is loosed for a few hours only. The full moon on the winter solstice will open the gateway through time again."

"Moira, I, ah . . ." Douglas stuttered, not really knowing what he should say or what he wanted to say. Going home was a stronger possibility now even if the way he found out was completely unbelievable.

"Ye must go now, Douglas. Caitlin needs ye."

"Caitlin? What's the matter with her?"

"She is at Iain's home. She needs ye now, Douglas, dinna delay."

He took a few steps toward the arch and realized she was gone. He tried to get his bearings and began to run toward the castle's gate. Passing it a few minutes later, he continued through the village until he found the place where Iain and Mildread lived. Stopping for a moment to try to catch his breath, Douglas was surprised when the door was opened for him by Iain.

"Please, Douglas help her. I ken what ye did for Bonnie's lass. Can ye help Mildread now?"

His stomach began to turn at those words. He stepped

into the cottage and saw Caitlin kneeling beside Mildread's pallet near the fire. With one look, he could tell that the young mother was dead. Her eyes were open but glazed and long past feeling. From the absolute whiteness of her skin and her recent traumatic childbirth experience, he guessed she'd bled to death.

He must have made a noise for Caitlin noticed him and ran to him. Taking his hand she pulled him to the fire.

"Come, Douglas," she whispered. "Ye must help her as ye did little Rose. Her heart has given up but I ken ye can make it beat once more."

Her desperation tore at him, he wanted to take her in his arms and sob along with her. But surprisingly, Caitlin was clear-eyed and completely confident that he could perform the miracle she asked.

"Caitlin, I cannot do what you ask. You don't understand, I can't make someone live again."

"Surely ye can, Douglas. I saw it happen. If ye would just make her heart beat again, I will try to heal the bleeding in her womb now."

He took her by the shoulders and forced her to look at him. She had such faith in him, and faith in her gifts, more than he ever had in himself. But she didn't understand—he did not have the power of life and death in his hands. Oh, he had cheated death a few times and brought patients back from death's door, but the final decision never lay in his hands.

What she had seen him do this morning was outside her experience and now she wanted him to repeat it. And Iain stood by waiting as well.

"Caitlin, sometimes if the heart has just stopped and the life is still there, I can start the beating again." She nodded and looked at Mildread's body and then back at him. "This is not one of those times. She is dead, Caitlin, and there's nothing I can do."

"If ye willna even try, then I will," she cried and pulled from his grasp. Kneeling next to the dead woman, she tilted

the head back and tried to blow into her mouth, the way
he had into Rose's. Because the position was wrong, it
didn't go in. Then she tried to perform the chest compres-
sions of CPR and was again unsuccessful.

Douglas's own heart ached for her. Caitlin had worked
so hard to keep Mildread alive and now couldn't face her
death. He knew the experience well but he knew his feelings about losing a patient were nowhere near as deep as
what Caitlin felt right now.

He stepped over behind her and wrapped his arms around
her, lifting her to her feet. He held her tighter as she struggled to get free of his hold.

"No, Caitlin, you cannot do anything else for her. She's
gone," he whispered fiercely into her ear. She stilled and
after a moment, she nodded.

"Ye can put me down now, Douglas. I maun prepare her
for burial."

"Isn't there someone else to do that, Caitlin?"

"And who would do it? I am her friend and will take
care of it."

He let her go slowly and watched as she approached Iain,
now with words of comfort. The two of them knelt down
and together they straightened Mildread's covers and closed
her eyelids over those sightless eyes.

Douglas waited nearby as Caitlin poured water from a
pitcher near the fire into a bowl and began to wash her
friend's body. A few minutes later, the task was done and
Caitlin was ready to leave. As they walked from the cottage, Caitlin stopped to speak to a small group that had
gathered outside waiting. He'd not even seen them when
he arrived but then he was thinking only about Caitlin.

"What will happen now?" he asked as they walked toward the edge of the village.

"Peigi has just given birth and can nurse the bairn for
now. Iain's sister will care for them while he is on duty."

"And what about you, Caitlin? Who will care for you?"
His words were a surprise to them both. She stopped and

looked at him. It had been a stupid thing to do. Why ask when you don't want to know the answer? Or if you already know and don't want to hear it? He would be gone in two months' time and that would end his involvement in her life. He should make as little a difference in it now as possible.

But, after today's examination of conscience by the lake, he had to admit that he wanted to care for her. He wanted to be the one she turned to in time of need. He wanted to love her.

"My maither and faither care for me, Douglas. And the clan, too. We pull together in times of need."

"And that's how you'll live? With your parents for the rest of your life?" He grabbed her hand and pulled her close to him. "Don't you want a husband and family?"

She looked at him with bright but vacant eyes; too much had happened today for her to focus on his questions. Her friend was dead. She had given Mildread not just a healer's care, she had given a part of herself trying to help the woman survive. And now that part of her was lost.

Douglas put his hands on each side of her face and smoothed her hair back away. He leaned down and kissed her forehead and then each cheek and, finally, he reached her lips. He didn't mean to push himself on her, he offered her only comfort. After barely touching his lips to hers, he drew back and let his hands drop to her waist.

"I am truly sorry about Mildread, Caitlin. I wish there were something I could have done for her." A tiny shiver of guilt walked down his spine. Was there something he could have done? In spite of being in a primitive time without any of his normal gear or technology, could he have helped if he hadn't been so hell-bent on staying out of it?

"Nay, Douglas, 'twas nothing for ye to do aboot her. I was just, weel, overwrought when I saw her and thought ye could help. 'Tis my fault she's dead now—ye need no' carry the guilt of her death."

She was serious—she believed she was responsible for

her friend's death. That's when he noticed that she was still completely calm, no tears in her eyes or on her cheeks.

"What do you mean?" He was worried about the way she was denying her grief in favor of guilt.

"I hivna followed Mildread as much as I promised her I would. I did hiv a new potion for her to try, but I dinna get it to her in time. And then, I waited too long to use my gift."

"No, Caitlin, you did not cause her death. You did all you could to save her. I've watched you these past weeks— you give all you have to the people you treat, more than any doctor or nurse I've ever seen." He pulled her closer until she rested her head on his chest. "The final decision is always in God's hands, not ours. We can do all we can but there is a limit to our abilities."

"Even yers?" she mumbled as she rubbed her head against him. It sent all kinds of sensations through him. And heat, too—definitely heat.

"Especially mine. I feel so very limited because my knowledge only works if I have the tools I use in my time. I haven't learned to heal the way you do—by touch and smell and listening. We use tests, Caitlin, to find out the problem. Then we use—"

"Yer gadgets and *tek-knoll-o-gee* to heal people?" She raised her eyes to him once more.

He chuckled at the way she finished his sentence and by what she'd remembered from their talk weeks before. "That's right, my gadgets and technology. We've . . . I've lost the true art of healing."

"But touching is so important in healing," she whispered. Her hands now slid from his chest up onto his shoulders, bringing them into closer contact.

"Yes," he stammered, knowing he was losing his train of thought because of her closeness. All he could think about was touching her. Visions from the dreams returned and he saw her in that pool, in that cave again. Naked, waiting to touch and be touched. His hands itched with the need to feel her, to rub them on her bare skin, to explore her body. His mouth watered when he thought about tasting her, licking her, drawing her breast in his mouth.

The heat rose between them, he could feel its power and by the look in her eyes, Caitlin could, too.

"Aye, Douglas, let me show you aboot touching." She reached up and pulled his face down to hers. He needed no more urging, his mouth covered hers and his lips rubbed against hers even as his hips did the same.

She opened to him and let his tongue sweep into her mouth. He touched and tasted and teased her tongue until she did the same to him. Barely a breath was taken as the kiss went on and on. As she pressed her belly to his, she took one of his hands and placed it on her breast. He opened his eyes in surprise. He was more startled when she spoke into his mouth.

"Touch me."

He did. His palm slid over one breast and he caught the already hardened nipple between two of his fingers and pulled it gently. He felt her gasp against his lips. He smoothed the nipple with his palm and then tugged again on it, loving every moan she made. She thrust herself into his hand more with every stroke. He moved his hand to the other breast and repeated and repeated the motion until she was panting against his mouth.

He was not unaffected. His erection rubbed against her hips through only the layer of plaid he wore. Waves of heat poured over him and he pulsed with desire for her. He wanted her so badly. Too many years of waiting and too many dreams of her to hold back now.

Dear God, what was he doing? Shuddering with the effort, he reined in his desires tightly and lifted his mouth from hers. She was seeking comfort and he was offering her passion. With everything else that had happened today, the last thing she needed was another burden to her conscience. And this, passion without love, would be a burden to her. He knew that for certain.

"Caitlin, let me see you home."

"No, Douglas, please. . . ." She clutched his shirt trying to hold on. He took hold of her hands and peeled her off himself. He needed some space and some air between them to cool his ardor.

"Please stop for a moment and hear me. I want you, I want you very much as you can probably tell." He paused and took a breath. "But if we continue and do what this will lead to now, we will be doing it for the wrong reasons."

"I understaun, Douglas, ye dinna want me. . . ." She started to pull away but he held her close.

"Now, stop right there, Caitlin. It's obvious you don't. If you understood, you'd know how much I want to tear off your clothes, lay you down with me and kiss and taste and feel you until we can't breathe. And how much I want to be inside you, so deep that I can feel the breaths you take, so deep that I'll be a part of you and you me. And I want to make you moan and scream while I'm there."

She looked at him with those green witch's eyes and he saw her swallow deeply. She was an innocent with no idea of what he wanted to do. Maybe now she had an inkling?

"But, Caitlin, when we do those things I want it to be for the right reason. Not in answer to a plea for comfort over losing your friend. I want you to know exactly why I'm kissing and touching you when it happens."

Her mouth, reddened from his kisses, just opened slightly. She was panting from his attentions and his words. Good. So was he.

"Now, let me see you home. Tomorrow promises to be a difficult day for both of us and you'll need your rest."

"Aye, Douglas, I fear ye hiv the right of it aboot tomorrow. Will ye hold my hand as we walk?"

He drew her close and put his arm around her shoulders. They walked without speaking the rest of the way. Douglas let the night's crisp air cool down his body and he was reasonably comfortable when they reached the cottage at the edge of the village.

As they approached, the door swung open and Pol stood in the doorway.

"So, ye found her?" His deep voice rumbled through the quiet night.

"Aye, Da, he did. Give me a moment." Pol stepped back inside but the door remained open. There was no sign of Moira. "Thank ye for bringing me home, Douglas, and for being wi' me when I needed ye to be."

He lifted his arm from around her and watched her step away. Before she could get far, he reached out and touched her cheek. She stopped and looked back at him . . . waiting. He didn't leave her waiting for long. Douglas leaned over and touched his mouth to hers. This time it was for comfort and lasted a few seconds.

"Try to sleep tonight. And I will be here in the morning. We have work to do." She walked silently into the cottage and the door closed behind her.

He turned and headed back the way they'd come. As he trotted back to the castle, he thought he'd feel tired but instead he felt very much awake. Sleep would be long in coming this night, that much he knew for certain.

Chapter 17

THE MORNING DAWNED dark and dreary, incredibly appropriate for the burial of Caitlin's friend. Storm clouds rolled through the sky and thunder rumbled in the distance. Douglas pulled a part of the plaid up over his head in anticipation of the downpour soon to come.

A small group of mourners gathered at the side of the hastily dug grave and were, but for a few quiets sobs, silent watchers. Caitlin was already there, as well as her parents, Robert and Anice, Iain and his family, and Craig. Douglas hadn't seen Craig since that first day at the keep and that was fine. He just didn't like him.

He liked him even less when he walked to Caitlin's side and put his arm around her shoulders. She allowed it and, as he watched, she moved closer to Craig. They whispered back and forth and Craig leaned down and kissed her on the cheek. They stayed in that embrace for the rest of the service.

Douglas felt very much the stranger this morning. He didn't want to intrude into the family's grief even though he found himself wanting to be at Caitlin's side. Every time he looked over, she and Craig were still together. The only ones who met his gaze were Pol and Moira. Each time Craig moved closer to Caitlin, he found them watching his reaction, as though they waited for him to do something.

He did nothing except mumble along with the prayers of the visiting priest. They were a curious mix of Gaelic and Latin, but some of them sounded somewhat familiar to him. Soon the prayers were over and Iain and some men laid Mildread's body in the grave and began to cover it with dirt. Caitlin was sobbing and turned into Craig's arms. He held her tightly and rocked slightly back and forth as he whispered to her.

The beating of his heart almost overwhelmed him once more. His fists clenched and released. His jaw did the same, causing his pulse to pound in his head, too. Seeing Caitlin in Craig's arms was not a comfortable thing. Well, he'd better not think much about it since Craig would most likely be doing more than just holding her after he left. Douglas had no claim to her affections, but his heart didn't want to hear that.

The last shovelful of dirt was added and a tarp pulled over the grave were the signals that the sky was waiting for—as it was placed lovingly by Iain and patted down, the clouds released the torrents, as they had been threatening to all morning. Douglas pulled the heavy woolen covering closer to him and stepped aside for the family to leave. He waited for Caitlin but she and her parents walked off in another direction. Craig had released Caitlin from another embrace and, without knowing how close to a violent end he was, followed Robert and Anice back toward the castle gate.

If Douglas was going to live these next few months as if he were staying forever, he had things to do before seeing Caitlin. And, since he didn't think they had such things as bereavement days in medieval Scotland, his first stop would be at the smithy's.

• • •

Ducking under the low edge of the roof, Douglas entered the smithy. The building looked like a small house with a portico extending off one side and that side was open to the elements. Hides, used to control air flow and temperature within the working area, were rolled up on each edge of the portico. In spite of the weather and the season, two blacksmiths were hard at work. Shaking off the water, he dropped the plaid onto his shoulders and looked around.

"I've come to speak with Pol," Douglas said, not recognizing either of the men. Then he heard someone enter from the other side.

"Ah, Douglas, here ye be," Pol said.

"I need to speak to you," Douglas started, looking from one man to the next.

"Weel, then, speak. But first, do ye ken my brother Ramsey and his eldest son Kenneth?" Pol introduced them as he pulled a heavy leather apron over his head and secured it behind and around his waist. After tying his long hair back out of his face, Pol picked up the tools of his trade.

Douglas nodded to each man and then turned to where Pol stood. "I need some tools but I have no money to pay for them."

All three men exchanged glances and then burst out in laughter. After a few moments of it, Pol looked at him.

"Ye are a learned mon, Douglas, and yet ye hiv no understauning of our clan. Tell me, will these tools be for the good of the clan?" He stood with his huge hands on his hips, legs spread wide.

"Yes, they will be," he said. The tools would help whoever the healer treated with them. He'd seen Caitlin struggle with simple surgical procedures that would have been made easier with the right tool.

"Weel then, tell me what ye hiv need of and we'll see if we canna get them for ye."

Douglas spent the next half hour describing to the blacksmiths what he had in mind and they surprised him in both their knowledge of design and cooperation. With some de-

cent scalpels, forceps and finer needles, Caitlin's and his
own work among the injured would be easier. Her skills so
far had impressed him and with a little guidance she would
be even better. More lives could be saved, or at least im-
proved.

After shaking hands with all three, Douglas pulled the
plaid back up on his head and turned to go.

"They've been friends since they were bairns," Pol said.

"I know that Mildread's death has hit Caitlin hard."

"Dinna misunderstaun my meaning. Craig and Caitlin
hiv grown up together."

So the cool, calm exterior he'd practiced for years was
neither cool nor calm. An interested father had read him
easily, through a heavy rain and darkened skies.

"And he wants her for a wife," Douglas answered. "I
know that also."

"That haes been settled, Douglas. She'll no' be a wife to
Craig. His parents ken and accept."

"But does he?" Douglas wasn't sure of the reason for
this. He knew that both Moira and Pol had studied him
throughout the burial. After seeing their embrace last night,
was Pol waiting for a declaration of some kind from him?

"Weel, the lad haes been hiving a bit of a hard time
accepting it so far. But, he will. For the good of the clan,
of course."

"Wouldn't Caitlin be good enough for him? Or do his
parents look higher for his bride?" Douglas knew the marriage customs of this time. As heir to the clan, Craig should
have a highborn wife, one that would bring wealth or land
or connections to him and to the MacKendimens.

"Robert and Anice are no' the ones looking higher for a
bride for him, nor Craig himself. There are others, elders
in the clan, who want alliances to come from the marriage
of the tanist. But after what Robert and Anice went through
with their own marriage, they would defend to the death
Craig's right to marry as he will."

Douglas started to ask a question but Pol's expression

stopped him. "Weel, lad, ye hiv things to do as do we," Pol looked pointedly at his brother and nephew, "And those tasks will no' get done on their own. Come to supper tonight and we can talk more."

Talk more? This was the most he'd heard Pol say in the month that he'd been there!

A rumble of thunder and flash of lightning caught his attention. Readjusting the plaid to cover more of his head, Douglas walked to the edge of the smithy.

"Thank you all for your help. Ramsey, Kenneth, it was good to meet you. Pol, I'll be there this evening."

He would spend the day with Caitlin. There were many things he could learn from her, and he intended to do just that.

She ruined the ointment for the third time. After measuring and grinding and mixing four different herbs together, she could still not remember whether she'd added more comfrey to the paste this time than she had the last. Frustrated by her inability to concentrate on the tasks before her, she put the bowl down with a huff.

Gathering her shawl up on her shoulders, she walked to the hearth and pushed the smaller cauldron of water over the flame. Mayhap a cup of tea would help her to focus on the tasks at hand, if she could remember how to brew one. A simple infusion of betony with honey would feel good against the chill of the day.

Finding the wooden box where the betony was stored, Caitlin chose a few stalks of it and crumbled them onto a porous cloth. Gathering its edges, she laid it over the side of a large earthen pitcher and waited for the water to boil. She stared into the flames and her thoughts drifted.

The last few days had been a trying time for her. Her feelings for Douglas were so confusing. She felt like she was being dragged up one side of a mountain and down the other. Before he came to her village, she knew her place in the clan and expected no more and no less than the kind of life her mother had—treating the sick and injured, having a husband and family, living among the clan.

Even though she had refused Craig's most recent offer of marriage, a part of her was accustomed to the idea of marrying him. He would not be faithful to her like her father was to her mother, but Craig would make a good husband and laird when the time came. She could continue her healing work and they would grow old helping their clan. A fitting life for the daughter of a healer and a blacksmith.

Then Douglas had crashed onto the scene and her life and heart had been turned upside down. She knew now that the dreams had set up some unrealistic expectations for her. She'd wanted to believe that she would meet the man, they would fall madly in love and be together. Instead, she and Douglas had spent most of their time denying the attraction between them and denying that their feeling ran deeper than just that of the flesh.

Oh, there was that. His kisses drugged her more than her mother's concoction of poppy juice and valerian root. She wanted them to go on and on. And his touch created such a heat in her. Memories of the night before and the waves of heat and magic his hands made when they touched and rubbed her breasts. She was sure that her breasts swelled as he held them in his palms. And tingled. Oh, they tingled more than in the dreams. She noticed the wetness and throbbing between her legs as they walked home. Just as in the dream.

She shook her head and realized she was watching the pot boil. Using the end of her skirt against the heat, Caitlin lifted the pot and filled the pitcher with steaming water. Soon the fragrant aroma of betony filled the cottage. As she watched the water swirl around in the pitcher, her thoughts turned back to Douglas.

She couldn't hold his desire to go home against him. After all, she would feel the same if this incredible thing had happened to her. To be separated from all you knew and loved had to be somewhat confusing. And the man was definitely confused.

She knew he must be skilled to be a doctor in his time yet he refused to use those skills now. Oh, he claimed not to have the right tools but she knew that was an excuse. Somewhere along the way he had lost his calling. He'd begun to rely on those gadgets and *tek-knoll-o-gee* instead of his instincts but his desire to heal was still there, buried deep.

Was that why he was here? To find his calling to heal again? And then he would leave, called back by the Fates the same way he'd arrived?

Sighing, she removed the cloth bag from the pitcher and poured a small amount of honey into the tea. Caitlin poured some of the steaming brew into a mug and held it in front of her, enjoying the smell of her favorite drink. Her thoughts always seemed clearer after betony, but what herb would help her heart after Douglas left?

Caitlin was certain of one thing—she and Douglas were linked somehow. They had saved each other's lives for some purpose. Was it only to restore his lost faith? She thought not. Her mother had not told her much but she knew her own part of this was yet to come. Maybe he had to believe in her gift, too? In something he could not see or explain even with his knowledge from the future?

Well, in her heart she also knew that she would not hold back her feelings from Douglas. She'd watched his inner struggles enough to know he cared, for her and for people in need of help. 'Twas only his uncertainty about changing things yet to come that held him back.

She would be there when the feelings became as clear to him as they already were to her. She would be there for whatever came. She would be there for him.

Chapter 18

"I NEVER THOUGHT you to be a lazy wench."

She gasped and then laughed when she finally saw him standing inside the cottage already. She'd been so lost in her thoughts, she'd never heard or seen him come in.

"I amna but this day is a bit different than most." She was determined not to cry anymore. She grieved for her friend but more tears would not help anyone. Finding a way to save the next woman from death after birthing her bairn would be a fitting remembrance of Mildread and her struggle.

He came to her where she sat at the worktable and took her hand, entwining their fingers in that way he always did. Blinking a few times to clear the tears that still threatened, she looked at him and smiled.

"Is there anything I can do for you? Anything I can say?"

"I am fine, Douglas, truly I am. I should be accustomed to death but I thought we had cheated it this time." He squeezed her hand and then let go, taking a seat opposite of her at the table.

"What are you drinking? It smells good." He inhaled a few times, testing the scent.

" 'Tis betony tea. Would you like some? I made a pitch-
erful and 'tis still hot." At his nod she took another mug
and filled it with the aromatic brew. "I added a bit of honey
for sweetness."

"Betony? Is that one of your herbs?" He sipped the tea
slowly as she watched.

"Aye. Did ye learn nothing of the healing abilities of
herbs and plants in yer training, Douglas? Hiv they been
forgotten in yer time?"

"I've had extensive coursework in pharmacology," he
started and then laughed. "You're frowning again. Pharmacology is the study of chemicals and drugs and how they
work in the body."

" 'Tis sorry I am that I canna understaun all of yer
words."

"Please don't worry about things like that. Herbs have
substances in them called chemicals. Unfortunately, I don't
think I've learned about many of yours."

He put the mug of tea down and took a small packet of
parchment out of his shirt pocket. Unfolding it carefully,
he reached for the pen she kept nearby. She moved the pot
of ink closer to him.

"Where did ye get that?" Caitlin nodded at the parchment. 'Twas hard to come by and not usually seen outside
the laird's study. Her own sheets had been a gift, protected
and carefully scraped clean and reused—not a fragment
was wasted.

"I asked Robert for it. He said to ask if I needed any
more." Douglas *couldn't* know how unusual his request or
the granting of it was. "Now, tell me about betony."

"Betony is excellent as tea," she started. "Mix half again
as much and steep it for twice as long and 'tis verra helpful
for headaches."

"Half again as much and for twice as long as what? How
do you keep track of how much to use?" He was frowning
now. Well, turnabout was fair play!

"I couldna resist the urge to tease ye, Douglas. Now ye

ken why I use my notes to record my recipes."

He laughed. "That is an excellent example to follow. I'm ready now—tell me all about betony."

"Mayhap I should tell you in a different way? If ye name an affliction, I can tell ye what we use for it."

"That would work, too. All right," Douglas looked pleased as he divided his parchment sheet into a grid of squares.

"Ye are no' planting a garden, Douglas."

"You just wait, Caitlin, you'll see. Now, start with fever." He was smiling and waiting, so she began.

"I use daisy or bogbean mostly, borage when we hiv it. They seem to be most effective against fevers when I dinna ken the cause." She looked up onto one of the shelves over the table for her supplies of those three.

"And how do you use them?" Douglas was scribbling across the parchment as she spoke.

"The leaves are steeped to drink for fever." She stood and walked to those shelves, looking for her own precious lists. Finding them, she sat down next to him so she could look over his shoulder. The writing on the page was nothing she'd seen before. The letters all looked like little square shapes, not flowing together at all. She looked up and found him staring at her.

"I can't write in Gaelic, I'm afraid. This is in English."

"English? Like the Sassenach use?" Her tone must have told of her Scottish dislike for anything English.

"Well, we call it that but it is nothing they use . . . yet." He laughed at her again and went on, "My medical colleagues tease me about this, too. Most scribble everything down and it's so tangled that it cannot be read. I started printing like this," he pointed to some of his words, "in block letters. I've done it now for so long that I'm pretty fast with it."

"If ye say so, Douglas." Although from the look of it on the parchment, she'd never be able to read his words.

"Now, what do ye want to speak of next?"

Before she knew it the morning was turned to noon. Her mother coming through the door was the first warning that so much time had passed. Almost all of Douglas's squares were filled in with his newly found knowledge of plants and herbs.

"Mam, I hivna started our meal yet." She jumped up to help her mother with the bags she carried. From the smell of it, at least one held food. Her mother removed the heavy cloak she wore and hung it by the door.

"No bother, lass, no bother. Yer da eats with his brother and I must go back out to the castle soon. There are freshly made bannocks in the sack and plenty of cheese in the cupboard."

Caitlin opened the sack and removed the oatcakes. She smiled at the aroma. She hadn't even thought about food all day; now her belly grumbled at the smell. Douglas retrieved their pitcher of tea, still warming on the hearth, poured a cup and handed it to her mother.

"I thank ye, Douglas. The tea will be welcome on such a day as this."

"Has the rain lessened at all, Mam?" Caitlin put a wheel of cheese, along with the oatcakes and a crock of butter and one of honey on the smaller table. Douglas and her mother sat down as she did, carrying their mugs with them.

"No' at all, lass. And how do ye fare this day?" Her mother reached out and rubbed her cheek, giving Caitlin a sad smile as she touched her.

"As weel as can be expected. Did ye see Iain in the village?"

"Nay, but I will see him later. The bairn is wi' Peigi for now."

No one spoke through the rest of the meal. Caitlin was lost in her thoughts and could think of nothing to say to them. And, thankfully her mother and Douglas seemed to know that she had no desire for conversation. When they had eaten their fill, her mother pushed back from the table and walked to the worktable to fill her bag of supplies.

"Douglas, Pol said ye visited him this morn after the burial?" Her mother did not look up as she asked.

Caitlin looked to Douglas for his answer. He *had* seemed in a different temperament as they worked together.

"I asked him where I could get some surgical tools." He looked at her and smiled. She was still confused.

"And tell me why would ye be needing those? I thought ye were but biding yer time here?" Mam knew something but Caitlin wasn't sure what that was.

"How do you know these things, Moira?"

"What things do ye mean, Douglas?"

Caitlin turned to and fro between the two of them waiting for a real answer. This seemed to happen frequently when they started talking to each other.

"I was wrong to 'bide my time,' as you put it, Moira. Someone challenged me on it yesterday and I finally realized that I could be doing some good while I'm here. Then, I guess," he paused and looked over at her, "Mildread's sudden death made it clear that we do not always know how much time we have left. And squandering it by standing idly by didn't seem like the thing I should do."

"Really, Douglas?" Her throat tightened with emotion.

"Really, Caitlin." He smiled and all she could do was smile back. "Your father and uncle are making some surgical tools that could make some of the procedures you do much easier. When they're ready, I'll show you how to use them in what you do."

"Will I need one of your *charts* to keep them straight in my mind?" She felt like crying, now even more than when Mildread was buried. He had so much to offer and now he would. And she would be a part of it. This must be what the Fates had in mind for them—working together for the good of the clan.

"No, you'll need no chart after what I've seen you do already with the few knives and needles you have."

"Weel, if ye two hiv things to do, I'll see to my tasks." Douglas picked up his parchment and held it out to her.

"I still have another side to it, surely there are more conditions to be treated and herbs to be used?"

Caitlin knew that the rest of the day would go by just as quickly as this morn did. And she looked forward to it.

"So tell me about Robert and Anice."

He'd waited until they'd all finished eating before he'd asked. Pol had piqued his already heightened curiosity about the laird of the clan and his wife. From the man's earlier cryptic comments, Douglas knew there was more to this story.

"I put an end to yer questions this morn because we werena alone," Pol started to explain. "I wasna certain what ye would ask and didna wish to speak of certain things in front of others."

"Yer own parents were here for the beginning of the story," Moira added. "Yer faither was mistaken by most for the old laird's son and heir, Alesander MacKendimen. The Lady Anice MacNab was betrothed to marry the next MacKendimen laird."

"My father and this Alesander looked alike?"

"Lad, didna yer parents tell ye any of their adventure?" Pol shook his head in sad disbelief. "Did they tell ye nothing of the history of yer clan?"

"Well," Douglas started to explain, "they may have told me but I don't think I believed them."

Moira let out a screechy laugh and pounded on the table. "Ye thought 'twas a bedtime story for bairns, did ye no'?"

"That's exactly what I thought," he answered, more convinced with each day that she, like Mairi, could read his thoughts.

"There is one thing ye maun agree to, Douglas," Pol began. "Ye maun promise that what ye hear from us aboot the laird and Anice goes no further than us." Pol looked around the table at his wife and daughter and then at him.

"Doesn't Caitlin already know this?" he asked. Caitlin shook her head as her mother answered.

"No' the whole of it she doesna. We hiv never spoken of much of the sad story," Moira explained, "and we dinna want this spread aboot."

"Agreed." Caitlin added a quiet yes to his.

"After yer parents were here and gone, Anice was left with Sandy, as he wanted to be called. Sandy wasna happy with the thought that she haid been looking forward to marrying the wrong mon."

"My father?"

"Aye, ye faither. He and Sandy were nigh to impossible to tell apart. Struan, the old laird, arranged for Sandy to go back with the king for another year to try to give him time for his anger to lessen and for Anice to prepare."

The hairs on the back of his neck rose. He already didn't like the sound of this.

"The delay in their marriage did no good—Sandy was even angrier when dragged back for the wedding. He savaged and beat puir Anice near to death on their wedding night and when he left, she was so distraught that she tried to finish his work."

"Mam," Caitlin gasped. Her face paled at this information. This was no doubt bringing back memories of her own attack. Douglas would have liked a few minutes with this Sandy character.

"Dinna worry, Sandy left here bound and gagged and a bit worse for the wear himself. Anice discovered she was pregnant."

"Wi' Craig?" Caitlin interrupted.

"Aye, wi' Craig. Robert Mathieson, who was raised as the steward's son, was called home to help Anice in her tasks as chatelaine."

"So, Robert is not a MacKendimen?" Douglas still didn't see how this had happened. The laird of the clan was not of the clan?

"He is, Douglas. Robert was Struan's natural son, but he was raised Dougal the steward's son. When the truth was revealed to Dougal, Struan arranged for the lad to train and live wi' the MacKillops in Dunbarton."

Pol took up the story. " 'Tis a longer tale than we hiv time for and ye shouldna be privy to all of their business. Let's just say that Sandy was killed by villains on his way home for the birth and no one was unhappy aboot that."

"So Robert ended up married to Anice and laird of the clan?" He was still amazed and knew many, probably most, of the details had been left out.

Moira laughed. "That is the long and short of it, Douglas, but 'twas much more than that. And, all haes turned out weel for the Clan MacKendimen. Robert is more laird than his faither was or his half brother could ever be."

"Well, thank you for appeasing my curiosity. I guess I should've paid more attention to my parents' bedtime stories." He started to laugh but realized the others were looking at him solemnly. "I thank you for the meal," he said, standing and stepping away from the table. "I should get back to the keep—there are people I need to speak with this evening."

Caitlin rose with him and walked to the door. He was reluctant to let this day end. For her own reasons, Moira left the two of them alone the whole day, other than the noon meal. He'd spent that time enjoying Caitlin's quick wit and gaining a true respect for her healing abilities. That was her gift—the knowledge she'd gained through her years of study and practice with her mother. She had no need to claim something more mystical—she was a healer.

Now this day was over, but with his decision to apply himself while he was there, he anticipated many more days with her. They would work together, laugh together, and maybe even . . . Douglas shook his head at the direction of his thoughts.

"Will you come again in the morn?"

"I'll be here but later than today."

"Douglas, stop at the smithy on yer way here. I should hiv some of yer tools done for ye."

"I will do that, Pol," Douglas said as he stepped into the shadows created when the door was opened. Drawing Caitlin a bit closer, he couldn't help but take advantage of the darkness by touching his lips briefly to hers. Too briefly. Caitlin's answering sigh inflamed him and he fought the urge to pull her from the cottage for some real privacy.

" 'Till the morn then, Douglas," Caitlin stood on her toes and repeated his kiss.

"Oh, aye, the morn," he answered and stepped through the door.

She knelt to bank the flames in the hearth before retiring for the night. Soft snores already came from her husband's pallet and she longed to join him there. But yet again the wisdom called to her and she could not resist. Staring into the flames, she emptied her thoughts and waited. Soon the hearth glowed with colors and the light and heat in the room grew. As the fire became more wild, she felt the calm descend.

A cave in the night, lit with a torch and heated by the fire rocks below it. The churning water. The growing heat. Two lovers clinging and writhing in passion's first embrace. A young lad in need. Another bairn fighting into the world. Denial. Rebirth.

Taking in a deep breath, Moira sat back to consider what this vision had brought to her. Should she stop it? Should she allow her daughter to become Douglas's lover without warning her about the dangers? Had she ever been able to interfere with the wisdom? Nay, 'twould do no good since the Fates had their plans for all of them.

She stood and settled the fire down for the night. Going about her last tasks silently, she thought about her own gift. Sometimes, as a mother, 'twas a difficult thing to accept. Mayhap 'twould be better not knowing what was to come.

The Fates had decided otherwise and as always she had no say in the matter. 'Twould be as 'twas meant to be.

Chapter 19

H E ENTERED THE yard without being noticed and made his way to the place where the swords were kept. He shushed the boy handling them and drew his own dagger from the sheath inside his boot. The sun peeked from behind thick clouds casting his shadow for many feet on the ground in front of him. He stopped and waited for the clouds to move again, to cover his movements forward. Now, creeping closer, he positioned himself twenty yards from the warrior and waited. Aindreas was engaged in a mock battle with Craig and didn't see him approach from the side.

Craig did and his face would have given Douglas away if Douglas hadn't decided at that moment to begin his battle cry. Aindreas never paused and turned from Craig's attack in the front to answer Douglas's blows from the side.

The fight went on for a long time; Douglas lost track of how long as he was met blow for blow by his equal in skill. Aindreas had been able to best him in their past contests because Douglas had not been trying to win. This morning, he was and it showed. Soon the yard was circled by other soldiers and villagers drawn to the sounds of the battle. Craig, not the equal of either man in battle skills, simply lowered his weapons and watched.

Each fighter began to have supporters and the crowd's noises grew and grew until anyone in hearing distance came to see what was happening. Douglas focused his attention on his opponent, who was not giving him an inch to maneuver if he didn't force it from him. Power surged through him even as the sweat poured down his body. He was enjoying this more than he had any other mock battle, and he was trying to win.

Actually, he was winning. Then Aindreas's foot slipped into a small hole and he ended up on his back, looking up at his adversary. Douglas took advantage of it just as Aindreas would have if it had happened to him. They were panting and blowing so hard from their exertions that he couldn't fashion the words demanding surrender. Instead, he too collapsed on the ground.

After a few moments, a bucket of icy water thrown on them forced them to sit up. Laughing, Aindreas motioned for more and someone obliged by throwing yet another bucketful on them. Douglas used both hands to clear his hair from his face and sluice the extra water out of it.

"If that was how ye greeted those MacArthurs in the forest that night, I can see how they couldna stand against ye," Aindreas offered. "And that was how I imagined ye could fight if ye ever felt the need or want to." The older man pushed himself to his feet and then reached a hand down to him.

A noise from nearby distracted Douglas from answering. He looked into Craig's very pale face. There was more to his part in the forest that night and Douglas knew he'd find out eventually. He already knew it was Craig's blow that laid him low—what else could there be? Aindreas's hearty blow on his back got his attention and when he looked back, Craig was hurrying out of the practice yards.

"I want ye to show me that last move ye used, the one when yer dagger went under in this direction . . ." Aindreas demonstrated the move he was interested in.

The next hour was spent in holds and maneuvers and steps and blows and parries. Finally, Aindreas let him go with his promise to return the next day and challenge him again. As he walked from the yard, many of the onlookers added their own handshakes and pats on the back as he walked by them. Scots liked nothing as much as they liked a good fight and his with Aindreas had given some entertainment to all.

Now, he needed to get to Caitlin's, but his first stop was at the smithy's.

"Now. . . ."

"I ken, Douglas, cut the skin afore it tears. 'Tis much easier to repair the cut than the tear."

He smiled as she did what he'd shown her how to do— with the fine scalpel Pol had made, Caitlin made an incision and opened the wound a bit wider for easier access to the bone inside. She amazed him with her ability to learn these surgical techniques so quickly. He knew second- and third-year med students who didn't have the skills that this uneducated young woman did.

Of course, his own license to practice medicine would be lifted if the medical authorities found out he was teaching unqualified personnel how to make incisions and place sutures. And assist in the surgical reduction of a compound fracture. Yet since the authorities he was responsible to wouldn't be around for several hundred years, he thought he wouldn't stop now. He must have let out a chuckle, for Caitlin looked up at him with a questioning frown.

"Hiv I done something wrong, Douglas?"

"No, Caitlin, you are doing just fine. Are all the fragments cleaned away?" He leaned closer to her work area and checked the wound. The fractured ulna bone would need to be set now that it had been cleaned. Once awake and other than a few weeks of recuperation, young Gavin

would be no worse for the wear and might even avoid
jumping off those rocks in the future.

"Aye," she said, moving aside for him to see. At his nod,
she moved the muscle tissue back in place over the bone.
With an expert's touch, she laid the layer of skin back in
place and reached for the thread to suture the wound closed.
Her stitches were small and even and would leave very faint
scars after the healing.

She paused before wrapping Gavin's arm to wash the
area again. Caitlin looked to Douglas and he smiled. She'd
learned so much in this last week. One of the first lessons
he'd taught both Caitlin and her mother had been about
infection control. They both had a basic understanding of
it that came from years of trial and error. Now their knowledge would aid in their patients' regaining their health.

He reached over to their supplies, spread out on the table
and picked up the small bowl of ointment. Douglas held it
out where she could reach it and found himself the recipient
of a frown.

"What is it?" he asked.

"Aye, Douglas, what is it?" she asked right back.

So, that was it, now it was his turn to be quizzed. And
his parchment was not handy.

Holding it close to his nose, he sniffed. Some of the
herbs were becoming more familiar to him by their scent,
some by their color. He tried to remember what they'd
mixed into this concoction.

"Comfrey?"

"Are ye asking or telling?" Caitlin smiled at his discomfort. He was nowhere near as fast a learner as she was.

"Telling. Comfrey and a bit of marshmallow to soothe
the incision and torn skin."

"Verra good, Douglas. Then what will we use?" She
dipped into the bowl he held and applied the creamy ointment over the boy's injury. When he hesitated, she looked
up at him.

"A poultice of crushed comfrey roots and wrap it tightly

until the skin heals. Then we'll try out my new plaster."
Their new treatment would replace the old one of wrapping
the broken bone tightly with a plank of wood for support.
Caitlin had laughed when he'd explained about using plaster like the house builders used to harden around the bone
until it healed.

He looked up in time to see a guilty expression in her
eyes. What could that be about?

"Ye are learning as weel," she said as though she spoke
to a five-year-old. Well, he probably deserved it for his
attitude, and his comments could still be a bit pompous
when he didn't pay attention. "He still sleeps?"

Douglas moved closer and checked the boy's breathing.
Slow, deep and quiet. Lifting one eyelid, he saw the very
dilated pupil and knew the boy would sleep for a while.
Poppy juice, which he still was reluctant to use, was very
effective in making their patients sleep. It worked faster and
stronger than Moira's valerian root tea so he used it carefully. And he used it sparingly since Moira didn't produce
it from her own stores or garden.

Caitlin had explained that once or twice a year, Moira
and Pol traveled to a monastery on the coast to trade for
those herbs her mother couldn't or didn't grow herself.
Since the abbot and monks were hesitant to deal with a
woman, Pol traded his skills as a blacksmith for what they
needed. Robert's written greeting and generous donation to
the monastery always smoothed the way. Herbs, tree and
plant cuttings for cultivation, and new recipes were Moira's
goals during the trip. From what Caitlin had said, she never
came home empty-handed.

"He will sleep for a while more," he answered, and then
smoothed the boy's hair back from his face.

"Here, Douglas, help me with the bandage."

Together they coated the boy's arm with the comfrey
paste and then wrapped it tightly with long strips of linen.
A few minutes and they were done. Caitlin gathered the
used cloths and lifted the bowl of bloodied water and car-

ried them away from the boy. After emptying the used water out the window, she rinsed the cloths and washed her hands.

"I will sit with him, Douglas. He willna awaken for a bit."

"Are you sure, Caitlin? I could carry him back to his mother?"

"Come now, ye ken he shouldna be moved right now. Do ye begrudge me a few moments of leisure now and again?" She laughed and patted his arm. That undercurrent that came with her touch was there again . . . always.

"If you don't mind waiting here, I'll run some errands and be back in a little while."

"I will wait here for his father to come for him."

Douglas covered the bowl and put it on the shelf. He stoppered some flasks and cleaned up their—her—worktable and walked to the door. Caitlin knelt next to the sleeping boy, straightening the plaid over his still form. Douglas took his cloak and threw it over his shoulders, preparing to meet the now-cold November winds.

Pulling the door tightly against its frame, he started down the path to the smithy. He had to get Pol to take a look at the blade on one of the new scalpels and the grasping edge of the new forceps. He gazed down at his empty hands and realized that he'd left the cottage without them. Wait until Caitlin heard this—she'd laugh at his forgetfulness. A few more paces back the way he'd come and he was at the door he'd just closed.

Easing it open quietly not to disturb the boy's rest, Douglas stepped inside and stopped. Caitlin knelt now on the boy's right side and faced the door, but she stared across the room at Douglas now with unseeing eyes.

What was this? Douglas wondered. She never reacted at all to his entrance into the room and as he walked closer, she didn't even appear to be breathing. Her hands lay on Gavin's injured arm. First she was completely still and then she slid her hands over his arm. He spoke her name quietly, then louder, gaining no response either time.

Douglas approached the two of them and crouched down at her side. Reaching out to her hands, he was shocked at the heat in them. He let his hand hover near hers to test it again. Hot, very hot, and yet Gavin never whimpered at all at her touch even though he had several times during the dressing of his wound.

He waved his hand in front of her face and watched her eyes for a reaction. Nothing. She never even blinked! He moved across from her and continued watching for a few more minutes. Finally she started to stir and he heard some mumbled words.

" 'Twill be just fine now, Gavin. All is weel."

Her breathing became more noticeable and less even and her eyes began to blink. As he watched, she began to sway ever so slightly. He quickly moved back to her side and supported her.

"Douglas, what are ye doing here?" Her voice was barely a whisper.

"I came back for things I'd forgotten and found you over the boy. Are you sick?" He touched her forehead and found her to be a bit clammy. "Here," he said holding her by the arm, "sit back and try to relax now. And tell me what happened."

"Caitlin." Moira's voice filled the room, startling him. He never heard the door open either, he was so intent on Caitlin and whatever was wrong with her.

"Aye, Mam," Caitlin answered, meeting her mother's gaze.

"Douglas, if ye would help the lass to her feet?" Moira moved in the other direction—to the worktable and the cupboard of stored herbs and concoctions.

Her weight was almost nothing to him and he lifted her from the kneeling position by Gavin and helped her to a nearby chair. Her face was now pale and her eyes were glassy. This all looked familiar but he couldn't place where he'd seen this before. He pushed the hair back from her

face and tried to get her attention. She clasped her right
arm tightly to her chest and rocked to and fro as he
watched, completely mystified by what he'd seen.

"Can ye walk, lass?" Moira handed a mug to Caitlin and
she drank down the contents without ever asking what it
was. It was apparent that this was a common occurrence to
them. He was the only one in the dark about it.

"Aye, Mam, wi' some help."

"Douglas, if ye will support her from that side, we can
help her into her pallet."

He did so, but released his hold when she moaned in
pain. "Dinna touch her arm, Douglas, hold her under it."
He slid his hand down to her waist and guided her toward
the small bed in the alcove where she slept. Then, watching
more like a helpless man than an experienced caregiver, he
watched as Moira settled her daughter down to sleep.

He was following Moira back to the main area of the
cottage when Caitlin's whisper reached him.

"I didna think ye would be back so soon, Douglas. I
thought I haid more time. . . ."

"For what, Caitlin?" he asked, running his hands through
his hair. Puzzled at why she would want him gone, he repeated his question again. "Had more time for what?"

"The healing." But it was Moira who'd answered his
question from across the room.

"But we were done our work on his arm. . . ." Then it
hit him.

The healing.

Chapter 20

HIS OWN HANDS shook as he unwound the recently placed bandage from the boy's arm. Not quite sure what he'd find, he held his breath. He didn't believe that Caitlin could heal with her touch but he also couldn't begin to explain what he'd witnessed a few minutes before. How could he shatter her belief in herself? What could he say?

Moira watched from across the room with those eyes that saw everything and knew even more. She believed in her daughter's abilities to heal. What would she say when this sham was exposed?

The last layer of linen came loose from the still-moist ointment and Gavin's arm lay before him.

Unmarked.

No swelling.

No sign of the surgery that he and Caitlin had performed.

Not willing to accept what his eyes saw, he lifted the boy's arm and turned it, examining it closely. Douglas searched for the marks of the scalpel and needle, for the tear in the skin over six inches long from the rock.

Nothing. The skin was as flawless as the day the child was born, soft and unscarred.

And he knew he must be losing his mind. He'd accepted many things, very strange things, in the last month but this stretched him more taunt than he could stand.

Douglas squeezed the area where the break had been, applying a moderate amount of pressure and waiting for the boy to rouse due to the pain. His breathing hitched once or twice but he never stirred. How could this be? How?

" 'Tis her gift, Douglas, as I tried to tell ye afore."

Damn her! Moira read the question in his mind again. Well, he must have been here too long for he was actually beginning to accept all manner of paranormal experiences. Or this was a bad dream and he would awaken from it soon, feeling tired but none the worse for wear.

He closed his eyes and shook his head, not quite sure if he wanted it all to disappear or not. The cottage was the same when he opened them again—the boy lay sleeping in front of him and Moira stood across from him. Caitlin was still on her pallet recovering from whatever she'd done.

"You told me she was a healer."

"And, because ye were unwilling to accept my words on their face, ye took a different meaning from mine." Gesturing toward the worktable, Moira continued, "Ye thought I was talking aboot her gift as an herbalist. Ye hiv refused to see the rest of it."

"But, it doesn't work that way. Healing with the touch of a hand is impossible." His organized, thoroughly modern mind rebelled at the thought of something more than medicines and treatments.

"Impossible as traveling through time, Douglas?"

He was completely overwhelmed. Of course it was. Impossible. Shaking his head, he dragged his hands through his hair and held his head. What could he do? How could he survive in this bizarre place with its strange powers and gifts? How could he fit in at all?

"Yes. I mean no. Oh, I don't know what I mean!" Douglas moved away from the boy and strode to the door. He needed some fresh air, the room suddenly felt too close for him. Grabbing his cloak, he pulled open the door and escaped. And it did feel like an escape.

The wind whipped his cloak around him and slapped his now-long hair against his face. He walked unseeing down one path and then another. Not knowing, not caring where he headed, Douglas soon found himself in that place where he'd stopped the first day he was here. On the edge of a fairy-tale village, he stood in awe once more as the reality of the people and the place hit him.

Dear God!

He really was here and that young woman in the cottage back there healed people with her touch!

And all of his work over the last weeks had been worthless. Caitlin wasted his time and hers trying to show him how to get back to being a healer, someone who treated a patient and not a disease. He'd started caring again, about what he did, how he did it and those on the receiving end of his work. Caitlin, who had given him back his soul, had now taken it from him. Why bother learning about which herbs to use when she could place her hand on an injury and make it go away?

Wait a minute. Faced with the incredible ability to heal someone without medical intervention, he was feeling sorry for himself? He'd never felt so stupid and selfish in his life as he did at this moment. A young woman who defied all his knowledge and used her gift for others and he was worried about his wasted time?

If Mairi could see him now, she would tear him up one side and down the other. He'd really lost his soul in these last few years. In order to protect himself from the death and disease he treated, Douglas had built a wall around himself, around his soul. And he'd lost track of the reason he'd become a physician in the first place. He'd lived for the money and the respect and the good life medicine provided for him.

How could he face Caitlin? She lay suffering herself now from the effects of sharing the healing energy with anyone who needed it. Her only goal was to help others. And wasn't that why he'd entered medicine?

As he stood on the edge of that village, realizing his insignificance in this time, he shook from head to toe. And it was not the cold causing the ripples that went through him. It was fear. He feared not knowing his own place in this world . . . or in his own.

"You frightened me."

She'd just opened her eyes when he sat down next to her on the low pallet. Trying to sit up and failing, she stayed where she was. Carefully, she tested her arm to see if the pain had passed yet. Feeling nothing but a bit of stiffness probably from holding it so tightly against her, she stretched it out above her. Douglas's grasp startled her.

He took her hand in his and waited for the same thing she did. When the pulsing began, he rubbed up and down on her arm, massaging it, loosening up the muscles. After a few minutes, her arm felt so warm and comfortable that she hesitated to reclaim it. She dared to look at him as he worked. She'd seen his face for a moment when she came to after healing Gavin and wasn't sure she wanted to face him. Or his disbelief . . . or his questions.

"How did I frighten ye, Douglas?" He pulled on the hand he still held and helped her to her feet. She wobbled a bit in those first few moments but then felt much steadier on her feet. She let him guide her to the bench next to the table.

"I thought you were having some type of seizure when I came back in. Your eyes were empty and staring but you didn't see me."

"I thought ye would be gone for some time."

"So, you were trying to deceive me?" He crossed his arms and stood before her. His face was grim and she could see him clenching his jaws even from her seat.

"Nay, Douglas, no' trying to deceive ye but to avoid—"

"Avoid telling me the truth about you?"

"A truth ye werena willing to accept aboot me." She heard his scoffing words before and her heart hurt with each one he uttered.

"You're right, of course. I couldn't accept your truth. It defies everything I know and believe. Or should I say don't believe?" Douglas reached to the table and slid a mug over to her. "Your mother will have my head if you don't drink this before trying to go anywhere."

Taking refuge in the silent act of drinking the mixture that her mother had left for her, Caitlin dared a peek at his face. He didn't look angry; stunned was a better description of his expression. Poor man. After everything else he was again faced with something out of his realm of knowledge and experience. He had no faith in himself so he had no faith in anything else.

Now, after trying to help him find his faith in himself by finding the healer hiding deep within, she'd failed. He thought that belief in her gift wiped out anything he could accomplish through the use of his own healing skills. He was wrong, of course, but how could she tell him . . . show him?

"Douglas, I hiv always held back using my gift unless the time was right. Mam said it should be used only when our herbs and other healing ways didna work or when the person's life was in danger."

"Gavin was in no danger. He would be in pain but his life was not threatened." His jaw was clenching again. This was not going well.

"Ye hiv the right of it, Douglas. Gavin would suffer from some pain and a bit of bruised pride, but no lasting damage." She paused and patted the bench next to her for him to sit. It was difficult to explain this with his standing over her like a guard. He looked at her and hesitated. Finally, he uncrossed his arms and sat down. "I waited too long with Mildread. Her bleeding seemed gone so I didna use my gift on her. By the time I reached her that day, I was too late to do anything."

Her throat tightened and tears threatened. "I decided to not wait anymore, to try to use the gift anytime someone was in need, no matter . . ." She hesitated.

"No matter what?" he asked.

"No matter the cost to me. Saving someone else is worth the pain and exhaustion it causes me."

"Does this pain and exhaustion come every time you use your gift?"

"Aye, but it varies as to the task involved. A more serious ailment or injury takes more of my strength and more time to recover." She could feel her mother's brew taking effect—her head felt much clearer and her arm pained her no longer.

"So, when you did this to me . . ." His face paled as he realized that she had touched him in this way and suffered for it. "I'm not sure what to say to you? Thank you doesn't seem enough."

"Ye dinna hiv to thank me, Douglas. The gift is to be used. That's why I hiv it."

He stood and walked toward the hearth. Pacing back and forth a few times, he kept glancing at her and then away. Again and again, words seemed on the tip of his tongue but wouldn't come.

"What do ye wish to ask me?" The clan was used to her using the healing touch but it must be a great shock to someone who just a bit ago would never have admitted to the existence of such a gift.

"So, you choose whom you heal?" His eyes were the color of midnight now, so dark and intense as he tried to understand the way of it.

"Aye and nay. Like my maither and her gift of sight, I feel a call when 'tis time."

"A call? Did you have this when you healed me?" He was still trying to be open to this, she could feel his struggle.

"Aye. Ye were doing just fine with the herbs. Yer fever was lessening and Mam had repaired the gash on yer head." He nodded at her words. "Then ye began to fail. Ye fell deeper and deeper into that unhealthy sleep and I kenned that I must do something right then to call ye back."

"I heard you!" She'd thought he'd lost all his color before but now he was truly ghostly. "Through the flames. In the dream, I heard your voice calling my name. How?"

"I amna certain how it works, only that I clear my mind and think aboot the healing. I place my hands on the injury if there is one and speak to the person." Some of this was not clear even to her; when she began the healing, she lost all touch with the world. She saw and heard only the person she laid hands on.

"You didn't speak when you healed Gavin," he pointed out to her. His eyes showed his confusion. He stayed on the other side of the room as though not sure of her.

"I called to him." He shook his head in disagreement.

"Aye, lass, but ye speak only in yer thoughts and no' with yer voice."

"Mam." Caitlin stood to face her mother. "I'm trying to explain to Douglas aboot the healing."

"I ken, daughter, but is he ready to hear ye?"

"Ready as some and no' as ready as others, Mam," she answered as both she and her mother looked at him.

"Did you feel the call to heal Mildread?" he asked, his question bringing back memories of her friend's death.

"Nay, I didna feel it, Douglas, and so I hesitated too long."

"That's why you said her death was your fault?" He didn't wait for her answer, they both knew it was the reason. "But, can your gift work if you don't get that feeling, that pull?"

"I didna ken, the call has always been there when I've healed in the past." But she had not felt it for Mildread. Or Gavin. That's why she'd tried today with the boy. She hadn't used the gift since she healed Douglas and a part of her feared that it was gone. Caitlin had believed they were destined to be together and that her healing of him was the final step in that drawing together.

" 'Twas why I tried to heal Gavin—to see if I could call the gift to me. I was"—she looked at her mother and then at Douglas—"afraid that I'd lost it with yer healing."

"Lost it? But why would you lose this ability after my healing?" He ran his fingers through his hair in that gesture of bewilderment and looked up at her for answers she wasn't sure she had.

He blinked then and she saw him get tangled in his own thoughts. He was remembering something but she had no idea of what it was. Then he shook his head and finally saw her again.

"I need some air. I'll see you in the morning." Caitlin watched as he grabbed his cloak by the door and left.

Her heart felt as if it were tearing apart. She'd told him the truth about her gift and he'd left. Clasping her hands together to stop their trembling, she raised tear-filled eyes to her mother. He didn't understand.

"Give the lad some time, Caitlin. We've thrown so much at him in the short time he's been wi' us. It will settle in his mind and all will be weel."

"And the archway? Ye hiv seen it open again?"

"Aye, lass, on the night of the solstice the arch will open for him. 'Tis his destiny."

"And mine?" She held her breath, wanting and not wanting to hear her mother's answer.

"And yours as weel."

Chapter 21

THE DREAMS ARE the call. One awaits ye, needs ye to survive and ye will need her to survive as weel.

Mairi's words echoed through his mind as he sat at the edge of the lake. Alone and in the dark, Douglas sat for hours watching the moon rise over the smooth surface. Through the pristine air and with no competition from other light pollution, the waning half-moon shone some significant moonbeams toward the ground. He only wished that those beams of light could pierce through his thoughts the same way they did the darkness.

He picked another stone and sent it skimming over the lake. The rings caused by the rock spread out larger and larger, moving slowly and after a few minutes they crossed the entire pool of water. He thought about how quietly Caitlin had affected him in just the same way, silent and deeply.

As he watched her battle her own fears and try to justify her actions to him, he'd been overcome with shame. This young woman, blessed with a gift beyond her understanding, or his, was attempting to take on his problems. He knew she was trying to bolster his faith in himself and in his abilities, all the time hiding her own.

She'd prodded him and questioned him and manipulated him into feeling good about what he was. She'd helped him find his lost sense of caring and purpose. She'd offered all that she had to help him in his quest.

Caitlin never asked for anything for herself except a share of his knowledge of the healing arts. And that was for her clan, her people. He'd never met anyone so compassionate and unselfish.

And somewhere through all of their time together, he'd fallen the rest of the way in love with her. He surprised himself by finally recognizing it for what it was—he'd been so busy trying to figure out why he was here and what his role was that he didn't notice her sneaking up on him or into his heart.

Douglas knew he'd been half in love with the dream version of her for years, but nothing compared to how he felt about the real woman. He owed her at least an apology for hurting her, for he knew his thoughtless words about the gift she prized so much had hurt her feelings.

There was much more he'd like to give her but he only had six weeks left here. When the archway took him back to his own time on the solstice, he would leave her behind. Going home held mixed feelings for him now, for he would go back with a renewed sense of himself, but without the one woman he'd sought for these past three years. Would these emotions and desires for her lessen now that he'd fulfilled his trip to her time?

As if his thoughts of her had conjured her up, Douglas saw her. Carrying a lit torch, Caitlin made her way around the edge of the lake and walked off into the woods. Where could she be going at this time of night? And alone? Wouldn't she learn about the dangers? He stood, stretched his cramped legs and picked his way to the path she'd taken.

It led away from the main body of the lake and followed a stream through the forest a distance and into the hilly area that was the source of the lake's water. He'd lost sight of her for a moment and then she was gone.

He retraced his steps and was about to give up when he saw the flickering light of the torch through some trees. Ducking under some low-hanging branches, Douglas followed the weak beams and was surprised to come to the well-camouflaged entrance to a cave. This must be where Caitlin was.

Douglas quietly pulled the bushes and foliage back from the doorway and stepped inside. Then he stopped. A wave of heated humid air hit him from the next room of the cave. Then he noticed the sound of running, gurgling water. A hot spring? From the size of this room, he thought that this cave must run for some distance into the hills.

This cave . . . *the cave*.

It couldn't be, could it? A look into the next area would prove him right or wrong. If it was the cave in the dreams, there would be a large, deep, heated pool of water that ran off into several smaller shallower ponds. The steam would rise from the surface of the water and heat the cooler air. The walls and floor of the cave would also be warm from the heat source far below the surface.

Pulling his outer cloak off and taking the few steps through this entrance chamber, Douglas felt his heart start to pump harder. His breathing increased, due to the steam and the anticipation. If this was like the dream, she would be there, too. Naked. In the water. He closed his eyes and fought the urge to go forward. Part of him knew that with each step he was coming closer to a decision that would impact both of them. Each step brought him closer to openly acknowledging his feelings for her, to her.

Could he? Knowing that he would leave in just six weeks, could he complicate this by admitting his love for her? And, if he admitted his feelings, how could he leave her untouched after the endless nights of sharing passion in those dreams?

He stood at the opening to the next room and put his

hand on the wall, both for support and to test it. It was warm to the touch.

Stepping into the next room, his vision was blurred momentarily by the thick cloud of steam above the water. The water mixed and churned in the pool and briefly looked empty. Light from the torch, perched up high in a sconce dug into the wall of the cave, lit the chamber in a cascading wave that moved with the steam.

Then he saw her. Naked. In the water.

His breath caught as he saw in reality the perfection of form he thought was only a dream. As she stood in a shallow section of the water, he saw her long hair hanging in waves down her back and covering the curves of her hips and buttocks in an enticing way. She turned toward where he stood and he glimpsed the shapely curves of her breasts and waist and hips before she slipped down under the water once again. A nest of black curls at the meeting of her thighs drew his attention as she stood once more.

As she raised her arms to lift and twist her hair into some kind of knot at her neck and he saw the way it lifted her breasts even more into the light, Douglas realized he was already hard and throbbing. With her eyes still closed, she backed up a few steps until she reached the side and then slid down until only her head, shoulders and the upper curves of those pale, full breasts were above the waterline.

Even as his mind entertained thoughts of discreetly leaving without her knowing he'd been there, his body was preparing him for other things. His erection became harder and more noticeable with every second he spent watching her. It forced its way up and out and would be evident even in a kilt. If she opened her eyes, she'd probably pass out in shock.

Caitlin opened her eyes. He couldn't imagine what he looked like standing aroused and lusting hungrily in the doorway. Her mouth formed an "o" and she started to stand. His rock-hard penis pulsed and throbbed, understanding the erotic sign her mouth gave even though she probably didn't. Her gaze moved over him and at the sight of his arousal, she sank back into the water.

"Douglas," she whispered in that voice that haunted him. He closed his eyes and let the magical tones sweep over him. "Douglas," she said again, and it was his undoing.

"Caitlin, I, uh . . .," Words failed him even though he had so much to say. Where should he start?

"I hiv dreamed this, Douglas. Hiv ye as weel?"

"I have, too. A cave just like this. You in the water and me . . ." He couldn't voice the rest—he was afraid it would end.

"And as in the dream, will ye come into the pool wi' me?"

"Ah, Caitlin. I'm afraid to. I've waited so long and seen this happen so many times in my mind and in the dreams. If I join you there in the water, there is no turning back."

"Douglas, there was no turning back the moment ye answered my cry for help in the night."

"But I answered without thought of the consequences that night. Now, I can't do that."

She stood up and came closer. Oh, God, why did she do that? Her breasts tempted him almost beyond reason. He'd felt them, rubbed them through her blouse that night Mildread died and his hand itched and his mouth watered for more.

"And what consequences are those, Douglas?"

"I leave here in six weeks, Caitlin. Is it fair to you to involve you in this way and then leave you behind when I go home?"

"Is it fair no' to share this wi' me afore ye leave? I would rather have memories of this between us than regrets that canna be changed."

He closed his eyes again and took in a deep breath. *Tell her*, his heart whispered. *Tell her now.*

"I told you before that when this happened between us it would be for the right reason, Caitlin. I want you to know why I want this . . . why I want you."

He paused and bent down to untie the straps around his shins, loosening his leg coverings and low boots. He tugged his shirt free and pulled it over his head. Reaching for the belt holding his plaid in place, he stopped and looked at her. Caitlin smiled and nodded, and he unhooked the only thing holding up his kilt. Well, not the only thing.

Her courage appeared to desert her and she glanced away as he stepped down into the water. He took the few paces to reach her, sliding his feet along the bottom, feeling his way. The water didn't reach the same place on his body and the proof of his feelings was visible above the water-line.

He reached her, put his hands on her shoulders and brought her to stand with him. Lifting her chin, he looked into her eyes. The flaming green that he also remembered from his dreams was there for him.

"You have helped me find myself again, Caitlin. During these weeks, you've given me a renewed purpose and reason to be a physician, *a healer*. And, you never ask anything for yourself. You give and give everything you can. And I love you for it."

She gasped at his words. His hands drew her in until he could finally reach her mouth with his. "I love you, Caitlin, and if we only have six more weeks, I want to be with you as much as and in every way possible."

"Oh, Douglas," she whispered. "Aye, 'tis what I want, too." She lifted her mouth those last few inches and offered herself to him. He touched his lips to hers and she was lost.

She felt his hands encircle her waist as their mouths joined. He lifted her against him and his heated flesh met hers. The kiss, as in the dream, went on and on. They were gasping for breath when he moved his mouth away. Caitlin wrapped her arms around his shoulders and began again this mating of the mouths.

His tongue slipped into her mouth again and she touched and tasted it with her own. Even as she met every stroke of it inside, she felt him against her, in that place that pulsed and throbbed. An ache grew there until she wanted him to ease it for her somehow. She rubbed against his hardness and moaned at the sensation it caused down there. It was wonderful.

He slid his hands under her buttocks and lifted her higher. 'Twas then she felt his fingers move into that swollen area, she tried to close her legs but his hands held her spread wide. Then his fingers touched where it ached the most and she gasped. Even if they were not in the water, she knew it would be wet there. He opened the folds of skin and slid his fingers along the sensitive area, seeking, searching for something.

He was gazing into her eyes when he touched it and she let out a long, keening moan. She had no control over the sounds or the feelings raging through her. Caitlin only knew she wanted him to touch her everywhere. His fingers continued rubbing against her, and a heavy feeling spread through her, from the tips of her tingling breasts to her core. Never had she felt anything like this before. And he showed no sign of stopping.

A tightness began inside her and she felt it winding like a spring waiting to be released. His chest against hers and his hardness teasing the spot where his fingers played made her ache even more. She moaned louder and longer as the intensity grew. She could feel something building but didn't know what it was. She knew their mating would not be over until he was inside her but he showed no sign of doing that. He just stroked and stroked until she felt something let go.

He took her mouth and he pressed his fingers against and in her, rubbing in slow strokes until her body exploded under his hands. Nothing she knew could have prepared her for what happened to her inside her. Her body pulsed to her heartbeat and breathing became impossible. Wave after wave passed through her and still he did not stop. She arched against him over and over until the tightness lessened and she could breathe again.

Leaning her head against his chest, she panted. He removed his hands from under her and let her slide down his body. 'Twas obvious that whatever had happened to her did not happen to him. His arousal was still huge and hard against her belly.

Confused, she looked up at him. "We hiv no' joined. Do ye stop now?"

He frowned, his brows furrowing at her words. "Have you ever done this?"

"This touching? Or mating?" This was all very strange, she never imagined speaking of it.

"Mating. We call it making love. Are you a virgin?" His eyes darkened as he asked. His hair damp from the humidity hung around his face in a dark frame.

"Aye, I am. 'Tis a problem for ye, Douglas?" Most of the men in the clan would not care or ask if she was or wasn't. Virginity was highly prized by the noblewomen but not those of her place in the clan. "What is it that bothers ye?"

"I thought that maybe those men . . . the ones in the forest that night . . ."

"Ye thought they had taken me by force?"

He seem to choke on the words. "Yes. I thought from your reaction in the practice yard that day that they had raped you."

"Oh, nay, Douglas!" She pulled out of his embrace and took a step back. "They put their filthy hands on me but didna force me to . . . to . . ." She couldn't put words to that deed.

"Did I hurt you just then? Touching you like that? I never even considered that you might be tender there." Douglas was concerned for her for no reason. There'd been no injury there.

"Ye hiv wiped away any memories of their touch wi' yer own, Douglas. I will remember your hands there and remember the throbbing you created in me."

Her gaze on his erection nearly undid him. She stood a

pace away and stared at him, her mouth open slightly. But when she reached for him and touched his penis, it was his turn to moan.

"Did I hurt ye?" She started to pull her hand away but he placed his over hers to stop her.

"No. Please don't stop."

"If ye are certain?" A frown marred her brow. She licked her lips as she looked at their joined hands. From the startled look he knew she'd felt the result of him seeing her tongue move over her lips.

"Yes," he said as he pulsed once more hard and hot against her palm, "I am very certain."

"Oh," she whispered yet again and that shape of her mouth gave him all kinds of ideas. Unaware of most of them, she followed his lead and began to stroke his erection. He knew he would come if she continued this so he lifted her hand from him. Keeping hold of her hand, he took several steps backwards until he felt the side of the pool at his back.

He let go of her and pulled himself up to sit on the side of the water. The stone beneath him was warm as in the dream. He pushed back a little and then reached for her, lifting her out of the water and onto his lap. Her legs straddled his and her core nestled near his erection. With his hands on her buttocks once more, he eased her closer and closer. Caitlin was panting again and so he slipped his hand between her legs and touched her once more.

Using one finger and then another, he parted her legs wider and entered her, feeling her tightness contract around his hand. He looked at her face and almost died at the look of arousal she wore. Douglas leaned over and kissed her neck and then moved his mouth ever closer to those engorged nipples. Tasting and licking his way down her breasts, he let his fingers explore the heated area between her legs. Soon he was panting too and wanting so desperately to be inside that hot, velvety tightness.

His mouth drew her nipple inside and he licked it, around

and around, mimicking those movements with his fingers. She tasted of salt and minerals from the water of the springs, and arousal, and something else he could not identify except that it was clearly her own. The bud grew tighter in his mouth as his tongue moved over it. He suckled harder and drew it in further. She was moaning again, inciting him to have her . . . now. Delaying for another moment, he moved his mouth to the other breast and teased it the same way. Then he leaned back and looked at her again.

"Are you ready?" This was her chance to say no, although he would die right now if she did.

"Join with me, Douglas. Now."

And so he did, sliding just inside her tight sheath and letting her take him in the rest of the way at her own speed, which turned out to be an exquisitely torturous slow movement down his shaft. Then he was in her as deeply as he'd ever dreamed of being and it was all he'd hoped it would be.

For a moment, he felt complete and content as he never had in his life. This woman was always meant to be his and now she was. He moved inside her to prove to himself that he was there. Her answering moan was such music to his ears that he almost cried.

Douglas guided her with his hands until she was moving over him, easing herself up and down him, increasing the tension and tightness and heat. He slowed her for a moment and took her nipple again in his mouth, licking, stroking it with his tongue and then worrying his teeth ever so slightly on it. He'd waited to taste them and he would not miss this chance. His penis swelled inside her and together they began rocking up and down.

He could feel it coming, his testicles becoming as hard as his erection was inside her. And as she reached her climax again she dropped her back and let out a loud cry that echoed through the cave. His release began and he pulsed inside her, mixing his seed with her own moisture. He groaned at the power of it and let out his own cry into the stony chamber.

Douglas leaned back and took Caitlin with him, lying on the heated stone floor and keeping her draped over him. He needed a few minutes to recover from what was undoubtedly the most satisfying experience of his life. Physically spent, emotionally drained and fulfilled, he drifted off with Caitlin in his arms.

Chapter 22

AS THEY PICKED their way through the forest, Douglas grasped Caitlin's hand and squeezed it again. It was obvious his nervousness was increasing with every step toward her parents' cottage. Never before had a man faced her father after being with her as Douglas had. Oh, a few stolen kisses and touches, aye, but no man had been her lover and she was not sure how her parents would react.

Deceit or hiding the step they'd taken was not an issue—her mother already knew or would know very soon what had happened in the cave between her and Douglas. He stopped once more and pulled her close. They'd shared dozens of kisses since he found her at the cave and each one sent the same ripples through her.

"We will never reach home if ye keep stopping along the way, Douglas," she scolded. Of course, she was just as anxious and willing to put up with his kisses.

"I don't think I want to reach your home, Caitlin. Maybe we should go back to the cave?" He jokingly pulled her in the opposite direction.

"Why no'? 'Tis late and my parents will be asleep."

He snorted in response. "Your parents will not sleep until

you do on your own pallet. They will be waiting for you tonight." That look of tension crossed his face once more. Facing Pol was a daunting task.

She lifted their clasped hands to her mouth and kissed his. " 'Twill be fine," she said again.

He mumbled some words as they started walking. "What did ye say?"

"I said that I would geld a man who came home with my daughter wearing a smile like the one I can't keep from my face," he said smiling that smile. "I would feel better if I could tell them we're engaged but I can't do that."

"Douglas, dinna make offers ye canna honor. I understaun what happened tonight and I ask ye for no more than ye hiv given me already."

"And just what have I given you tonight except more to regret when I leave?" The smile left his face and sadness entered his eyes.

"Oh, nay, dinna think that way. Ye gave me yer love which I will keep with me always."

"And when I leave? Who will care for you? Who will hold you? Who"—he looked deeply into her eyes as he asked—"who will love you?"

"I canna say or know what will happen after ye leave. I will make my way among the clan as their healer as my maither haes and her maither afore her. And, I hope in time to pass on my knowledge to my daughter that she may serve the clan as weel."

He paled at her words and she realized what she'd said. A daughter. She always hoped for a daughter to carry on her family's gifts—her mother's second sight, her healing touch. Her older sister, Jean, God rest her soul, had shown great promise as a seer before her death.

"Oh, God, Caitlin. I hadn't even thought about that. You could be pregnant even now." His face was gray now and not a pretty sight. He rubbed his hand across his brow and down his face. "When did you have your last period?"

"Period?"

"Monthly . . . courses. Your woman's time."

She wanted to laugh at him and his discomfort. But because he was so serious and concerned for her, she wouldn't.

"Dinna worry, Douglas. I amna going to bear a daughter from our joining."

"And how do you know that? Do you know some way to prevent it from happening?"

"My maither has seen my first child being born, a girl with MacKendimen blue eyes and black hair. She said it will be my husband's child born after I wed." Her heart hurt with the thought of lying with someone else and making a child who would not be Douglas's.

"And you trust your mother's visions enough not to worry about being pregnant?"

"I hiv faith in her gift, Douglas. Now, are we going to my home or not?"

"Well, then, let's get you home. The faster we get there, the faster I'll find out if I'll live to see the winter solstice."

"Dinna worry. Da haes no' killed anyone in a long time."

From the pained look on his face, her words had not comforted him at all.

It was much more difficult for Caitlin to face the silence of this morning than it had been to face it last night. Douglas was wrong—her parents were not waiting for her. They were asleep in their bed and she hadn't see them until just a few minutes ago.

"Did ye sleep weel, lass?" her mother had asked as she pushed a platter of oatcakes closer to her on the table. Caitlin reached for one, feeling the heat enter her cheeks. She couldn't look at either one of them. She stood and walked to the hearth to pour a cup of tea. It gave her a minute to gather her thoughts.

Sleep, did her mother ask? She had not a moment of it until the sun's light crossed the barrier of dawn and flooded her room with its warmth. Then she had fallen asleep.

The dark hours of the night she'd spent tossing and turning and remembering and reliving every touch, every taste, every sensation that jolted her body and soul and joined them together in love. There was not a part of her that didn't ache for more or from too much of the soul-searing passion they'd shared in the cave.

Her breasts tingled and swelled and that place at her core throbbed to be filled with him once more. Could there still be anything left to share with him? After they'd dozed a bit, they bathed together in the pool. Lathering the soft soap onto each other, touching and swirling it over the hard and soft places, had led to another coupling.

This time she had laid back onto the heated floor next to the water and he'd knelt between her legs, touching and rubbing her most sensitive area. Then without warning he placed his mouth and tongue where his fingers had been and she screamed with the pleasure of it. When she tried to move away from the intensity of it, he'd lifted her legs over his shoulders and done it again. Unable, nay, unwilling to stop him, she felt each stroke of his tongue against the now-sleek folds. Once his tongue even went in her and she stopped breathing because of the tremors it sent through her from her core to her heart.

Then, as the trembling began to subside, he placed his own hardness there and filled her once more. The sense of completeness and contentment was like nothing she'd ever felt and she could have kept him in her like that forever—joined physically and emotionally.

She tensed her leg muscles together and felt the aching wetness there even now. Her breaths were more labored, as well. At the clearing of someone's throat, Caitlin took notice of her surroundings and wanted to crumble; she was standing in front of her mother and father filled with desire and love for a man not there.

"So, did ye sleep?" Her mother repeated her question.

Caitlin poured the tea into her mug and then faced her parents, her face and body flushed with heat and memories.

"Nay, Mam, I didna sleep much at all." She sat on one of the benches and looked directly at them waiting for them to speak their minds.

"Was it yer choice, Caitlin? Did he force or hurt ye in any way?" Her father's gruff words were somehow comforting to her.

"Nay, Da. 'Twas of my free will. He gave the chance to say no but in truth, I didna want to stop him."

"Will he offer for ye?" Her father put his mug down and waited for an answer.

"Pol, I hiv told ye—" Her mother started to interrupt.

"Nay, Moira, I want to hear my daughter's words on this and no' yers." He waved off her mother's reply.

Caitlin looked at her father, surprised by his vehemence. He always accepted her mother's wisdom and never questioned it. The insult to her visions was apparent on her mother's face and in the way she crossed her arms against her chest and turned to face her.

"Da, he wanted to make an offer to me afore we . . . ah . . ." At his brisk nod, she skipped over trying to name the act for him. "Wi' his future so uncertain, I wouldna allow him to ask for anything more than what we already share."

"And what is that?"

She stood straighter and responded as the adult and not the child any longer. "We love each other and have shared that love between us."

"And ye dinna feel dishonored by what has passed between ye? Some in the clan would call it that."

"Did ye feel dishonored by what ye shared wi' Mam afore ye two were wed?"

" 'Twasn't the same, Caitlin."

"Aye, 'twas."

"Yer maither was a widow and I was a single mon. There was no one to gainsay either of us."

"And did that make it right, then? Ye lived in her cottage

and were lovers afore the whole of the clan. I hiv heard the stories of the passion between ye."

"And when he leaves? What then?" He was not making this easy as he turned the subject of the questions back to her. They touched some of the sore spots in her own heart. She stuck out her chin and took a deep breath.

"I will go on wi' my life."

"And marry?"

"If someone will hiv me as wife, aye, I'll marry."

He lifted his mug and drank deeply before he said anything more. Wiping his mouth with the back of his sleeve, he stood and walked to her side of the table. He pulled her to her feet and tilted her head back to look directly at her. She felt the burning of tears in her eyes and in her throat.

"Only yer actions can bring dishonor to ye and I see none here. But try to protect yerself against being hurt and be ready for those who see this as sinful."

He wrapped her in his powerful arms and held her tightly. Caitlin took comfort from his embrace and closed her eyes.

"I will geld him if he harms ye, Caitlin. Make sure he kens."

She chuckled as her father repeated Douglas's own words. "I will tell him." She opened her eyes and looked into Douglas's own as he stood just inside the door. "Or ye can tell him yerself since he is here."

Her father released her slowly, kissing her on the forehead before letting go. They turned as one to face Douglas. And, as men do, the two of them stared hard and their gazes sized up the opponent before them.

"Ye are courageous or foolhardy to show yerself here on this morn."

"I did not want Caitlin to face your anger alone. And, I thought you might want to speak to me."

Her father nodded and snorted. "Aye, I would hiv words wi' ye."

The silence stretched on and on. She looked to her

mother to intervene but her mother shook her head at her. No help there.

"I dinna approve of what haes happened between ye and my daughter but she is a woman grown and I willna interfere," he paused and looked at her first and then Douglas. "But, I willna hiv her disgraced or embarrassed afore her family and clan. Ye will leave her behind when ye return to yer own time and place. Make certain ye leave her dignity intact or ye may no' make it back to yer home alive."

"I understand, Pol," Douglas answered.

"Good. Now, I maun be on my way. Moira," he held out his hand to her mother. "Walk wi' me a bit of the way?"

Her mother hesitated for a moment and then gave him her hand and they walked quickly from the cottage. She and Douglas stood in the silence and stared at each other.

Chapter 23

T HE URGE TO run to her almost overwhelmed him.

Douglas stood at the door as her parents left and just watched her. He saw her pale face and the circles around those luminous green eyes told him that she'd tossed and turned as he had since they parted in the night. He ached to hold her again, to be part of her once more, to fill his own emptiness by becoming one with her. But fear held him back.

If he moved or breathed or blinked, he feared she would disappear in a mist as his dreams of her always had. He had trouble convincing himself that his dreams had come alive in the cave last night. He woke constantly through the short night, each time believing that he would be in his own bed at the manor house in modern-day Dunnedin and she would be gone.

That's what he hoped for, wasn't it? He wanted to go home. He was really just a visitor and he would go home and leave her behind in her own time and place. After last night, how could he do that? But, even after last night, did he have a choice?

Caitlin stepped toward him and stopped. Fear. It was

there in her eyes, too. They were both caught up in the same feelings of hope and fear.

"Douglas, kiss me afore I believe 'twas only a dream again."

He ran the few yards that separated them and swept her up in his arms, swinging her around and around. He slowed and gathered her tightly to him, enjoying the feel of her against him. She was real, flesh and blood and in his arms.

She lifted her face to him and closed her eyes. Leaning down, he pressed his lips to hers. He felt her sigh against his mouth as she opened once more for him. His tongue dipped inside to taste and feel. He raised his face from hers and smiled.

"Betony tea with a drop of honey?"

Laughing, she reached up and kissed him lightly. "There's a fresh pot on the hearth. Can I get ye some?" Turning and walking toward the fireplace, she added, "Hiv ye eaten yet? Some of Mam's oatcakes are on the table."

"I meant that's what you taste of," he said as he licked his lips. "But, yes, I'll have some of my own as well."

The routine they'd created over the last weeks took over and soon he sat on this extraordinary morning after an incredible night, drinking betony tea and eating oatcakes. Eating and drinking as though his world had not turned upside down and back again. As though he had not found the woman of his dreams and made her his, and become hers. As though he belonged here, in this room and in this time.

For a brief moment he let himself imagine how it would be to wake with her every morning of his life. How would it feel to take his place by her side as a healer and work for the good of the clan. How would it be to marry her and have children with her and live a long uncomplicated life with her as his wife.

Now, he was dreaming. Whatever force had brought him here would be taking him back soon. It would be better to enjoy what time they had together, teach her as much as he could to aid her in her duties and then return home with as few regrets as possible.

"So what do we have to do today?"

"More herbs to crush and store. Those"—she pointed at the left side of the rack over their heads—"are ready."

"Why do you bother with those? Can't you just use your gift to rid the clan of disease and injuries?"

"Is yer disbelief back, Douglas?"

"No. I saw what you can do. But, I feel like you've been wasting time these last weeks teaching me about your herbs."

"I canna fix all the ills that face my clan. My gift is for those who canna heal wi'oot it."

"So, you will use what I show you?" He left off the "after I leave."

"Oh, aye, Douglas. Everything ye hiv taught me will be so helpful to what I do."

He'd truly misunderstood this gift of hers. She guarded it and used it carefully as the precious thing it was. The techniques he could teach her would make her life as the clan healer easier. For all she'd given him, it was the least he could do.

"Do we visit as well today?"

"There are a few who need our attention. And I'd like to look in on Gavin."

"Are you tired?" he asked quietly, changing the subject without warning. He'd wondered at her thoughts about last night. She'd said nothing that gave him any hint. Now, he smiled at the blush that spread up her neck and face, even to the tips of her ears.

"Aye, I am tired this morn," she whispered.

"Do you hurt?" She may have been manhandled by those miscreants in the woods that night but she was a virgin to all they did last night. He'd lost control over his desires and couldn't stop touching and loving her in the hours they spent in the cave. He should've been more sensitive to her lack of experience and stopped after the first time. But, when he held her and felt her, alive and welcoming, he could not hold back the passion that had built for years.

"I do ache, Douglas, but more to hiv ye again than from anything we did. I maun say that my bath is no' usually so eventful."

She wanted him again? He thought maybe she would be sore. Instead she wanted him!

"Maybe we can meet at the cave again, tonight?" He wanted to hold back and not let this physical need for her get the upper hand, but he cold not resist her invitation.

"Tonight is the *ceilidh*, Douglas, for the villagers. Did ye forget?"

"I did forget." And he would like to ignore this village dance and keep her all to himself. God, what was happening to him? He was acting like a teenager with no self-control. She did this to him. "So, a long day will be even longer."

"At least we will sleep tonight."

"Or collapse before," he added.

With the endless day looming before him, he stretched his arms and rolled his shoulders to loosen the muscles. If there was a God, he wouldn't have to dance at this village party. But Douglas had a feeling that the Fates Caitlin swore by were women. The night would tell.

The Fates were definitely female.

Douglas could almost hear their laughing as he stumbled around yet again in what he would describe as a medieval game of torture. His clan in Scotland would rather hear it called a country dance but he knew better as his feet threatened to tumble him to the floor at any moment. Only the warm look in Caitlin's eyes could have induced him to take part in this.

Brodie trotted by, hand in hand with his wife Rachelle, not looking embarrassed at all by the silly steps he took in the circle. Of course, he never took his eyes from his wife's so he would never know if anyone was taking notice of him or not. Maybe that was the trick, look into Caitlin's eyes and ignore everything else.

Before he could try out his new strategy, the music ended and the dancers separated, most out of breath as he was from the fast pace. He tried to hold onto her hand, but she was pulled from his grasp by a chattering group of young women. As he watched, Caitlin whispered and laughed along with them. She reminded him of his younger sister and her friends when they were in high school.

They'd spent so much time alone together that this was the first time he'd seen her with people her own age, her friends in the village. Their age difference stared him in the face for the first time. Thirty suddenly felt ancient as she stood surrounded by the other girls. Well, it didn't matter since he would be leaving the village soon. Maybe if he was staying, it would be a problem. So, he stood, watching every smile that lit on her face and feeling very much an outsider.

"So, 'tis true?" A large thump on his back caught him unaware. Turning around, he faced the laird.

"Robert," he held out his hand in greeting. "I didn't see you. Is what true?"

"Ye hiv developed tender feelings for that lovely lass over there. 'Tis the talk of the *ceilidh*."

"It is?" Shaking his head, Douglas wondered how to stall this kind of gossip. He had been too obvious in his behavior tonight.

"Actually, I've heard of it before this night." Robert laughed. "Yer wear a scowl on yer face, Douglas. 'Twas it to be a secret?"

"Nothing can come of my feelings about Caitlin, as you must realize. And, if I do anything to ruin her standing in the clan, I won't live to return to my own time." He rubbed his face, hearing Pol's words in his mind. *I willna hiv her disgraced or embarrassed afore her family and clan.*

"So, Pol has made his position on this clear to ye?"

"Absolutely clear." He would have to step back from

Caitlin, at least in his dealings with her in public. Rumors of their involvement could make it very difficult when he left and she remained. He had to think this through and watching her in the midst of family and friends made it impossible to do so.

"Robert, I need to leave for a while. Tell Caitlin I'll see her in the morning?"

Robert nodded his understanding and stepped aside. As Douglas passed by, Robert caught his arm.

"Sorry I am that ye canna stay with us and let this relationship with Caitlin proceed. But I think ye do the right thing in keeping it a private matter."

"But, if you already heard of it, then it's not so private."

"Dinna worry, I heard it from a very discreet source. Anice would not spread gossip about that would injure Caitlin, she's too fond of the girl. And, we're both so indebted to her mother that we could do nothing but protect her."

Douglas nodded, not completely convinced of the limited scope of the news. Robert released his arm and he walked out of the great room, not seeing or hearing much else.

Following a long hallway, he turned into the stairwell and climbed to the third level. His room was the second chamber. Taking a candle from the small table, he lit it from a torch in the hall and entered the place he'd been assigned for his stay.

It was really only an antechamber for the larger unused room next to it but it afforded him much more privacy than staying in the men's barracks did. The room was clean and well-kept at the orders of the Lady Anice. And with the brasier lit, it was warm in spite of the swirling November winds outside.

Douglas walked over and stared out the tiny windowpane. From his place, he could see the front gate and most of the courtyard between the keep and the castle wall. And none of this would be there when he returned home.

The castle would be scattered ruins, the village would grow and spread away from this area and be rebuilt many times over the centuries. When he thought of it in those terms, this all seemed incredible. And what about the people?

All of them would be long dead and forgotten when he was home. Moira and Pol, Robert and Anice and Caitlin. With the scarcity of records from that time in history, finding out their fates would be an impossible task. So, they would cease to exist—actually they'd ceased centuries ago.

How had his parents coped with this sense of loss? They'd known many of the same people he'd met in his time here—Moira and Pol, Brodie and Rachelle, Anice and others. He cursed himself for not paying more attention to those bedtime stories.

That's how his parents had coped! By telling those stories over and over, they kept alive the people in them. Like the ancient Egyptians who believed that a person was not truly dead if their name was uttered, Maggie and Alex MacKendimen had never let go of the spirits of those they'd met in their trip to this time. They'd kept their friends alive by talking and telling about them.

He turned away from the window and leaned against the wall. The coldness of the stone seeped through the wool he wore and into his skin. He raked his overgrown hair with his hands and sighed. Who would he tell?

Certainly he could never share the details of this experience with his friends in Chicago. And his medical colleagues would wonder if he hadn't cracked under too much stress. There were always his parents and family, however. They would listen and know the truth of it. He could tell his parents what had become of the friends they'd known.

But who could he tell about Caitlin and what she'd brought to his life in such a short time? About the way his heart felt when she smiled at him with those magic green eyes? About her touch and the chills it sent racing through his blood? About the way his name sounded when she whispered it in the middle of making love.

"Douglas."

He closed his eyes and let the sound of it pass over him. He would never hear his name said that way again after he left her and this time behind. Only in his dreams would he hear her or touch her again.

"Douglas."

Once more he heard her voice and he tried to memorize the sound. Opening his eyes, he looked across the room and into the face of the woman he loved.

Chapter 24

"ARE YE UNWEEL, Douglas?"

The tears burning in his throat and eyes prevented him from speaking. He gazed at her, imprinting this vision in his memory so he would never forget. The low light given off by the candle framed her against the darkened hallway behind her. Waves of ebony hair cascaded down over her shoulders all the way to her hips. Her pale skin made even more luminescent and her fiery emerald eyes more shimmery in the candle's flickering glow.

She stepped farther in and pushed the door closed behind her. He finally shook his head at her but she was already too close. If she touched him, he would lose his resolve to do right by her. If she touched him, he might not be able to let her go. Shaking his head again, he stepped back and ended up against the hard stone behind him. He could go no farther.

"Are ye ill? Ye look pale," she whispered as she reached up and touched his forehead—always the healer, always caring. "Ye hiv no fever."

"But I feel like I'm on fire, Caitlin. I feel it every time you touch me or every time you look at me as you did in the cave last night."

His words caused exactly what he was trying to prevent—both of them remembered the passion of the night before. Her mouth opened slightly and he could hear her breath in the silence of the room. She licked her lips and he could feel the slide of that tongue over his skin once more. He became as hard as steel in that instant.

"Douglas, love me again now. Here," she said as she walked to the side of the small, rope-tied bed and tugged on the laces of her blouse.

"But, Caitlin, that's what we need to talk about. . . ."

"Nay, Douglas, no words tonight. I can see in yer eyes what ye wish to tell me but I amna ready to hear it yet." She sat on the narrow bed and gazed at him.

"We shouldn't do this." He was amazed that the words came out at all. Apparently his conscience was still working but definitely losing the battle as his body responded to her words and the hungry look she gifted him with from her place by the bed. They'd made love several times last night—in the pool, on the steam-heated floor and even in the shallow pond—but making love in a bed brought even more erotic images to his mind.

"Do ye love me, Douglas?"

"Yes, Cait, I do. You know that, but—"

She held her hand up to stop his words. "Then love me now afore ye say farewell to me."

"I'm not leaving yet. I still have about six weeks."

"Oh, but ye are. What ye will ask me to do is say goodbye. Ye want us to go our own ways in the next weeks and no' be together as lovers again. Is that no' what ye plan to tell me?"

He looked at her, amazed at her insight. Maybe her mother's mind-reading talent had been passed down as well as the healing?

"It would be for the best." What else could he say?

"And if I dinna want what's best? If I want us to continue as we started last night?"

Why did she have to make this so difficult? He'd like

nothing better than to take her in his arms and love her every waking moment until the day when he had to walk through that damned archway and leave her. But that would make leaving even that much more impossible and might lead to other things as well. They had used no protection when they'd made love in the cave last night and he wasn't sure that Moira's visions were enough for his peace of mind. Caitlin seemed convinced but that was no reason for him to be irresponsible and take the chance that he would leave a child behind.

"Then let this be our farewell, Douglas." He saw the stubborn set of her chin and knew he'd not change her mind in this. "Please?" Her voice trembled as she asked again.

How would he ever love any other woman after this one? They were more than lovers—they were soul mates. He felt it through his being. A yearning always to be with her that was destined not to be satisfied. So, just once more. . . .

She could tell the moment he gave up fighting this feeling between them. She could feel it tugging him toward her even as she sat on the bed. She untied the laces on her chemise and then loosened the ties holding her skirt in place. When she stood, the skirt slid down her thighs and pooled at her feet.

Douglas swallowed deeply several times as he watched, his eyes as hot as coals, as hungry for her as she was for him. When he stayed as still as a statue, with only his gaze moving over her, she leaned over and gathered the edge of the long chemise. Standing up, she pulled the hem up her body and over her head, leaving her body naked to his stare.

He started fumbling for the edge of his belt and his plaid was soon on the rushes at his feet. It took but a moment for his shirt to join the woolen tartan on the floor. They stood a few paces apart but their souls and hearts would be linked forever. Douglas took the first step that would bring them together.

Opening his arms, he stood before her, inviting her in.

Caitlin stepped into the warmth and love of his embrace. The curly hair on his chest tickled her as he drew her closer. Her breasts already tingled and ached for his touch and her nipples tightened as he rubbed against her. Their bodies touched from chests to bellies to thighs—his hard muscles to her soft curves. She felt his rigid flesh pressing against her and an ache started in the core of her and grew.

Finally he kissed her.

Kiss was too tame a word for the possession he took of her mouth in those few moments. Their lips were open and their tongues danced, tasting and teasing each other as their bodies molded together in a heated embrace. She would die if he didn't touch her soon, she craved the magic his fingers would make on her body. Lifting her mouth from his, she found herself panting from this excitement.

"It is different than in the water."

"Oh, aye, 'tis." She looked into the midnight eyes, enjoying the throbbing that pulsed through her body. "But, I am wet, Douglas."

His eyes flared at her words and he kissed the breath out of her once more. When she thought she would swoon, he released her mouth. His hands that had caressed her back and arms and hips now moved down her belly and into that wet place. His fingers opened her to his touch and she moaned as he finally slipped into those sensitive folds between her legs. Grabbing his shoulders for support, she let her head tilt back and watched him as he awakened the hunger and fire inside her even more.

The tension coiled in her belly and in her chest and she could hardly breathe from it. But, before she could reach that wild crashing place Douglas had taken her to in the cave, he stopped. Easing his hands from her, he bent down and lifted her in his arms. A step or two and he lowered her onto the bed, joining her without hesitation.

"Love me," she begged him, running her hands in his hair and drawing his face to hers.

"I do, Cait. And I will," Douglas answered, lowering his

mouth to hers yet again. And, for the next while, he did what she'd asked him to do.

"Here, let me do that for ye." She reached for his belt to secure the plaid around his waist. "Ye are taking forever to fasten it."

He chased her hands away from his waist. "I *can* do this, it just takes me longer than most."

Caitlin turned back and finished her own tucking and adjusting, glancing at him every so often. He might be skilled as a surgeon, but he was the worst she'd ever seen at wrapping the plaid. And his hair, now much longer, kept falling in his face, obscuring his vision.

"At least let me help ye in another way?" He grumbled and then nodded. "Here, sit on the bed."

Caitlin stood to one side of his long legs and took a section of his hair in her hand. Dividing it into sections, she wove it over and under until a well-formed braid began over his one ear. Holding the braid, she pulled a leather thong out of her skirt pocket and asked him to cut it in two with his dagger. She secured the end of the braid with one and then moved to his other side and repeated it.

Douglas shook his head but the hair stayed well back from his face. Smiling, he touched them.

"It was getting harder to keep it out of my eyes. It hasn't ever been this long."

"Now mayhap ye can see to put yer plaid on?"

"Well, I'm not sure that even seeing will help. I have a bit of trouble making it stay on."

"That sounds interesting. So ye hiv haid mishaps?"

"Mishaps . . . a good word. I call them humiliating moments myself." They laughed and she helped him with the unwieldy length of wool. Soon, it was wrapped securely around his waist and over his shoulder.

As she finished, he took her hand and entwined their fingers together. Kissing it gently, he looked at her with those resignation-filled eyes.

"I love you, Cait, and I'll always remember you."

Tears threatened and she brushed her eyes to clear them. "We hiv plenty of time for farewells, Douglas. Dinna make me greet like a bairn now." There would be time enough for crying later, after he was gone and when all she had were the memories.

"I'm sorry, love. Shall we go back to the party and you can help me trip through another dance?"

He swung open the door to his chamber and pulled her along the hallway toward the stairs. Down the steps and to the great room they went and music and loud chatter greeted them as they entered. He dropped her hand as they walked into the *ceilidh* but they remained close together. The piper and drummer began another song and she looked to Douglas for his consent. At his nod, they took their places in the circle for another round.

He was much better at dancing than at wrapping the plaid. He did have a certain male grace in spite of his protests that he could not follow the steps. Laughing through the movements, they left the dancers and stopped at one of the tables holding the refreshments. Pouring a mug of ale for each of them, Caitlin stood panting as her breath returned to normal.

She turned with her hands full and faced Craig.

"Craig, I didna see ye here."

"Ye canna see anything but him," Craig answered, his belligerence clear.

"Him? Ye mean Douglas? He was my partner in the dance."

Caitlin placed one of the mugs back on the table. Pushing her hair back off the sweaty plane of her forehead, she drank deeply from the other mug. Douglas was still speaking to one of the men at the table.

"He is yer partner in more than that, Caitlin. I saw ye." Craig's voice rose and the surrounding crowd quieted. "Haes he made ye his whore?"

She gasped at the insult. Her face burned as she realized

that those all around had heard his words. She wanted to strike out but held back. Craig was drunk and 'twould best be handled quietly.

"Craig, ye hiv drank too much ale this evening. Mayhap yer brother can help ye to yer chamber?" She nodded at young Struan and the boy started forward.

"I dinna need help," he shook off his younger brother's hold. " 'Tis true, then? Ye wouldna give yerself to me and I promised ye marriage. I am the tanist, in line to sit at the head of the clan. But ye threw yerself at this outlander. He came here for his own reasons, used ye and will leave ye behind when he goes."

Caitlin looked around at her friends and family. Their red faces showed their embarrassment at being forced to hear this. She looked for Douglas and saw him nearby. He stood like a statue, his face was rigid. She noticed his jaw and fists clenched in time as was his habit when vexed. But he didn't speak.

"Was it because of what happened in the woods that night?" He was yelling, his deep voice carrying throughout the hall. She looked around for someone to intervene but there was no one.

"Craig, I told ye I understaun aboot what ye did that night." She tried to take him by the arm to lead him out of the room to privacy but he shook her off as he had his brother.

"Oh, Caitlin, I offered ye marriage and you held back from me. Does he offer ye the same?"

The crowd parted and Douglas approached where they stood. She knew he could not make an offer but a part of her begged silently that he do just that. Now that Craig had made his accusations in this gathering, it was no longer a private matter. Glancing around the room, she wondered where her parents were. And where could Robert and Anice be?

"Weel, do ye, outlander? Ye hiv taken her as yer lover, will ye take her as yer wife?"

The only thing that stopped her from lifting one of the heavy tankards of ale and aiming it at his head was the look of absolute anguish on Craig's face. He did love her in his way and couldn't know or understand what was between her and Douglas. Most of the time, she didn't understand it herself.

She turned to face the two of them in this distorted triangle. Knowing the answer before it was spoken didn't help her prepare for her clan's reaction.

"I cannot." Douglas answered the question as she knew he would.

"Ye cannot?" Craig bellowed. "Isn't she good enough for a physician from the university? Would she bring shame to ye if she went back wi' ye when ye left Dunnedin?"

"She will not leave her clan and I must." His face was like stone but his eyes gleamed with anger and impotence. She trembled with sorrow for the things that could never be for them. Wishing a hole would open beneath her feet, Caitlin took a step toward Craig.

"Please, Craig, let us go into yer mother's solar and finish this."

He looked from her to Douglas and back again to her. His eyes were filled to overflowing with tears. His throat was clogged with them and he sobbed out his disappointment. "But did ye hiv to whore for him, Caitlin? Ye should hiv been mine."

The pain of his words pierced through her attempts to remain calm. Her heart screamed in agony—the truth of his words and her actions struck too close. The guilt over her refusal of his offers of marriage that had lain so quietly on her conscience now raised itself to her thoughts.

Standing in shock with tears spilling down her cheeks, Caitlin watched as Robert finally made his way to where they stood.

"Here now, Craig, this is no' the place for this talk." He gestured at Brodie and another man who took hold of Craig. "Take him to his chamber for the night. We can sort this out in the morning." Craig was dragged off, the only sounds breaking the silence were the words he shouted once more.

"Why him, Caitlin? Why him?"

No longer able to hold back, she sobbed openly. An arm went around her shoulder and a soothing voice spoke in her ear. "Come now, lass. Let's go home, for the night is over for ye." Her mother guided her steps away from the fracas and out into the cool night's air. She let herself be led through the claming quiet of the village to their home.

She never asked about what happened to Douglas.

Chapter 25

THE SUN FAILED to rise the next day, or so it appeared in the village and keep of Dunnedin. Douglas was sure he'd never seen as gray a day as this one. And his mood fit it quite well.

The *ceilidh* didn't recover its vitality and fun after the scene with Craig. Craig was shuffled off by Robert's orders and Caitlin was spirited away by her mother. *Spirited* was a good way to describe it, for when he turned to try to explain to Caitlin, she was gone.

But what could he have said?

Douglas approached the practice yard hoping that some exercise would rid him of this nervous energy. Several small groups of men worked out in mock battles with swords. A few skilled horsemen put their mounts through their paces in the yards near the stables. Younger boys and teenagers ran here and there gathering up weapons or ladling out water from buckets they carried. Everything was just as it was every morning there.

Until he entered the yard.

Each and every man there turned to face him. He could feel their anger and animosity. He was, as Craig had called him last night, an outlander. After the initial wave of hostility, they turned from him, ignoring his presence. All but one, that was.

Craig, appearing no worse for his overindulgence, stared at him as he walked the perimeter of the yard. When Douglas reached for a sword from the rack holding them, Craig grabbed his wrist.

"Why did ye no' speak last night? How could ye let someone like Caitlin be shamed by yer actions?"

Douglas flung the man's hand off his own and glared back at him.

"If you have something you wish to settle with me or something to prove, why don't you challenge me man to man without bringing her into it?"

He waited for a few moments and when no such challenge was issued, he turned away. He underestimated Craig's rage, for no sooner had Douglas turned away that the attack came. By sheer force, Craig tackled Douglas into the dirt and began punching and kicking him. No finesse, no weapons other than fists and feet were employed in this grudge match.

"Ye . . . are . . . a . . . learned . . . mon.   Why . . . did . . . ye . . . take . . . advantage . . . of . . . the . . . lass?" Craig delivered one blow after another, accentuating his words with each. Douglas rolled from under his attacker and gained his feet. His head swirled with dizziness from the unanswered punches as he tried to balance.

"I will not answer to you about her. You are not family to her," Douglas panted as he spoke. "You have no claim to her."

"But, at least I will be here for her, ye bastard. Ye will leave wi'oot a care for her or her place after yer gone." Craig began to circle around him. "I offered her marriage, ye offered her nothing but yer bed."

Craig gestured to one of the boys nearby and a staff was thrown to him. Shifting it in his grasp, Craig continued to move around him, waiting to strike. Douglas looked at the men watching. None offered him a weapon to use to fight back. This was not to be a fair fight—this was to be punishment for daring to take Caitlin as his own.

The attack came and Douglas did what he could to fend off the blows with his hands and feet. Although he managed to get in one or two punches of his own, Craig was fueled by pure rage. Fighting on behalf of Caitlin's honor in the clan, he was unstoppable. And, maybe a sense of guilt on Douglas's part made his responses a bit slower than they would have been.

The first few blows hurt as they landed on his arms and back and shoulder, but with each one, Douglas became less and less aware of them. Soon, unable to see through the sweat and blood that dripped into his eyes, he lost his balance and ended up on his knees in the mud. Craig stood over him.

"Ye will stay away from her for the rest of the time yer here in Dunnedin," he yelled, loud enough to be heard out of the yard and through the village beyond. "Do ye hear me?"

Douglas nodded, unable to speak. Craig kicked him once more in the ribs and he landed in the dirt. He could feel consciousness fading and thought he felt the earth move below him. Craig grew dimmer and a new face entered his limited and hazy field of vision.

Pol, the blacksmith, stood over him, all in black, like the harbinger of death. Pol, the incensed father, would give the final blow. He knew with a certainty that he was a dead man, so he closed his eyes to meet his end.

Dying should not be this painful.

When he'd closed his eyes with Pol standing above him, he thought his end would be swift. One blow from those powerful hands and it would be over. He tried to open his eyes but another wave of pain and nausea swept through him and he gagged. Soon his stomach clenched and the bile rose to his throat. Rolling to his side, he tossed up what little food he'd eaten that day and then groaned with the effort it took to lie back down.

" 'Tis a good thing I saw where ye were aiming."

The voice was familiar but he dared not look at Moira. Every inch of his body hurt, from his swollen-shut eyes to his throbbing ribs to his bruised back and sore stomach. The man had been thorough in his assault. He could only hope that Caitlin's honor had been salvaged.

Fingers and hands poked and prodded and his answering grunts and moans gave her the answers she needed. Soon, a cool compress smelling of . . . betony, borage and comfrey was laid on his forehead and ribs. He chuckled, which set off a round of spasms in his chest and stomach. Even half dead, he remembered Cait's lessons.

"Here now, lay still and let me tend to these," Moira said. "Ye are covered wi' dirt and filth and these will fester if left untreated." He felt a warm solution on his torn and bruised skin as she washed his injuries.

"I thought"—he whispered through teeth clamped against the pain—"Pol wanted me dead. Why do you help me?"

"Pol doesna want ye dead. Ye must be daft or the blows hiv done more damage than I thought."

"I saw his face. He was there to kill me as he promised to do if I hurt Caitlin before the clan."

" 'Tis yer own guilty conscience at work, lad. My Pol wouldna hurt anyone. Here now, lift yer head and sip this." She slid her hand under his neck and lifted his head. "What is it?" he asked as the cup touched his lips.

"A bit of valerian root and feverfew for the pain and to help you sleep and mugwort for the spasms in yer belly. Is that according to yer liking?" She held the brim at his mouth and waited. He nodded and she tilted the bitter mix so he could drink it.

"This is better if swallowed quickly." He followed her instructions, knowing it was better than fighting her.

Douglas forced one eye open to look at her. Moira sat

at the side of his bed, measuring and mixing from various vials and pots. He was in his bed? He had no memory of being brought here or by whom. Looking across the room, he noticed the darkness outside the small window.

"How long have I been here?" His head dropped back onto the rough pillow. He'd used too much of his meager energy in holding it up.

"Since Pol brought ye here after yer fight," she answered without looking at him.

"Pol? Pol brought me here?"

"Aye, he did. But his outrage at yer behavior kept him from telling me until just an hour ago." A smile played on her lips. "He kenned he would tell me but at his own time."

"So he left me here all day?"

" 'Twas better than what he really wished to do to ye! Only the knowledge of my displeasure at him beating ye kept ye from more by his hand."

Douglas shifted on the bed, trying to get comfortable or at least out of pain. The groans slipped through as he did.

"Dinna try to move until the concoction does its work, Douglas," she warned. "Just lie still now."

He had but one question. He felt a rush of warmth move through his veins and knew her herbs were at work. The heat and dulling swirled through his head and his thoughts began to scatter out of his mind's reach.

"Caitlin? Does she know?"

"Oh, aye, she does. The whole of the village kens."

"What did . . . she . . . say?" He could feel and hear his words slur and didn't know if he'd even finished his question out loud.

"She said she should kill ye herself for being so foolish as to get into a fight with Craig and for losing."

Smiling, he could hear the words in Caitlin's voice. He drifted off into a drug-induced sleep never knowing Caitlin had uttered the words to him herself.

●　　●　　●

"Such tender words of comfort for the mon ye love? 'Twould no' hurt to really tell him how ye feel," her mother laughed.

"What do ye expect me to say?" Caitlin crept closer to his side and winced as she got a closer look at his injuries. She reached out to touch him but let her hand just rest in the air above him. "Wi' his skills and Craig's lack, he should never hiv lost."

Moira snorted this time. "His loss in this fight has smoothed yer way in the clan, lass. It assuaged Craig's pride and outrage at his taking advantage of ye."

"He didna take advantage of me. Ye ken that as I do," she argued.

"I do, but let his pain and suffering be for some good, Caitlin. Ye shouldna be here at all. Go and see to yer faither's meal. I will join ye soon."

"Ye will leave him here alone?" He could be sick again or need more of her mother's mixture for pain. She shivered at the thought of him, here in the dark and cold and lying in pain with no one to look over him.

"Nay, lass, the lady Anice has someone to check on him. Now, go before ye are seen and Craig hears of it."

"I dinna answer to him. And at this moment, I dinna think I care what he thinks."

"Craig is a good mon, Caitlin. 'Twill be a good laird for us after Robert. He just canna see his way yet."

"Verra weel, I'm going. Did ye want me to tell Da anything?" Caitlin pulled her shawl up over her hair and wrapped it tightly around her shoulders.

"Just that I will be there shortly."

"Mam?" Her mother looked over at her. "Shouldn't I try to ease his pain?"

" 'Tis yer gift to use as ye see fit. I wouldna tell ye aye or nay."

"But, I accept yer wisdom in using it, Mam. What do ye think?"

"I think that he is in pain and will be fine, wi'oot the

use of yer gift. His pride will be battered more than his body in this. Douglas needs this lesson in how the clan's honor works. 'Tis important he learn it now."

Not certain that she agreed, Caitlin nodded acceptance of her mother's advice. She tugged at the door and opened it, checking in the hallway before entering it. Staying near the wall, she made her way along the corridor and down the back stairs. Weaving through alcoves and the shadowed halls, Caitlin left the castle and the keep.

The sight of him lying on his bed, battered and bruised for her, had left her shaken. Her first impulse had been to cry for him or to heal him but the need to throttle him for acting like such a stupid . . . *man* . . . won. Her mother was correct, though. Craig's pride would be salvaged as well as her own in front of the clan. Douglas could stay on but he would not feel the welcome he once had.

Now, all she had to do was stay away from him in all but some social situations. Could she do it? Could she honor the price he'd paid for her reputation and future? She would try but she would make no promises about it.

Chapter 26

TWO WEEKS PASSED and he ached for her every waking and sleeping moment. The dream was back. Almost nightly as he slept now, they were together in the cave, but now the feelings were so much stronger than before they had actually lived the experience. He woke panting and soaked with sweat.

He caught himself walking though the village trying to catch a glimpse of her as she visited those who needed her care. Once or twice he'd been successful but it was not enough. She passed close by him in the hall and he struggled with the urge to reach out to her. It wouldn't have hurt as much if he hadn't caught his glance and if he hadn't seen the same struggle and desire in her eyes.

It had to be this way, it had to. To do otherwise would leave her open to ridicule and shame when he left. But, he was tempted—oh so tempted—to reach for her hand and draw her into his arms.

One morning as he was eating breakfast, he received a summons to the solar from Anice. Surprised and curious, he answered it without delay. The heavy wooden door opened before he could knock. The lady Anice stepped in front of him and prevented him from entering. Taking his arm, she led him a few steps away to a small alcove.

"I have need of your help, Douglas," she said in flawless English.

He blinked in surprise. "I didn't know you could speak English." He'd been speaking Gaelic here since his arrival and had never heard anyone speak anything else.

"I learned many years ago and rarely have the chance to use it here in Dunnedin."

"What is it you need from me?"

"I know of the difficulties between you and my son over Caitlin. She's been a part of his life since he was a child, even through his betrothal to Margaret MacKillop, and he finds it impossible to let her go."

"Not to be rude, but I know all this. Your son made his position quite clear in the yards a few weeks ago. See," he pointed to his still-bruised jaw and eye, "I still bear his mark."

His defeat by the heir of the clan had been rubbed in his face daily. He would take it because of the protection it offered Caitlin, but he didn't have to like it.

"Please, I do not mean to insult you. You and I both know that you could have won that particular battle if you had wanted to do so."

Her assessment and honesty surprised him. The lady Anice was clearly not blinded by a mother's love. He nodded for her to continue.

"He was on his way back from the MacKillops' holding and was ambushed by outlaws."

"Ambushed?"

"Yes. Our men chased off the attackers but Craig took an arrow deep in his arm. He's lost much blood and they haven't yet removed the arrow."

"You want my help?"

"Of course! You are a trained surgeon and know more than any healer here and now. I'm afraid he'll lose the use of his arm if the arrow damages more on its removal."

She stepped closer to him. "Please? Please help my son?"

His instincts took over then and he nodded.

"Yes, certainly I'll help. Where is he?" Already his thoughts were filled with thoughts of what he'd need for this procedure. "Can Connor run for me?"

"Connor, come here to me," her voice carried through the hall and the slapping of feet on the stone floor told her the boy had heard her call.

"What is it you need, Douglas? Connor, do as he says."

Douglas ran down a list of supplies he'd need and directed him to Moira's cottage. Then he followed Anice into the solar. Craig lay on a raised pallet by the fire. His face was a pasty white from loss of blood and his arm still had the arrow stuck in it.

"No, Mother, not him," Craig yelled out as soon as he caught sight of him.

"Cease this tirade, Craig. You willna allow me to call Caitlin or Moira. You will allow Douglas to see to this wound."

The man had used up his energy trying to make his stand and he wilted back against the pallet. Douglas approached and laid his fingers against Craig's neck, testing the strength and speed of his pulse. It was rapid and erratic. Until his supplies got here, there was not much he could do.

"I will need plenty of linens, hot water and soap first," he said to Anice, who stood nearby. She gestured to a servant girl who ran to get it.

Taking his dagger from his boot, Douglas cut through the rest of Craig's shirt and pulled it from him. He tested the position of the arrow and grimaced as Craig paled even more.

"It is lodged in the bone, I'm afraid."

"Do ye think to take my arm?" Panic filled the man's voice and face. He began to struggle to rise.

Douglas held his shoulders down on the pallet. "Nay, Craig, I won't take your arm. You will just require some surgery to remove the arrow without more damage."

"And ye would do this for me?" Craig's eyes were wild with pain and fear.

"Of course I would. Now lie back and be quiet."

When the linens and soap and water arrived, Douglas washed the wound. Standing up, he took hold of the arrow. Craig's face lost the little color it had as he broke the shaft off closer to where it had entered Craig's arm.

A knock sounded at the door and a servant opened it. Finally his supplies and tools had arrived. He turned to thank Connor and instead found Caitlin standing before him.

"I'd like to help ye in this, Douglas, if ye'll let me."

It was the first he'd seen her up close since the fight. Her face was lined with fatigue and her eyes were dulled. He started to reach for her face and realized where they were and who was with them.

"You look ill, Caitlin. Are you certain you're up to doing this?"

"I am just tired. Tell me what has happened to him?" She pointed at Craig, who looked horrified at the thought of the two of them treating his injury.

That look on her face struck something in his memory. She didn't look tired so much as used up. "You did it again, didn't you?" She'd used her healing gift and worn herself out.

A slight smile was her reply. "A gift is to be used, Douglas. Someone had need of it and I couldna refuse them."

"But Caitlin, look at what it does to you. It pulls the energy from your body and your soul. How can you—"

"Douglas. Why don't you finish with Craig and then you can have this discussion with Caitlin outside?" Anice interrupted.

Douglas looked at Anice and then at Craig who watched with interest the exchange going on over him. "You are right, Lady Anice. Caitlin, here is what I want to do."

He leaned over and explained to Caitlin how he wanted to proceed. She listened and agreed and offered suggestions for what they would need to do. In a few minutes they were ready to begin.

Douglas watched as Caitlin brewed a mixture of poppy juice and held it out to Craig. Not sure if he wanted to partake or not, Craig sniffed at it and wrinkled his nose. Anice stepped forward and gave him no chance to refuse, pouring it into his mouth even as he objected.

Trying not to laugh at the similarities between the lady Anice and his own mother, Douglas set out the surgical tools that Pol and Ramsey had completed so far. As he looked up, he caught Caitlin staring at him. She reached out to touch his face and froze. He smiled back, knowing exactly what she was feeling.

Craig grew a bit drowsy so Douglas began probing around the wound. Before he could go much further, the door slammed open against the wall with a thump and Robert strode in with Brodie behind him.

"How is he? Douglas? I'm glad ye are here to tend him. Caitlin, too? God be praised, the lad is in good hands, then." Robert slapped Douglas on the back and winked at Caitlin. "Can I help ye at all?"

"Actually, you can. We've given him the poppy juice to make him sleep but he will fight what we will do. Can you hold him down?"

With a nod to Brodie, they took places at Craig's head and feet and waited for his signal. Anice stood near Caitlin, twisting a piece of linen between her shaking hands.

"The good news is he'll survive with his arm intact," he said motioning to both men. "The bad news is he'll probably still feel this. . . ." Douglas made his first incision into the skin on Craig's arm, opening the area surrounding the arrow. Caitlin followed his every move, dabbing and wiping the blood away so he could see. Craig moaned in his stupor and tried to pull away from his grasp. Robert and Brodie were prepared and held him down.

Douglas worked quickly, though doing this without gloves still felt strange—like walking around naked. He cut

through the skin, layers of muscle and fascia, and deeper
still until he uncovered the arrowhead lodged in the bone.

"He's lucky. The head missed the major artery in this
area. He could have bled to death if this was half an inch
to the other side." He pointed the artery out to Caitlin and
she took a closer look. "We'll need to cauterize that bleeder
there." He touched a damaged blood vessel that still
spurted.

Caitlin called to Anice and gave her some instructions
and some of their instruments. Anice blanched but did as
she was asked, heating the tools in the open flame in the
hearth. Douglas continued his work, cutting out the arrowhead, cleaning the area of bone fragments and other debris
and preparing to make his repairs. He marveled that she
kept pace with him through each step of the procedure, at
times she was ready before he was.

"Are ye ready for these?" she asked.

"Yes. Let's do it quickly now."

Holding out his hand, she placed a long, sharp-ended tool
in it and he touched the bleeding vessel, sealing it with the
hot contact of the superheated metal. They exchanged instruments and he repeated it in different locations until the
bleeding had stopped. His electrosurgery unit at the hospital
would have done a cleaner, finer job, but this rudimentary
system worked once they got their selection and timing
down.

A few minutes later and they were ready to suture the
outer incision. Douglas stepped aside and let Caitlin do it
since her stitches were far better than his. He followed her
movements, dabbing and patting the surgical site so that
she could see her way. Soon they were done—an ointment
and tight clean bandage finished the job.

Caitlin stood and stretched her back as she stepped away
from the pallet. She stumbled as she turned and he reached
out to support her. They stood, looking into each others'
eyes, completely ignoring the world and people around
them. He savored every moment of holding her near to him.

He would have so little chance to do this again before he left.

"You have not even recovered from using your gift. I should have sent you home to rest."

" 'Twas important for me to see how you did this, Douglas. I need to know as much as possible afore ye . . ." Her voice trembled and she never said the word. He heard it though. *Left.*

"Caitlin, here lass, let me see ye home." Brodie stepped closer and took her by the arm. Robert walked over to whisper to Anice as Douglas stood by watching, unable for so many reasons to stop their separation.

"Douglas, the ointment is there," she called over her shoulder. "Give it to Anice with instructions."

His throat was too tight to answer so he simply nodded. Gently pulling the bloody linens from under Craig's sleeping form, he began cleaning up the surgical instruments. He would take them from here to finish the scrubbing and sterilize them as best he could afore returning them to Caitlin. Anice came to his side and tapped on his arm.

"There is no reason for you to do this. Come, let Suisan clean this up."

He followed Anice away from the pallet where Craig now lay sleeping peacefully. She gestured to a chair and he sat down heavily on it. A servant girl collected the bloody sheets and bandages, rolled them up and carried them out of the solar. She returned and gathered up the instruments. She looked to him for guidance. He pointed at the pail sitting on the floor next to the bed. She nodded and made quick work of getting everything ready for him to take.

"Douglas, I can not thank you enough," Anice said, speaking in English once more. Robert came to stand next to her and stared at her as she spoke.

"You are welcome, both of you," he answered, also in English. Robert frowned at him. Apparently the laird did not speak it or know that his wife did.

"I feared that you would be unwilling to help him."

"Anice? I didna ken ye could speak to him like that," Robert said. "Another secret?" His tone was very much a teasing one, one that spoke of the secrets between him and his wife.

"I fear so, Robert, I fear so," she answered in Gaelic once more. "Please, give me a few minutes with Douglas?"

Robert turned in answer and walked to the bedside to check on Craig's condition.

"You worried that I wouldn't help him because he won our fight?"

"Well, there is that . . . and my treatment of your own mother when she was here."

"I don't understand. What has my mother got to do with this?" Douglas searched his memory for any mention his mother may have made of Anice. Only a few vague comments came to mind.

"I was not so kind or accepting of your mother. I even had her—"

"Beaten?" Anice wouldn't meet his gaze so he knew that was it. "Now I remember." His parents had mentioned Anice many times—about how she had beaten his mother and tried to seduce his father, whom she thought was her fiancé. But his parents always ended any comment about Anice with their wish that they could have brought her back with them.

"I am still shamed by my actions against your mother. Even more so when I found out the truth of who your parents really were."

He could feel her pain and remorse and took her hand in his. "They always ended any story about you with their wish that they could've brought you back with them."

Tears filled her eyes and spilled onto her cheeks at his words. She dabbed at them with her handkerchief and then looked at him.

"Now I am truly ashamed. I can see now where your sense of compassion comes from, Douglas. Thank you for helping my son"—she glanced at Craig across the room—"both today and in your dealings with him about Caitlin."

"You make me sound so altruistic, lady. I do what I do for Caitlin." And he didn't like it one bit.

"Then I will thank you for your actions and for those of your father, whom I never had a chance to thank."

"I don't know what you mean."

"Your father suffered physically for my benefit just as you chose to do for Caitlin's." She wiped her eyes once more and looked at him.

"But my father wasn't successful, was he?"

A flash of pain, shame and fear crossed her face and was gone so quickly he didn't know if he'd really seen it. Then he remembered Moira and Pol's words about Craig's father and what he'd done to Anice on their wedding night.

"Your actions will be," she answered, evading his real question and standing. "Now then, it appears my husband is anxious to have words with me. So, tell me what Craig will need."

Douglas walked with her to the pallet and explained the ointments and what she should do in the next day for Craig's injury. After checking the surgical site and Craig's breathing, Douglas picked up the pail with his tools and prepared to leave.

"Douglas?"

He looked over at Anice, who stood clutching Robert's hand.

"Remember me to your parents when you speak to them. Give your father the thanks I could not."

"I will, when I see them."

That day, if all went as Moira thought it would, would be just over a week away. He should be happy about his own time and his own life but his happiness was dimmed by the thought of Caitlin being left here.

Douglas pulled the solar's door closed behind him and went out through the great room and into the kitchen. He would scrub and clean the instruments before returning them to Caitlin.

Then it hit him . . . maybe Caitlin could return with him to his time? He didn't know why Anice had not returned with his parents, but maybe Moira did. He hurried to finish so he could track down the woman and ask her.

Chapter 27

"WHY CAN'T SHE?"

He'd finally found her at the smithy, delivering food to the hungry men working there. She'd tried to avoid his question but he persisted. Finally she grabbed his arm and dragged him outside into the frosty December afternoon. Gray clouds piled on each other to block the sun's rays and warmth from making it to the frozen ground beneath his feet. Occasional snowflakes blew through the air, adding their own chill to the cold.

"Ye are mistaken if ye think 'tis my own hand that guides this, Douglas. I hiv no say in who can pass through the gateway and who does no'."

"I didn't say that."

"No' with yer words so much as the manner in which ye spoke them. The Fates control that archway—I can sometimes see their plans, but that is all."

She was furious at him, he could see it in her face and the ways she nearly spit out her words at him.

"Do ye no' think that sometimes I would like to be able to change the things I see? To save someone marked for death or to be able to do differently something that will harm or injure someone else? Sometimes this gift is a burden." She gasped and covered her mouth with her hands, apparently just realizing what she'd said. "But 'tis mine and I will bear it."

"It must be difficult to know and not be able to help or change what's to come. Have you ever tried?" he asked softly, tamping his own anger down.

"Aye, I hiv tried more than once. 'Tis a hard lesson to learn." Moira stared off into the clouds for a few moments, obviously remembering one of those times.

"So, Caitlin cannot return with me?" The solution had been there in front of him all the time. He would return when the winter solstice and full moon together reopened the door to his time and he would take Caitlin with him.

" 'Tis no' that it canna happen, Douglas. 'Tis just that I havna seen it in the bits of wisdom granted to me."

"So it could, then?"

"I hiv seen her give birth to her husband's child, Douglas. Here, in this time, in this village. I do no' think she will be with ye in yer own time."

"Do you think she would try to return with me?"

"Ask her yerself, for she stands over there."

"Caitlin?" he whirled around to see her standing near the smithy, listening in on their conversation. Her face had more color than earlier but her eyes still looked fatigued. "Would you try? Would you come back to my time with me next week?"

"Douglas. . . .'tis no' Caitlin's choice, either," Moira warned.

"I understand that," he said through clenched teeth, "I need to know if Caitlin would be willing to try."

Caitlin stepped closer, misery etched into her features. She reached for his hand but stopped and let her hands drop to her sides. The wind blew some of her hair free of its tether and the blackness next to her pale face just accentuated the dark circles under her eyes. He knew her answer already but wanted to hear it from her own mouth.

"I canna, Douglas, even though I'd like to see yer world in yer own time." A sad smile lit on her face as she continued. "I canna go with ye, kenning that my people, my family will suffer wi'oot me. My skills as a healer and my gift are all that my clan has to help them when they are ill or injured." She did touch him then, she reached out and placed her palm against his cheek. "But I would go wi' ye if I could."

His eyes and throat burned at her words and at his sense of loss. So this was all a game? He'd been returned to this past to learn about himself and to gain a better hold on his reasons for becoming a doctor. And only to return to his life and be miserable? This didn't make sense at all.

"Can I stay?"

The words were out of his mouth before he could stop them. Would it be better to be miserable in his own time or to stay here and be with her? Her look never changed. He turned to Moira.

"I hiv seen ye under the arch on the night of the solstice."

"And you are never wrong?"

"I see what is shown, what is set. I dinna always see how it comes to pass."

"I would stay, Caitlin, if I could." He wasn't sure if his words made him feel better about this or not but she smiled at him.

"Yer words mean much to me, Douglas. I will keep them and you close to my heart forever." She stepped back and then looked at her mother. Then, before he could saying anything else, Caitlin pivoted and ran away from them and the smithy. A sob carried back to him on the winds and tore at his heart again.

"So that is that? She cannot go and I cannot stay? It doesn't seem fair."

"Life and the Fates are rarely that, Douglas. Ye maun ken that already. And all we can do is make our way through it all."

He looked away, unable and unwilling simply to accept

that this was the end of it, the final word. "Will I see her again before I leave?"

"Aye, ye still hiv work to do together." At his look, she held up her hand to stop the question he was ready to ask. "I dinna ken more than that so dinna ask. 'Tis more of a mother's feeling than true knowledge anyway."

He asked no more questions of her. Moira turned from him and reentered the smithy but not before giving him a sympathetic glance. An overwhelming sense of powerlessness surrounded him, something he'd never felt in his years as a physician. There was always something to try, something to do before giving up hope. Here, now, he had no clue of what to do.

He walked back through the village ignoring the cold winds that pulled at his cloak and his hair, ignoring the greetings called to him, ignoring his heart that clenched in pain in his chest. He could not stand by idly but he just didn't know what to do.

She stumbled along the path, the wind and tears stinging her eyes as she sobbed. Coming to a group of close trees, she stopped and leaned against one for support.

She wanted to go with him. She had, for a single moment, in the deepest part of her being, decided to leave this village and its people behind to accompany him to his world.

Caitlin wanted to be with him, live as his wife, give him children, be part of his world. She'd never desired anything in her life as much as she wanted this man and what he offered.

Not to be alone anymore. Douglas understood how her gift held her separate from others, how it made her different in ways the others couldn't understand. But Douglas did.

Could she go through the arch with him? Even her mother didn't know if it was possible. And her mother had seen Douglas in her visions enter the arch on the night of the solstice. As much as Caitlin believed in her own gift, she had faith in her mother's. Douglas would pass through the arch and return to his own time in less than a week's time and be gone from her life.

Except in her dreams. He still lived there. The cave dreams had returned, now made more vibrant, more real because they had been there, doing everything she saw. There was a new one in these last few nights. She felt the heat in her cheeks as she remembered all they did together in the steaming cave, both in her dreams and in their true experiences.

In the new dream, he'd arrived first and was in the deeper pool. She watched as he dipped under the water and then stood, sluicing his hair and face and opening his eyes. His body glistened with the wetness and in the steam and she ached to run her hands over his chest and to feel his muscles ripple beneath her touch. He'd hold out his hand to her, inviting her in to be with him and inviting her to something *else*. Something more. Something different.

His gaze would become hungry as she shed her clothes before him, he would watch every movement she made until she stepped into the pool and into his embrace. Then, as they kissed for that first time, he would dip them both under the water and they would come up wet and hot and together.

Caitlin shook herself free of the lethargy of the dream. She yearned for nothing more than him, in her life and she in his. But, as the Fates had decided, it was not meant to be.

She could no more give up her place in the clan than she could stop breathing. She could not ignore the gift bestowed on her long ago, not even for Douglas and her own dreams. Even as much as she'd like to at times like these. The gift was part of her, it was her.

The frigid wind finally battered its way through the heavy cloak she wore and reminded her of a task left undone. She rubbed her eyes with the heels of her hands and pulled the hood shawl down tighter on her head. Looking around, she found the right direction to take her home and she walked the short distance to the cottage.

After wiping the rest of her tears away with the corner of her tartan shawl, Caitlin opened the door to the cottage and held onto it as the wind threatened to pull it from her grasp. Winter storms were on their way, these winds told her. The clouds grew thicker and darker by the minute. Winter was full upon Dunnedin and the nights were now longer. She longed for the warmer days and colors of spring and summer.

Once inside, she hung her heavy cloak by the door. The smell of meat and vegetables stewing wafted across the room to her. Caitlin picked up some of the cooking herbs her mother had left on the table and added them to the cauldron over the fire. Stirring to check the consistency, she added two more ladles of water and then pushed the pot back to steep some more. At least a hot and filling meal was promised at the end of this day.

A knock interrupted her kitchen work. Pushing on the door, a small girl crept inside.

"Cora, what brings ye out in this cold wind?" The girl had only six years but was a bright lass.

"My maither said to tell ye 'tis time."

Beitris, Aindreas' young wife, was carrying for her sixth time in as many years. She had become Caitlin's friend the year before.

"I will gather what I need and come to yer cottage. Does yer faither ken yet?"

"No," the little girl shook her head as she answered, "Mam said no' to tell him until the bairn comes."

Caitlin laughed. Aindreas, for all his bulk and strength, was helpless at the sight of his wife in labor. He'd even fainted at the last birth. No, 'twas best if he was not there until the end.

"I will join you shortly. Will ye hiv someone put a pot of water on to boil?"

Caitlin opened the door to let the child out. Cora nodded

and scooted under her arm and out the door. It now looked as though the night would be even longer for her than the day had already been. Caitlin picked up her bundle of herbs and a few other supplies and left for Beitris's home.

The night was even longer than she expected. By dawn, in spite of intense laboring, the babe was still nowhere close to being born. Caitlin had summoned Moira since her mother's childbirthing skills were far superior to her own. Not even that helped Beitris's bairn move from her womb. Now, as dark approached for another long night, she faced the prospect of losing both mother and child.

Aindreas stood before her, arms crossed over his chest and grim-faced. What could she say to him? I'm sorry but your wife and babe will die soon? Even her mother's attempts to turn the babe to allow it passage through the birth canal met with failure.

"What can ye do?" he asked, his strong voice quivering with unspoken love for his young wife.

"Aindreas, I dinna ken what else there is to do. The babe haes turned the wrong way and canna come out. My maither haes tried to turn it to get it in the right position for birth but twice the bairn has slipped her grasp."

The big warrior whitened at mention of what her mother had done. If he'd seen it, Aindreas would have been on the floor in a dead faint. Beitris had held on through the painful attempt, screaming only at the very worst part, but she'd made sure her husband had been sent on an errand before allowing it.

"There is nothing else ye can do? Do ye sit and wait for her to die?"

"Please don't say that where she can hear ye. Beitris needs all her strength and all the fight she haes left to birth this bairn." She pulled him away from where his wife lay exhausted from the last two days of labor. She wasn't ready to give up and didn't want Beitris to, either.

"Mam has gone to talk with the other midwives. Mayhap she will hiv a plan when she returns."

Caitlin walked over to sit near Beitris. Aindreas paced back and forth, making their small cottage seem even smaller. Beitris touched her arm and struggled to lean up.

"Nay, Beitris, save yer strength."

"I maun tell ye, Caitlin," she whispered. "Ye maun save this bairn. I ken I'm to die but ye maun save the babe."

The ailing woman clutched her sleeve and pulled her closer. " 'Tis the son he's always prayed for, yer mam saw him. Ye maun save the babe."

"Aindreas loves ye," she whispered back. "He wouldna want to lose ye for a bairn, even a son."

"But I want him to hiv a son. I've been able to bear him only daughters and just three still live. This . . . is . . . a . . . son . . . for . . . him." The words were barely out when another strong contraction was on her. Too tired to fight it or work with it, she lay back, moaning in spite of her efforts to remain quiet.

Aindreas lost what color he had left and started to sway on his feet. Catching himself, he strode to the door and opened it, taking big gulps of fresh, cold air to revive himself. Caitlin watched, helpless to do anything for either of them.

Her mother came through the open door and closed it behind her, taking in both Aindreas's complexion and his wife's condition. She gestured to Caitlin to join her away from both of them.

"And what hiv ye found?"

"No one haes any other ideas that we hivna tried already."

"There maun be something left to try!" Caitlin would not, could not lose another friend this way. After watching Mildread die just weeks before, Beitris's death would be unbearable.

"Ye canna heal this, Caitlin. We canna take the bairn

until she dies or is close to it and ye canna heal her if she dies."

"I ken, Mam." Desperate, she searched for another idea, another plan—something they hadn't thought of to use to save her friend's life. Douglas. He could help, he could do something with his skills. She would go to him and ask for his help.

"He is at dinner wi' the family now."

She smiled at her mother and at her mother's other gift, the one she rarely talked about, the ability to read someone's thoughts. "I will go to him now."

She stopped Caitlin from leaving. "Everyone will see ye going to him. Mayhap I should send someone to get him?"

"Nay, I need to speak to him first. He still haes the new tools Da made for him."

"Go, then, and hurry. Her strength is fading and the babe canna wait for much longer."

Caitlin grabbed for her cloak and ran the entire way through the village and through the castle gate. Not even the biting wind slowed her steps. Soon she reached the stairs into the keep and was in the great room. Douglas sat with the family this night on the dais where all could see. Craig, pale but recovering, sat at the other end of the long table.

She hesitated only to catch her breath before walking quickly to the front of the hall. Douglas had caught sight of her just after she entered and kept his gaze on her the whole way up to the dais. She went directly to him, never stopping or noting anyone else at that table.

He could not refuse her request, at least she hoped she knew him well enough to know he wouldn't. Of course, with everyone watching, the very act of approaching him was inviting trouble to befall him and her. For her friend and her friend's life, she would risk the anger of the entire clan if that's what it took to save them.

Everyone in the hall watched her in silence as she leaned over to Douglas and held out her hand to him.

"Come with me?"

Chapter 28

HE STARED AT her as though he didn't know who she was. Then he blinked and nodded his head. Standing, he dropped the napkin that had been on his lap onto the table and stepped away from the bench. Walking around the end of the table, he took her hand and followed her back the way she'd come. She stopped outside the hall and faced him.

"We will need the rest of yer tools," she explained. "Do ye hiv them here?"

"Someone is injured?" He turned back to the stairs.

"Someone is dying and I need yer help to save them."

He stopped and waited for her to explain but there was no time. "Please hurry. Beitris can't hold out much longer."

A smattering of talking began in the hall behind her and pretty soon everyone was back to the business of eating. She stood impatiently tapping her foot on the stone floor waiting for Douglas. He was Beitris's last hope.

"I'm ready," he said, racing down the last few steps with his canvas bag under his arm. "Lead the way."

She trotted just ahead of him, leading him back to Aindreas's cottage where Beitris fought for her life. When they reached it, she stopped outside and stood before him. He needed to know what awaited him inside.

"Aindreas's wife is in labor."

"I'm not an obstetrician, Caitlin."

She didn't know what that word meant; another one of his strange-sounding words from the future. Shaking her head at him, she asked, "What is that, that you're no'?"

"An obstetrician," he said again, "is a doctor who delivers babies. It's not my specialty."

"Douglas, my friend is in there, losing her verra life trying to hiv this babe for her husband. I dinna need ye to deliver anything; I need ye to cut the babe out so I can heal her afore she dies."

She thought she'd been clear in her meaning but he scrunched up his face and then stared wide-eyed at her words.

"Cut the babe out? Are you crazy?"

"Douglas, the babe willna come out. Mam haes turned it twice and still the stubborn little thing slips back to where it wants to be. Beitris is losing her strength and soon will no' survive the babe being removed. Ye maun hurry or I willna be able to help her."

"You want me to cut her open and take the baby? A Caesarian section without any medical equipment or support? Caitlin, I'm afraid this won't work."

He stood by the door of the cottage shaking his head. He looked confused by her request but she could see he was thinking it over.

"Please, Douglas. 'Tis her only chance. Otherwise, we maun wait for her to be near or at death's door and take the babe then. She willna survive that and the babe may no' either. Yer skills can get the babe now while she can still fight."

She was about to say something else when the door opened and Aindreas stood in the doorway.

"Good, yer back," he said. Reaching out and grabbing Douglas by the back of his neck, the large man dragged him into the cottage giving him no chance to argue. "My wife haes need of ye now."

She watched as Douglas went to Beitris and spoke to her in quiet whispers. He was quite a sight to watch when he finally accepted his role in this. He felt her friend's belly and then asked if he could check her elsewhere as well. Beitris was so far gone in pain that she wouldn't have known but her bulky husband was watching everything now.

"Aindreas, I need to check your wife—" he started.

"Then he should leave," Moira interrupted. "He doesna do weel in these times."

"On the contrary, he should be right here," Douglas pointed at the spot next to him. "This is his babe and his wife will need his strength in what's to come."

She almost laughed as Aindreas turned a nasty shade of green. But, as Douglas had asked, the man swallowed several times deeply and then went to his wife's side and took her hand in his. Douglas washed his hands in a nearby basin and then pulled a covering over Beitris's legs and lower belly. Quickly, he did the examination he needed to do and then washed again before leaving the woman's side.

"The babe is butt down and settled tightly," he reported to her and her mother. "I'm afraid the placenta is separating from the wall of the womb."

Caitlin didn't know what a placenta was but it sounded important.

"She is bleeding now from inside."

"Bleeding? Oh, God, no' that." Despair began to build, there was no more time. "What will ye do then, Douglas?"

"I have no choice—we have to remove the babe and we have to do it now." He began looking around the room. "I'll need her up higher, on that table if it will hold her." He walked over and tested the table with his weight. "Can you cover this while I tell them what we need to do? Moira, more candles?"

Caitlin found the pile of linens she'd gathered and cov-

ered the table with some, placing several layers and one of
the clean sheets on top. Then she went to wash her hands
again. She knew she would do this with Douglas and
wanted to be ready. Her mother started gathering as many
candles as she could find in the small house to light them
near the table.

She watched as Aindreas and Beitris calmly accepted
Douglas's words and agreed. Aindreas lifted his wife up
onto the table and stood by her head. Caitlin felt tears beginning to swell as she saw Aindreas lovingly caress Beitris's face and kiss her forehead. Blinking rapidly to clear
them, she waited for Douglas to tell her how they would
proceed.

"Caitlin, I am sorry I hesitated. I was back to thinking
about being a healer rather than just being one." He looked
at her and smiled. "I forgot what you've taught me since
I've been here."

Her own heart pounded at his words. He spoke to her
with so much love in his voice that she wanted to cry. But
she could do that after they were done here.

"We cannot wait for something like poppy juice or take
the chance of using henbane since a babe is involved, so I
will have to start and hope she passes out from the pain.
It's not how I want to do this but we have so little time."

Caitlin looked at her mother and saw her nodding in
agreement with Douglas's assessment.

"I need another very strong man or two to help hold her
down and maybe even control Aindreas during this. Is there
someone nearby ye can get to quickly?"

"Ramsey and Kenneth are close by. I could get them,"
her mother offered.

"Mam, no' Kenneth. His wife died in just this way.
'Twould no' be good to put him through this."

Douglas looked startled, almost disbelieving, at her
words. "Does every woman here die in childbirth?" he
asked incredulously.

"Many do, Douglas. 'Tis the most dangerous thing we

do as women," her mother answered. "Weel, I will find whoever I can and be right back."

"Quickly, Moira," Douglas called out but her mother was out the door already. "Now, here's how we will do this." As he laid out his surgical tools, he explained in a few words what he would do.

Within minutes, her mother was back with Ramsey and another large man, Tavis, in tow. He pointed out where they needed to stand and made the last of his arrangements. With a last look at each of them, Douglas was ready to begin. Beitris started to cry and Caitlin found it hard to breathe as she listened to Aindreas comfort his wife. After a few moments, the man nodded at Douglas to start.

The first touch of his blade on her belly was met with a loud, keening wail. Moira had placed a thick strip of leather between her friend's teeth and she could see Beitris clenching it as the pain and scalpel sliced into her. Her bucking was controlled by the many hands on her. A moment later she did faint, leaving the room in silence. Only the heavy breathing of those surrounding the table could be heard.

As she watched, Douglas deepened and widened the cut over her belly from top to bottom. She blotted the incision, trying to give him a clear path in his work. He went in deeper still through all those layers he'd spoken of until he reached a large dark mass that moved under his hands. This was where the babe was? This was what a woman's womb looked like? Amazed, she watched as he cleared his path and prepared to free the babe.

Again he paused to look around at his assistants. "Are we ready?"

"Aye," came Aindreas's reply. He knelt with his head on Beitris's shoulder and her hands clasped tightly in his.

"She may rouse because of the pain. Be ready." Ramsey and Tavis placed their hands lightly on the woman's thighs and ankles.

She followed his movements again as he cut into the womb and within moments, a babe appeared within view.

Tightly curled and frail-looking, it seemed to be tucked inside its mother, waiting to be freed. Douglas did just that, lifting the precious bundle up and out, pausing for a moment before handing it, *him*, to Moira for cleaning.

" 'Tis a boy, Aindreas, a very big boy that yer wife haes given ye this day." Moira wrapped the babe immediately and rubbed his face clean of the fluids coating it. Soon a raspy cry echoed through the room as the babe took his first breaths and found this outer world not so hospitable as the one he'd left behind.

Aindreas lifted his head to look at his new and first son. She could see his mouth moving near Beitris's ear. Caitlin looked at Douglas and for a moment let herself wonder what it would be like to have his child—to see that love and caring on his face as he told her the name chosen for their first son.

'Twas not to be, so Caitlin shook off the sadness and leaned over to help her friend once more.

"This is the placenta, it feeds the babe while in the womb," Douglas said as he pointed to the place inside where the long cord began; its other end was still attached to the babe. He took his surgical knife and cut it close to the babe's belly. "Now, we'll wait a few minutes for it to release completely."

" 'Tis the afterbirth," she said. "I didna recognize it from the inside."

"This is how it attaches to the womb," he explained as he tugged gently on it. "It comes free within a short time after the babe is delivered and then the womb shuts itself off, contracting and shrinking slowly."

"We knead the belly after the babe comes to help it get hard."

"You do? I didn't realize that was known ...," he stopped as he noticed the others listening. "Here. I didn't know you did that here ... as we do in ... the university."

"Aye, Douglas," she said with a smile at his discomfort, "we do that here in the little villages, too."

"How is the baby, Moira?" He looked over to where Moira stood, holding and cooing to the newly born little boy.

"Ramsey and Tavis, we thank ye for yer help in this," she said, ignoring Douglas's look.

Both men released Beitris and moved away. Aindreas murmured his thanks and the men left, looking very relieved to be going.

"Cait? We're not finished yet. I still have to repair her. And it looks like there are a few tears in the wall of the uterus. . . ." He lifted his hands from Beitris's belly and carried the afterbirth over to a pail on the smaller table they were using to hold his instruments.

"Would ye stay or go, Aindreas? I need to finish this birth."

"Is she . . . will she . . . die?" He could hardly force the words out. "She haesna even seen the bairn."

"Wi' God's blessing and if the Fates are wi' us this night, she will hold her bairn by morning."

"Cait, what are you doing?" Douglas reached out and took her by the hand. "I need to cauterize those vessels and suture this incision. Won't you help me?"

"Douglas, please close her belly and let me . . . heal her."

His face went blank and then the deepest frown replaced that dumbfounded expression. "You cannot think to . . ." He couldn't say the word.

"My gift will complete this, Douglas. Can ye hiv faith in me? In the gift I was given?"

"Cait, I can remove her uterus, her womb. She won't have any other children but she'll live. Let me do that." He started to pick up one of the tools but Aindreas stopped him.

"The lass haes a gift, Douglas. Let her tend to Beitris."

Douglas looked as though he would object but then he stopped. Love shone in his eyes. And faith.

"What can I do for you then, Cait?"

She took a deep breath to clear her thoughts. "Can ye catch me if I fall?"

Douglas smiled tenderly and moved away from the table where his work had just done such good. A bairn, alive and healthy. The boy that her friend wanted for her husband. Now she would try to save her friend's life so that she could share in that joy.

Aindreas released his wife's hands and stepped away, leaving Caitlin by herself but watching from a few paces back. She placed her hands over Beitris's belly and began breathing slow and deep. In and out, in and out, in and out. Thinking of nothing but the air moving in and out of her, she cleared her thoughts and sought the black, empty place where the healing came from inside of her.

Moving her hands over her friend's body, she found a certain spot and rested her hands there. With her eyes closed, she waited for the healing to begin. As the tingling and burning started in her hands, her mind looked deeper and deeper within, and soon she lost all awareness of everything but the healing.

Chapter 29

HE CAUGHT HER before she hit the floor as she'd requested.

He wanted to argue when he realized what she planned but then stopped. Although his modern-day mind told him it wouldn't work, his heart told him that Caitlin had the right of it. He wasn't sure of how serious a condition she could heal, but she was certain of it.

Knowing how deeply she cared for her friend, he knew Caitlin would never jeopardize her life. He knew that she would have allowed him to perform the hysterectomy if it was needed. But with the strength of her faith and of her gift, it would not be necessary.

He'd stood back and watched as she used her gift. He'd seen her standing over Gavin as she worked on him but this was different. One moment she was breathing in and out, he thought he heard her counting to herself, and the next moment she was gone.

He'd called her name several times, even stirring the babe from his sleep, but elicited no response from her. Her eyes were closed, her hands stretched out over Beitris, and nothing else moved. The silence and stillness went on and on for more than thirty minutes, he estimated but it was impossible to say without his watch. If Moira or Aindreas were concerned, they never showed it. Both stood by, waiting for the results they knew would come.

"Did it take this long for my healing?" he asked when her trancelike state began to worry him. Her breathing had slowed to almost nil and her complexion grew paler with every passing moment of this process.

"Nay, Douglas, yers was no' so long as this."

"Each one is different?"

"Aye, though the difficult ones take the longest."

"And she'll suffer more for it?" he asked in a whisper, not wanting to add to Aindreas's burden.

"The lass kens the cost of it, Douglas. Dinna worry aboot something ye canna control." Moira rubbed the sleeping babe's head and walked over to his father, who stood by the fire.

"Here, hold yer new son for a bit now," she said as she passed the precious bundle into his arms, guiding him in holding the newborn.

"Will it cause a stir?" He thought about men's role in childbirth and didn't think a father's presence was usual in this time period. Douglas gestured with his head at Aindreas, now holding the baby and looking as if he'd never give him up.

"Oh, aye, 'twill stir things up for a bit. The men in the village go the other way when a woman is giving birth. He did much better than I ever thought possible given his history."

She smiled at the very large warrior across the room who was now a virtual prisoner of the little one in his arms. "He haes usually been on the floor looking up at his wife and new bairns." Moira laughed loudly and Aindreas added a quiet chuckle to hers.

"It's true, Aindreas? You pass out easily?"

"I hope ye won't find it necessary to share yer knowledge wi' anyone else, Douglas. Moira, Caitlin and Beitris are the only ones who ken my abhorrence of the birthing of bairns and why."

"You have nothing to be ashamed of any longer then." He smiled at the incongruity of this brave warrior being taken down by a little pain or blood. He'd seen it happen many, many times in the hospital with emergency births. The bigger they were, the harder they fell.

For all his talk, his concerns never lessened about Caitlin. Still she stood next to the table in that same position.

"How do you know when it's over?" He walked to her side and touched her hands lightly. Heat pulsed through them.

"Ye will ken. Are her breaths still slow and even?"

Listening, it was hard even to hear her breathing. He reached up and laid one finger on the side of her neck to find a pulse. It was there—very slow and even. He counted and estimated that it couldn't be more than fifty beats per minute. He leaned forward and watched for the rise and fall of her chest since he couldn't hear her. Respirations were very slow, too.

He'd seen this before, in people who meditated and those in hypnotic trances. He'd seen one man slow his heartbeat down on command. Douglas wasn't sure which happened here first—the healing or the trancelike state.

He was getting restless just standing here but he wouldn't be anywhere else in the world. They had so little time left in which to be together. However, this was not how he'd like to spend it with her. Still, it was better than being tormented with worry about how or where she was. He would stay with her until forced away.

A few minutes later, he thought he saw her eyes move under their lids. Checking her pulse again, it was faster, though more erratic this time. He could hear her breathing now and watched as her hands trembled and shook and she began to sway. He reached for her at the same time Moira called out a warning.

She was dead weight in his arms and he struggled to get

a hold of her without stumbling against the table and against Beitris. Aindreas handed the baby off to Moira and helped Douglas lift Caitlin and carry her over to the vacant pallet.

All color had drained from her face and her breaths came in irregular gasps. She seemed to be in pain but didn't know how that could be. Of course, if the blood was rushing into her legs and arms after standing so still for so very long, he could understand those feelings. This was different— she lay clutching at her stomach and moaning.

Douglas was at a loss for what to do for her. He looked at Moira who seemed very calm considering the circumstances. Her daughter lay writhing in pain and she stood by and watched.

"There is no' a thing I can do for this part of it, Douglas, except to watch over her and keep her from harm."

"She's in pain? Does that happen?"

"Aye, the severity depends on the seriousness of the healed person's injury or illness."

"She's clutching her stomach?" He didn't like what he knew was coming as an answer.

" 'Tis the area where the injury or illness occurs."

"You mean that when Cait healed my head wound, she had pains in her head?"

"Aye, Douglas," she answered quietly. " 'Tis the way of her gift."

"Then I don't like her gift. It is a big burden for her to carry." He wasn't sure what kind of person could carry a burden like this one and do it successfully. Knowing that you can heal but will suffer physically for it? It took a very strong person to face that kind of choice.

And Caitlin had been doing it for years. Alone. And she didn't hesitate to use it when needed: for him, for a small boy with a broken arm or for a woman trying to birth a son for her husband and trying to live through it.

She moaned again and curled up tighter on the rough

bed. He needed to do something for her. Now. He looked to Moira for answers.

"She will rest easier on her own pallet. Can ye take her home now, Douglas?"

He began to collect his instruments until Moira waved him off. "I will gather yer things for ye, Douglas. Just take her home now."

"I want to check Beitris, if Aindreas says I may?" He looked to the man for permission before laying a hand on his wife. At Aindreas's nod, he lifted the covering Moira had placed over the woman's abdomen and looked at the surgical site.

It was gone.

The abdomen was nearly flat and no incision line or scar marred the smooth surface. He placed his palm on it and slowly, gently felt the surface and pressed against the skin. Firm. No swelling. No puffiness. No sign that she'd delivered a baby by Caesarian section less than an hour before.

This was absolutely the most incredible event he'd ever witnessed. His hands trembled as he continued to probe Beitris's belly, looking for signs of trauma. Nothing in his training or experience could match this.

"Douglas? Are ye unweel?" Aindreas asked. "Ye look as I feel just before I hit the floor."

He shook himself free of the stupor he felt and simply could not believe his eyes or his hands. He'd told Caitlin he believed in her ability to heal others. It was a lie. He believed that she believed in her gift. He'd held back his own true feelings, not wanting to admit to his doubts in her.

Now, faced with the truth of her gift right in front of his eyes, he believed. She would be crushed by his lack of faith in what she held so dear.

"Douglas, ye hold yerself guilty of something that ye are no' guilty of."

She was doing it again. Moira had appeared at his side and offered her calm words as if she knew the internal turmoil he was suffering. He turned to her and she wore that accepting expression he'd seen so many times on Caitlin's face. And on Mairi's.

"I didn't believe." He held his hands out over Beitris, pointing out his lack of faith.

"Lad, ye of all people haid many reasons to doubt. The more learned ye are, the less ye can accept the unknown or the unseen."

"She only asked me for a bit of faith in her gift."

"And, ye gave it to her tonight. Ye could hiv interfered and done what ye planned to save Beitris. Ye didna. Ye gave over when she asked ye to. Ye believed."

"But, I . . ." He couldn't say anything more. All he'd seen tonight was finally getting to him.

"Dinna fash yerself now. Take my lass home and ye can talk more when she wakes."

"How long will that be? Is there some way to tell?" He tried to remember back to his own healing but his thoughts were scattering rapidly.

" 'Twill be as long as she needs, no longer and no less."

"I see."

"Nay, ye don't, but yer too tired to argue wi' me anymore! Take her home and then get some rest yerself."

"Should I leave her alone?" Douglas didn't want to leave her in the dark and alone. Staying with her might not be an option, either.

"Pol will be there. Ye can stay if ye'd like."

He nodded and walked to stand over her. She moaned softly in her sleeplike state but didn't respond to his lifting her in his arms or when he said her name. Moira tucked a heavy plaid around her for the journey home.

"I will finish here and make certain all is weel afore I come home."

"Aindreas," he said as he carried Caitlin to the door. "Congratulations on a fine new son."

"I willna forget yer role in this, Douglas. I am in yer debt as weel as the lass'."

"Love her"—he looked at Aindreas's wife who slept peacefully—"and your debt to me is paid."

Douglas navigated his way out the door, stepping carefully as he held Caitlin so close. He breathed in her scent and recognized the soap she made for herself and her mother. She'd always smelled of mint, she had even tasted of it when he'd been with her in the cave.

It was a short walk back to her cottage by way of a shortcut he now knew. Soon he was knocking on the door and hoping that Pol was there to open it.

The door swung in and Pol stood in the doorway. When he saw who it was and who he carried, Pol tried to take her from him.

"I will carry her in, just open the door," he said.

"Here now, let me help ye," Pol moved out of the way and took the woolen wrap off his daughter. "Her pallet is over here."

Douglas followed him and knelt down to lay her on it. He covered her with the plaid that Pol held out and then tucked it around her to make sure she was warm. Caitlin continued to moan and clutch her stomach even through his ministrations. He touched his wrist to her forehead and cheek and checked for fever but there was none.

"This happens wi' each healing," Pol offered.

"So Moira tells me. Is she ever not successful?"

"Caitlin? In her healings?" He nodded. "She haes been successful in all but one."

"Really? What was the one that didn't work?"

Pol leaned over and brushed the hair away from his daughter's face. Standing up, he smiled. "She was. She tried to heal her own sprained ankle the night ye arrived."

"Her ankle? How did that happen?"

"She told her maither she turned too quickly on a rough part of the path and twisted her ankle. When she heard the outlaws, she tried to heal the sprain but her gift didn't work."

"All the others have? That's amazing."

"Aye, 'tis." He heard the father's pride. "Weel, 'tis late now. I'll look after her until Moira returns."

"I would like to stay a bit, if you have no objection. I want to make sure she is recovering."

Pol looked at him in the light given off by the hearth and few candles. " 'Twould do no harm if ye sat by her for now."

"Thank you. I won't stay long."

Pol went back into the chamber he and Moira shared and soon snores emanated from the room. He checked Caitlin once more, then threw his own cloak onto the floor near her and lay down on it. He planned to stay awake until Moira returned home.

Reaching over carefully, he took one of Caitlin's hands and entwined their fingers. That slight sensation was still there, much duller than their first touch but nevertheless there.

Since he didn't plan on sleeping, he was very surprised to be awakened by Pol's leaving for the smithy in the winter day's gray dawn. He looked around, confused at first by where he was and why. His hand, still entwined with Caitlin's, made things clear.

He released her hand and rolled to his back, stretching muscles sore from sleeping on the very hard floor and, from the looks and feel of it, in one position. Sitting up, he saw that Caitlin was still asleep and still as pale as when he'd laid her on the pallet. The thick covers were off her shoulders so he knelt over her and rearranged them to make sure she was covered. Then he sat back, leaned against the wall and watched her sleep.

How long would she be this way? Her heartbeat was still erratic but it was not as slow as when she'd done the healing. Her breathing, too. He watched her eyes moving now beneath their lids, much as in REM sleep. Maybe she was dreaming? Only an EEG could give him an idea of her brain activity and that machine was still centuries in the future. So he hoped and prayed that this was going along the way it should.

Moira had said she would sleep as long as was needed. He only had a few more days before the doorway through time was open again and he would leave. He added a prayer that he would have a chance to say good-bye to her before he left.

Sometime later his stomach grumbled, letting him know that he'd missed most of dinner last night. Moira was still not back from tending Beitris so he'd have to see to his own needs. He could go back to the castle for food but he didn't want to leave Caitlin alone this way.

He stood and left the alcove where she slept. Going to her worktable, he pulled out a wooden box that held some of her herbs and found the betony she'd already wrapped in material. He told her it looked like a big tea bag and she'd laughed, but not known what he'd meant. Going to the hearth, he stirred the embers and added a few new pieces from the wood pile. While waiting for the fire to burn hotter, he looked for the big cauldron and carried it out the well.

Taking a few minutes to handle his early-morning tasks, he went to fill the large pot with water from the well. A thin coating of ice covered the surface of the water and he heard it crunch when the pail hit it. A few dips of the bucket later and the pot was filled. Hauling it back into the cottage, he slid it onto the sturdy metal grating over the cooking fire and waited for it to heat.

Douglas searched through the stored pans and pots and found the one Caitlin used for her tea and placed it near the hearth, dangling the betony stalks over the side of it. A short while later, after checking on her condition twice more, the water began to boil. Pouring it over the herbs filled the air with the fragrant smell of betony. He inhaled the aroma and the steam and chuckled to himself over how much this simple act reminded him of Caitlin.

He watched her do this almost every morning they'd

spent together. A simple task but so intermingled with memories of her: her smile as she poured his tea for him, a grimace when she forgot to add the requisite drops of honey, the satisfied sigh when it was just right.

His stomach rudely interrupted his musings. Adding some honey to the pot, he placed it on the corner of the hearth to steep. Then, searching on one of the shelves, he found a large bag of oats. Mixing it with water as he'd seen Caitlin do, he soon had a small collection of the most unsightly, uneven oatcakes he'd ever seen. Cooking was never his forte so he was pleased with his results and placed a flat griddle pan over the heat. Already well-seasoned from much use, he placed the moist cakes on the heated surface and watched over them as they cooked. In spite of his close attention, some of them burned.

He scooped them onto a plate and brought them to the table. He poured a mug of tea and sat alone at Caitlin's table. Biting into one of the cakes, he laughed. If he'd been able to add some cinnamon along with the honey to the oats, it would've covered some of the burnt taste. At least he wouldn't starve.

It was sitting there, eating oatcakes and drinking betony tea, that Moira found him. The door opened and she entered with the cold December wind at her back. He ran over to help her get in the door and relieved her of the heavy sacks she carried.

"Thanks to ye, Douglas. I thought the wind would carry me away in spite of these."

"It does grow colder these last few days," he said, carrying the bundles to the worktable. He went to the hearth, poured another cup of the tea and walked it over to her. She removed her heavy cloak and hung it by the door. Accepting the mug and nodding her thanks, she went to the table and sat down.

"It haes been a very long night."

"All is well with Beitris and the babe?" He pushed the

plates of oatcakes toward her. Thinking on it, he also moved the crock of honey within her reach.

"Oh, aye. Beitris woke in time to give young Robbie his first feeding this morn."

"They've named the boy Robbie?" He bit into another cake and washed it down with a swig of tea—it was more than tolerable that way.

"Aye. 'Tis our custom to name the first son after his faither's faither. Robert was the name of Aindreas's faither, God rest his soul."

Looking at their food, Moira frowned. "Caitlin couldna be awake by now. Did ye make this?" She held out the oatcake in her hand.

"I'm afraid so. Be kind in your comments, it was my first attempt." He laughed, anticipating some caustic remarks.

" 'Tis much better than Pol's efforts, but dinna tell him I said so. He does try," she said as she bit once more into the cake. Chewing and swallowing, her expression became more serious. "Haes she stirred yet?"

"No. She is in the same position as when I placed her there last night. Her breathing and pulse is faster but not steady. Is this normal?"

"Aye, 'tis how it goes. She will need several days to recover from this one."

"Several days? But I don't have several days to wait for her to wake up." He'd be gone on the third day from this one.

"Ye canna rush this or she willna regain her own strength. Ye saw how she was when she rushed to Craig's side the other morn? She had just started to rouse when young Connor arrived with your request for your tools. She gained the whole story from him and ran off to help ye."

Douglas remembered her pale face and how little strength she seemed to have, even swaying on her feet near the end of their minor surgery.

"This healing took much from her, it still does. 'Twill take time to let her come back from it."

"I wanted . . ." He choked on the words.

"Ye wanted to say yer farewells to her afore ye leave?" He nodded, his voice refused to work.

"Mayhap, 'tis better this way. She will suffer from yer leaving and will long for ye. If ye leave while she sleeps, 'twill be easier in the run of things."

"Not to say good-bye?" he whispered. Was she crazy? A chance to share a few last minutes with the woman he loved, and he should pass it up?

"Douglas, I think the two of ye said what ye had to say in at the smithy the other day. Prolonging this with vows of remembrance and never-ending love will make it much more difficult on both of ye." He started to shake his head but she pointed at him.

"Ye will return to yer world and move on in yer life. There will be other women and ye will love again—'tis the way of things. Caitlin will remain here and soon be a wife and maither."

"I will never forget her," he argued.

"And, she will never forget ye. But she will pick up her life and go on and find her place in the clan as she was meant to do."

"Such a realist," he said sarcastically.

"Someone haes to be," she answered blandly. "In the meantime, dinna ye hiv something ye can tend to while ye wait?"

"Here?"

"Here or up at the castle? Ye should stay busy."

He looked around the room and saw that many of the herbs were ready to be ground and added to Caitlin's stores. His instruments, the ones that would soon be hers, needed to be cleaned and sharpened and wrapped.

"There are things to be done here, especially if Caitlin cannot do them herself. I would like to stay and do some of them."

"As ye wish," she said, standing up and walking to the worktable. "I hiv to check on some others in the village. I will return by noon."

"Should I try to feed her something? Broth, maybe?"

"Nay, she'll eat when she wakes. I'll hiv a tonic ready as weel."

"Does she need anything else when she wakes? Is there something else I can prepare for her?" He wanted to do something for her. He ran his hands through his hair and pushed the long pieces behind his ears. The braids she'd made had come loose long ago and his hair hung in his face again.

"She'll wake, drink the tonic, and then go to the hot springs for a bath. That's what she does when the healing takes this long and this much from her. There's no' much else for ye to do."

"Fine," he nodded at her. "I'll look after her and finish some work we started a few weeks ago."

Moira packed a satchel and threw her heavy cloak around her shoulders. With one more look at him, she tugged the door open and left.

Chapter 30

THE REST OF the morning passed slowly; Douglas alternated between sitting with Caitlin and grinding, sifting and sorting herbs. He stopped for another round of oatcakes for lunch, this time with some hard cheese and ale. The afternoon was showing every sign of passing as slowly as the morning when the door to the cottage opened.

"Moira," he said without looking from his seat at the worktable. "I expected you back for a noon meal. Did my oatcakes frighten you off?"

" 'Twasn't yer oatcakes, Douglas."

And it wasn't Moira. Douglas spun on his seat to face Craig who stood across the small cottage from him.

"I came to see Caitlin. Haes she roused yet?" Craig loosened his cloak and pulled it from his shoulders. Without hesitation, he walked back over to the door and hung it on one of the pegs. He obviously knew his way around here.

"No, she still sleeps." Douglas glanced toward the alcove where Caitlin lay sleeping.

Craig walked past him and into the next room. Trying to be nonchalant, Douglas followed Craig's movements without turning his head. Craig crouched down next to Caitlin and touched her cheek. Then he smoothed her hair away from her face and stood. After watching her for several minutes, he came back into the main room.

"Haes she been like this since the bairn was born yesterday?" Obviously he'd heard the news and the story behind it.

"Moira tells me this is the way of it."

" 'Tis the first time ye've seen her do this?" Craig asked.

"She healed a broken bone, but didn't use herself up like this." He gestured to where Caitlin slept.

"*Used herself up* is a good way of saying how the healing affects her. I worry for her when 'tis something more difficult like this time."

Douglas could hear the sincere concern in Craig's voice. Maybe Caitlin would be okay with him after all. But there was still the issue of what happened in the woods the night he'd arrived.

Gazing directly at him, Douglas decided to ask. "Why did you stand and watch that night Caitlin was attacked?"

Craig blanched at the accusation leveled at him and looked away. He took a deep breath and looked back at Douglas.

"I was watching her that night. She'd told me no' to follow her but I thought it would be a chance to get her alone."

"For what?" Douglas asked, although he was pretty sure he knew the answer.

Craig's gaze met his momentarily, then the man focused on something across the room. "To try to convince her to marry me. 'Twas damn difficult to talk privately wi' her faither always nearby."

Douglas laughed—he knew the feeling himself. Pol could be quite intimidating.

"So I followed but I lost sight of her when she turned off the path unexpectedly. By the time I'd caught up wi' her, the MacArthurs had taken her."

"And you did nothing?" He couldn't believe Craig would

stand by and watch her be kidnapped . . . or worse.

"For God's sake, I panicked! I've never been in a real battle and never faced three warriors to my one. I hesitated, God forgive me." Craig hung his head in shame. "I thought to challenge them and didn't. I thought about going for help but there wasna time. I did no' ken what to do."

"And?" Douglas wanted to know the whole story.

"I heard and saw ye come crashing through the trees," he added dejectedly. "I did no' ken who ye were, whether ye were wi' them or against them. So, after ye'd finished wi' two of them, I crept up behind ye and tried to hear yer words."

"I was no danger to Caitlin. Why did you strike me from behind?"

"By then I heard some of the MacKendimens coming up behind me and I needed to do something. . . ."

"So that they would not know you panicked?"

"Aye."

As much as he disliked hearing it, Douglas found the whole story very believable and sincere. The young heir of the clan was under much pressure to perform in battle. Fortunately for the clan, he'd not had the opportunity to be tested in that way since their part of the Highlands had existed in relative peace for years.

"And Caitlin knew this?"

"Aye. I came here when ye were still unconscious and told her. I thought everything would be the same between us. But it wasna." He gave Douglas a disgruntled look. It didn't take much to decipher that one.

"Me?"

"Ye. She fell in love wi' ye even while I tried to convince her we could still be married."

"Do you still want to marry her? Could you love her?" He might as well get this straightened out. Maybe he could go home easier if he knew she would be taken care of.

"I would marry her but I dinna think she will hiv me as a husband."

"Do you love her?" He had to know how it would be for Caitlin even if the thought of another man loving her tore at his insides.

"I hiv always cared for her and I still do."

"Even knowing that we have been lovers?"

Craig shifted on his feet and took a few steps toward the alcove where he could see Caitlin. "Aye, even knowing that ye had her first," he whispered. "I ken that she will be a faithful wife and I willna worry aboot what came afore."

"Will she be accepted as your wife?"

Craig returned to face him. "Caitlin is esteemed by the clan for her gift. We all ken what the price is to her each time she uses it to benefit someone. As my wife, she will be accepted in all ways."

That was what he needed to hear. Craig would not hold against her what they had shared. She would take her place as the next lady of the clan and the clan valued her for the gift she had and used on their behalf. She would not be alone. She would have the husband and the blue-eyed, black-haired daughter Moira saw being born in one of her visions.

A lump in his throat prevented him from saying anything else. Douglas stood and went to the hearth, trying to appear busy by moving pots around on the metal grate. He heard Craig walk over to the door. He cleared his throat and looked at the other man.

"I leave Dunnedin tomorrow night or the next day."

"Then I should thank ye now for what ye did. My arm feels better already." Craig lifted and rotated his injured arm in a circle. "Ye are verra skilled at caring for wounds. Robert speaks of nothing else but yer own gift for treating the wounded and ill."

"You are welcome. I ask only one thing in return."

Craig looked at him, waiting to hear his price.

"Love her well."

"I will. If she'll hiv me, that is," Craig answered, his

voice husky with the same emotion Douglas could feel in his own voice: love for Caitlin.

"You'll have to handle that yourself, Craig."

"She haes a way of making her own decisions aboot things, Douglas. I am no' certain she'll accept my offer."

"You might want to give her some time after I leave before you ask her."

Nodding, Craig held out his hand to Douglas. Douglas accepted it. Caitlin would do well with this man.

"Did ye note that she didna heal either one of us when we needed it?" Craig asked as he threw his cloak over his shoulders.

Laughing, Douglas realized he was correct. "I wonder why that was?"

"I heard her muttering something aboot 'pigheaded, stupid men' under her breath as ye cut the arrow out of my arm. Do ye think she meant just me or both of us?"

Douglas clapped him on the back. "I'm afraid she was talking about both of us."

Craig walked to the door, but paused with his hand on the wooden bar.

"One question." He nodded and Craig continued. "Why did ye let me win?"

"Who said I let you win?" All his pain and the time spent away from Caitlin would be for naught if Craig thought he'd let him win.

"Dinna insult me, Douglas. Just answer my question . . . why?"

"I think you know the answer, Craig."

"Caitlin?"

Douglas just nodded. Craig paused for a moment and then pulled the door open. " 'Tis sorry I am that ye willna be here for a proper challenge." And with that implied threat, Craig leaned down and ran out into the cold winds that swirled outside.

Douglas poured himself another cup from the pot on the hearth and put it on the worktable. He spent a few minutes clearing up the work he'd begun before Craig's arrival and then went in to sit with Caitlin again.

She had rolled to her other side but was still curled up tightly with her arms crossed over her belly. He adjusted the covers and replaced the pillow under her head, trying to make her as comfortable as possible. He brought the brasier closer and placed another peat chunk into it to make it warmer in her area of the cottage.

Her color was still ghastly so he checked her pulse again. It was still erratic but gaining strength. Her breathing was stronger, too. How long could she stay in this comalike state?

In spite of Moira's words, he wanted to see her to say a last good-bye. He believed that a clean break was necessary. He didn't want to be plagued with thoughts of what he should've said or could've said in the years to come. Living without her would be difficult enough.

Unfortunately, it would not be his decision. Her recovery from using her own energy to heal Beitris had wiped her out. She had taken almost two days to recover from his own healing. At that rate, she would awaken the day after he left.

She must have known. She must have known that she would miss his departure when she used her gift on Beitris. But wasn't that just like her? Always putting others first, always using her gift when needed. Never thinking about her own needs or desires. That was one of the reasons he loved her.

He would spend the night here again and hope against hope that she would wake in time. Tomorrow he would clear out of his chamber in the castle and say his farewells to Robert and Anice and a few others. He would be back here before dark and wait for the time when the fullness of the moon met the winter solstice. Then he would go home.

Without his heart.

Without his soul.

Without Caitlin.

Chapter 31

THE LAIRD AND lady greeted him in the solar. They'd wanted these farewells done in privacy so they could talk freely.

"So, this is the night, then?" Robert asked from his chair by the fire. Douglas and Moira had come, leaving Pol with Caitlin.

"From all the signs, 'tis the night," Moira answered.

"I wish you well on your journey, Douglas," Anice said. "And I thank you again for the help you've given during your stay with us."

"I'm glad that I could help. I will pass on your message when I see my father. My parents will both be glad to know you are alive and happy."

Anice looked to Robert and then back at Douglas. "I am that, Douglas. I am that," she said, placing her hand in her husband's. His parents would be glad to know there was a happy ending to Anice's story.

"I ken ye willna want to hear this but I am sorry to see ye go," Robert said. "I watched ye and Caitlin work on Craig and ken that ye would be good together. Not just for each other, but for the clan as weel. Yer skills complement each other's and would be of such benefit for us in the coming years."

"Robert, I . . ." Douglas couldn't go on. This was much, much harder to do than he'd thought it would be.

"I ken, lad, ye hiv yer own life to return to in yer own time."

"And no control over the coming and going," Moira added.

This lack of control was beginning to grate on his nerves. He wanted to scream to the heavens but it would do no good. This was the night.

He had to get out. Now.

"Robert and Anice, thank you again for your hospitality and understanding in this." He nodded at them and turned to leave.

"I'll meet ye back at the cottage, Douglas. Make yer way and ready yerself."

Douglas picked up the satchel that held his clothes and belongings he'd had with him when he arrived here. He would need to change before going to the arch tonight.

Leaving the solar, Douglas made his way through the great hall and out of the castle. A few stops to make and then he would spend his last hours in this time at Caitlin's side, awake or asleep.

He entered Moira and Pol's chamber to change into his own clothes. It took a few minutes and he was dressed as he'd arrived—jeans, shirt, leather boots and leather jacket. His hair was much longer but that could be handled easily enough when he got back to his own time.

The jeans felt very restrictive, tight around his waist and thighs. He hadn't gained weight while here—he'd probably even lost a few pounds—but he'd grown used to the loose-fitting kilt. He gathered his hair and tied it back. He slipped his watch on his wrist and checked it once more. It still didn't work.

He carried the satchel with his daggers in it and his

leather jacket into the main room. Pol looked him up and down and grinned.

"Verra strange clothes ye wear in yer time, Douglas."

"It feels strange to wear them again. I've grown used to the plaid."

"Can ye move aboot in them?" Pol pointed at his straight-leg jeans.

"Right now, barely. They will loosen as I wear them longer."

"Douglas, Caitlin is stirring. Ye might want to spend a few minutes wi' her afore ye go."

Douglas was overwhelmed by Pol's attitude. He had taken the man's daughter as his lover, without promise of marriage, and the man continued to be his supporter.

"Pol, I don't understand. Why do you allow this?"

Pol laughed. "Mayhap because I believe that love is stronger than even the Fates? I was a young mon once and loved where I should no'. I understand the pain ye suffer. Now go to her. I hiv to see Ramsey for a bit; I'll return later."

Pol turned and, as Douglas stared in disbelief, left the cottage. He was speechless. The blacksmith was really a romantic at heart? So it would seem. He wasted no time going to Caitlin.

Her color was getting better, now ghostly instead of ghastly. He touched her neck to feel her pulse and found it stronger, too. Still erratic, but definitely stronger. She turned her cheek into his hand as he touched it to check for fever. It was then that he noticed her eyes were open and looking at him.

"Douglas," she whispered. "I thought ye would be gone."

"But you gave up your own strength anyway and took the chance of not seeing me again, didn't you, Caitlin?"

Tears filled her eyes.

"No, please don't cry. I only have a short time before I leave. I wanted to talk." He crossed his legs and sat down next to her. "Can you sit up?" Taking both of her hands in his, he pulled her up gently to face him. Seeing her eyes begin to get glassy, he held her against him, laying her head on his chest.

"Give it a few minutes—the dizziness will pass. You've been laying down for a long time."

He sat, holding her in his arms, rubbing her back slowly. He would stay like this forever if only the Fates would allow it. Soon she lifted her head and looked at him. They spoke at the same moment.

"Caitlin."

"Douglas."

"Go ahead, Cait. You go first." The smile on her face, so full of love, nearly broke his heart.

"No matter what happens tonight, I am glad ye came to this time. I'm glad we could love for a while, even if no' for our whole lives."

"I feel as if I have loved you for my entire life, Cait. I don't remember a time when I didn't have dreams of you. And now that we've shared this time together, I know I'll always dream of you."

He leaned down and kissed her mouth. She opened to him and tilted her face to meet his mouth more fully. Rubbing their lips together, he tasted her again and again. He would never get enough of this, of her. And the memories would have to last the rest of his life.

Caitlin lifted her mouth from his and opened her eyes. "I will remember yer kisses for the rest of my life, Douglas. They make me feel so verra hot and cold at the same time," she said, smiling at him once more. "I dinna think that I will ever feel that again."

"I'm sure that Craig . . ." The words escaped before he could stop them. Damn! This was really not the time to speak of who would take his place in her life, in her heart, in her *bed*.

"What haes Craig to do wi' this?" She eyed him suspiciously.

"I shouldn't have said anything, Cait."

"Ye probably should no' hiv, but now that ye did, tell me the rest."

Douglas touched her lips quickly before telling her of his conversation with Craig. Her chin was already beginning to edge forward in protest.

"Craig came to see you while you slept. We talked about . . . many things."

"Such as?" The chin moved a bit more. He ached to kiss it but this would not be a good time.

"You. Me. The night I arrived in the woods."

Her mutinous look softened slightly. "So you did know the truth of it."

"Aye, I did. Craig and I talked of it while *you* slept."

"Tell me your version." She frowned at his words. "Tell me what happened."

"I was to go and find some certain herbs for Mam that night. They are ones best harvested in the night and they maun be picked in the light of the full moon."

It was his turn to frown and look confused.

"There are such plants, Douglas. No' many but a few that Mam and I use. That night was my last chance to get to them since the full moon was beginning to wane and the cooler air would soon damage the fragile leaves."

He nodded as she spoke. This was interesting. When he got home, he had many topics to research for more information.

"Craig haid been here and wanted to accompany me into the woods. I wanted some small measure of peace and quiet so I made certain that Da heard us outside."

He laughed. "You are a wicked woman, Cait. Setting your father on the *puir, wee lad.*" She laughed with him this time.

"Sometimes, I just canna help myself, Douglas. Da's size and stern looks can frightened even the bravest in the clan. So thinking Craig out of the way, I set off to the place where we grow some of our herbs. I maun no' hiv been watching my steps for I looked around me and realized I was lost."

"You went alone into the woods at night? Don't you worry about . . . well, exactly what happened to you?" This time didn't have the muggers and higher crime of his own but she must know there was danger.

"Nay, I was on MacKendimen land. I was safe. Weel, I thought I was. . . ."

He could tell by the movements of her eyes and the brief look of fear that she was remembering the MacArthurs.

"No, Caitlin," he said, rubbing her arms. "Don't think about that part. Tell me when Craig arrived."

She shook her head and cleared her throat before continuing. "Douglas, if ye haid no' come at that time . . ."

"Craig would have acted." At her frown, he added, "I am certain of it now."

"Weel, ye came screaming through the trees, throwing yer daggers like a berserker of old. 'Twas a sight to behold." She reached out and touched his cheek lightly. "Truly."

"Ye took out the two and approached the other who was holding me." She paused and swallowed deeply. He took her hands in his and held them. "I didna ken ye, I could no' see ye weel in the shadows as ye approached us. I was so frightened."

"I know. I couldn't see your face, either, your hair hung around it. And, from the training I've had in handling these kinds of situations, I didn't want to look at you."

"Training in what?"

"I've worked with the police before, Cait. Oh," he said at her scowl, "they are like your king's men—they capture criminals." She nodded, understanding his explanation. "In an emergency situation—in times of danger—looking at the victim or hostage can make you lose your concentration. So it's to be avoided once you assess their condition . . . once you know how they are."

" 'Twas then that I saw Craig, creeping out of the woods

from behind ye. He was watching ye and waiting. Then I heard more noises from the forest and kenned that the MacKendimens were coming. Craig hesitated as ye aimed yer dagger and then I screamed when I saw yer face. The last thing I saw afore fainting was Craig's arm raised behind yer head."

"Craig said he panicked."

" 'Tis the right of it, Douglas. Craig is more skilled as a lover than a fighter."

He choked at her words, coughing until his throat cleared. "You know of Craig's skills as a lover?"

"No' his skills, just his reputation. Although now, the words of his women make more sense to me. Since ye . . . since we . . . hiv . . . ."

"His women?" Douglas asked incredulously.

"Oh, aye. His nights are never spent alone. Suisan seems to be his favorite right now but most of the women who work at the castle hiv shared his bed."

"He does this while trying to convince you to marry him? Is he a fool?" He didn't know if he was more baffled by Craig's behavior or Caitlin's calm acceptance of it.

" 'Tis just the way of it, Douglas. Craig does care for me and would never shame me on purpose as his wife, but 'tis no' unknown for a husband to hiv lovers."

"And you would accept this behavior from him?"

"I amna married to him."

"If you were?"

"I would no' like it, but could no' stop him from doing it."

Maybe he'd have to rethink this—Craig didn't sound like the person he thought him to be. He didn't want Caitlin married to someone who would be unfaithful to her for the rest of her life.

"Do all men here, now, behave like that?"

She thought about it before speaking. "No' all, but surely most."

"Your father?" She grimaced and shook her head. "Robert?"

"Oh, nay, no' Da or Robert, of course."

"Would you know?"

"There is no' much that remains a secret from the clan. We protect our own but no' a thing goes unnoticed or unknown by some one or another."

"So, if you married Craig and he took a lover, ye would know?"

"Aye," she answered softly. From her quick reply, he knew she'd thought about this before.

"And the clan would know of it?"

"Aye," she said with a sigh. "The clan would ken. But I amna marrying Craig so it doesna matter."

"He still wants to marry you, Cait, after I leave. We talked of it."

"He is persistent."

"He would be good to you, Cait. I do get that feeling from him. And your own mother said he will be a good leader when he takes his place as laird. Will you think on it after I've gone?"

The reality of his leaving brought back, she sighed and looked at him, sadness etched in her features. "Aye," she whispered. "I will consider his words."

"Cait, this is not easy for me, either. I really don't want to think about you marrying someone else or being with someone else. But, I need to know you'll be taken care of."

"The clan will—"

"No, I mean you, as a person. I want to know that someone will be there for you, to care for you, to love you."

She looked at him with tear-filled eyes and touched his cheek again. "I will think on his offer, Douglas. But yer no' gone yet. . . ." She draped her hands over his shoulders and, pulling him closer, pressed her breasts against his chest. Lifting her mouth from his, she gave him a quizzical look.

"As we've been talking, I've been trying to understand the clothes ye wear. What is this?" She rubbed her fingers over his shirt, outlining his tank top underneath.

"This?" he asked pointing to his shirt. She was changing the subject—it was obvious she didn't want to talk of Craig any longer.

"Nay," she shook her head and unbuttoned the top three or four buttons of his shirt to get inside. His skin tingled at her touch. She traced the outline of his tank shirt on his neckline and on his chest, tickling the hairs as she moved her finger lightly over it. "This."

He shivered at her touch. "This is called an undershirt."

"And do ye always wear it in yer own time?" She continued the maddeningly slow motion of her fingers, over his collarbone and into the hair on his chest just above the line of the shirt.

"I, ah, do wear one most of the time, Cait."

"Why?" she asked as she leaned over and licked the place where her fingers had just traced.

He forgot what the question was, he forgot that he was leaving, he forgot to breathe. All he could feel and think about was her warm, wet tongue gliding over his skin. She pulled more buttons opened and lowered her head to reach more of his skin.

"Caitlin, yer father . . ." was all he could force out.

"Is gone and will be gone for a while." She laughed as she said it and now her warm, moist breath added to the heat building within him.

"Caitlin, you are not well . . . ," he tried again.

"I feel just fine, Douglas. Here," she said, placing one of his hands on her breast, "does no' this feel fine to ye?"

Waves of heat now pulsed through him. He was trying to be good—even honorable—since he'd pretty much turned her over to Craig's care. But his body wasn't behaving at all. The tightness of the jeans became even tighter as his erection pulsed inside them.

He caressed her breast and was rewarded with a sweet moan. Her mouth stilled on his neck as he stroked her until he could feel the nipple through the thin blouse she wore. His own mouth watered with the need to taste her once more. She arched into his palm again. Sitting as they were, he could not get closer to her. He sat back in spite of her groan when he let go of her.

"Caitlin? Are you sure about this?"

"Oh, aye, Douglas. 'Tis verra certain I am. Please love me once again afore ye leave."

He stood and pulled her up with him. Her hands moved quickly to open the remaining buttons; when she reached his waist she simply pulled the shirt free of his pants. Then she stood back and gazed at him in his own clothes.

"I could like these, Douglas. Look how this fits yer body." Her hands moved over his chest and stomach and then over his thighs and legs. Not content with just the front of him, she moved around him, letting her hands lead the way on his body. By the time she stood in front of him again, he was rock-hard and breathing heavily.

"Although the plaid haes its own benefits, these do as weel."

He tried to shift himself within the jeans but it was impossible. Caitlin seemed to know he was uncomfortable and tugged at his belt, opening it and exposing the button and zipper below. She looked to him for guidance. Douglas unbuttoned his jeans and slid the zipper down, freeing his erection.

"More clothes?" she asked, pointing now at the briefs he wore under the jeans. " 'Tis normal to wear this many layers of clothes in yer time?" Her eyes sparkled with humor. "I think I prefer our plaid and shirt to all these clothes."

He stood with his jeans unzipped and shirt unbuttoned and laughed. "Why don't I take these the rest of the way off?"

Her face took on a hungry look that spurred him to hurry in ridding himself of the recently placed clothes. He leaned back against the wall and tugged off his boots; his pants, briefs, shirt and undershirt followed quickly. Douglas reached for the laces of her blouse but she stopped him.

"Nay, Douglas, just stay for a moment and let me look at ye."

Chapter 32

HE STOOD BEFORE her and let her do as she asked. He could almost feel her eyes touch him as her gaze caressed him the way he wanted her hands to do. She must have inherited a bit of her mother's mind-reading abilities for she lifted her hands and finally touched him. The blood thundered through his veins and waves of heat washed through his body as her hands skimmed over his already-heated flesh.

Soon or hours later—he couldn't tell by that time—she slid her hands around his penis and stroked it, her fingers moving lightly over the length of it. Her fingers encircled it and he felt it surge within her grasp. It was torture to stand and let her do as she wished, but it was a torture he would have endured and yearned for forever.

"Douglas?"

He heard her say his name; it was impossible for him to say anything in response.

"In the pool at the cave . . . ye tasted me down there."

He looked at her and tried to comprehend her words and her intent.

"I would like to taste ye as weel."

Oh, God. The thought, the image in his brain of her mouth moving over his erection, licking it as he had done to her, brought him to the edge. She didn't wait for his answer. She first leaned closer and rubbed her teeth on his nipples. Then she nuzzled her face in the hair on his chest, her hands all the while weaving their magic spell on him.

Douglas felt her tongue sliding down his stomach and onto his belly and then closer and closer to that raging part of him that craved its touch. He could no longer hold in the loud moan that echoed through the cottage as she wet her lips and slid them over the head of his very erect, very aroused penis.

She hesitated once or twice and then proceeded to excite him as he'd never been before—she obviously had little practice at this but she made up for that lack by her enthusiasm for it. After wringing countless moans from him, he could stand it no more. He reached down and lifted her mouth from him.

"Cait," he gasped taking in deep breaths to forestall his impending climax, "you must stop for a bit and give me a chance to breathe."

"Did ye like it?" Her eyes were filled with passion, gleaming like green flames as he looked into them. Her mouth was swollen now from their kisses and the attention she'd given him. As he gazed at it remembering the feel of it on him, her tongue slipped between her lips, moistening them again. His body reacted again and he pulsed against her hands, which still surrounded him.

"Did you?"

"Oh, aye, Douglas, I did." Her breathless whisper invited him to her now. He untied her skirt and dropped it. Then he pulled her blouse over her head. With her arms still raised above her head, her breasts thrust forward at him and he leaned over to her.

Kneeling before her, he kissed her neck and then moved down and rubbed his face against the soft swell of her breasts. She gasped as it was his turn to taste her. He licked her nipples and sucked them into his mouth, over and over until she was panting and clutching his shoulders for balance. Wrapping his arms around her thighs, he moved his mouth down her belly and nearer to her core. Her knees buckled as his lips touched the springy curls on her mons; he caught her and eased her down onto the pallet next to them.

Now their heated flesh touched from chest to thighs and his erection lay between them pulsing against her belly. He turned them on their side and wrapped himself around her and kissed her mouth slowly. Soon she writhed against him wanting more. He lifted her leg up onto his hip and rubbed against her more deeply.

"Join wi' me, Douglas. Please. Love me now."

Her words pushed him over the edge. He eased into her as they lay together. Watching her face as he moved inside of her, their gazes locked as they joined one last time. Rolling her onto her back, still within her, he rocked in deeper and deeper. She closed her eyes and moaned from within her throat as he filled her with himself.

Then he stopped and waited. She opened her eyes and looked at him, waiting too.

"I love you, Cait. I love you and I always will."

"And, I love ye, Douglas. For forever and a day."

He surged into her now unable and unwilling to wait any longer. Cradled there between her thighs, he arched, sliding in and out, deeper and deeper, until he heard and felt her climax begin. Ripples of movement inside her sheath tightened her muscles even more around his shaft. Caitlin moaned louder and louder. He took her mouth as he thrust once, twice more. In the midst of kissing her, he felt his seed escaping to deep within her heat.

Panting, he eased to his side again so as not to leave all of his weight on her slighter frame. He moved slowly, not wanting to break their connection yet. After a few minutes of regaining their breaths, Douglas felt himself drift off to sleep, physically and emotionally sated.

Roused by the sound of tears, Douglas drew her closer against him and rocked her in his arms. Rubbing her back and whispering of his love, he tried to soothe her. Soon he felt her relax and knew she slept. When he thought she was soundly asleep, he eased away from her gently and slowly. Pulling the woolen covers up around her shoulders, he made certain that she was completely covered and warm enough.

Silently he got dressed once more and prepared to leave. Checking out the window, he saw that the full moon had risen already. Moira would be waiting for him at the arch.

He couldn't leave her just yet. He went to look at her once more. Kneeling down next to her, he brushed her hair from her face and kissed her again, first on her lips then on her forehead. She turned to him in her sleep but he moved away.

Standing over her, he watched her sleep for several minutes, yearning for all that could not be. With one last touch on her cheek, he turned from her. He put on his leather jacket, retied his hair and grabbed the satchel that held his daggers. Without looking back, he left the cottage.

Chapter 33

IT WAS ALL she could do not to scream to him and beg him not to leave or to plead with him to take her with him. He'd no sooner closed the door of the cottage than the tears flowed. She sobbed loud and long, helpless to stop their flow once they began.

Soon, they ebbed away and left her hiccuping and out of breath. Sitting up, she gathered her clothes and put them on. She stood and entered the main room of the cottage. A low fire burned in the hearth and a pot sat off to one side of the grate over it. Wrapping the edge of her skirt around its handle, she lifted it up and sniffed. Betony tea—almost a full pot and freshly made from the smell of it.

Pouring some into a mug, she sat at the table and held it in her hands, waiting for it to cool. She spotted a flask of the tonic her mother made for her—the one that helped her throw off the stupor after a healing. Sitting there, holding the warm metal mug, she realized that Douglas's lovemaking had worked better than any tonic she'd ever used before. Although parts of her felt sore and well-loved, her body felt alive and something else . . . full of . . . what did he call it?

Energy! Full of energy. Like the sensations she felt whenever he touched her skin to skin. Tingling and pulsing still moved through her. She would remember and treasure this feeling forever. She feared that it would never come to her again.

She sipped the tea and looked around the room. It felt empty, without him there. Just as she felt. Would this feeling ever pass?

Sighing, she looked out the window and saw the full moon above, shining wide beams of light down on her world. Soon the solstice would begin and, if her mother was right, the powers controlling the arch would allow Douglas passage back to his own time.

She would like to be with him at the arch, but didn't have the strength to watch him leave her behind. She feared that she would give up all—her family, her gift, her clan—and try to follow him through the arch. 'Twas that fear that kept her prisoner in her cottage while the moon rose and the solstice approached.

After finishing her tea, she covered the flask her mother had left for her and began to return it to the cupboard when she noticed all her jars and boxes were on the worktable. Looking overhead, she saw that all the herbs were gone. Opening some of the jars and drawers, she found her supplies had been replenished. Then she spotted the satchel that Douglas used to carry his surgical tools. Opening it, she found all the tools cleaned and wrapped and marked with the codes they had picked out to tell them apart without handling them—to prevent the spread of *germs*, he'd explained to her.

"He did it while ye slept, lass."

She turned and faced her father as he closed the door behind himself.

"Douglas?" she asked, already knowing the answer.

"Aye, Douglas. He sat at yer side as ye slept."

"The whole time I was asleep?"

"Weel, no' the entire time. He did eat and sleep some himself," her father said, laughing.

"From the looks of my supplies, he did more than eat and sleep. All the herbs are ground and stored."

"He wanted to keep busy." Her father stood at the hearth and rubbed his hands together over it. "He waited for ye to wake, hoping ye would afore he left."

She watched him from her seat at the table. Her father was taking this all too calmly. For a man who would scare off those young men or boys who tried to steal a kiss from her, this was all too strange.

"Da? Ye seem to be taking this better than I would hiv expected of ye."

Her father laughed long and deep. Soon he walked over to her and stood before her. Opening his arms to her, she took refuge in the one embrace that had always been there for her.

"Douglas said the same thing to me just afore ye woke," he said, smoothing her hair down.

"And that is funny?" she mumbled against his chest.

"No. What is funny is yer reaction. Did ye want me to pound him into the dirt for loving ye?"

She pulled back to see if he was teasing her, but his face was serious now. "No. . . ."

"Did ye want to throw him out while ye slept?"

"No. . . ."

"Then what is it ye think I should hiv done?"

"I expected that ye would yell and threaten and carry on, like any other insulted faither would."

"Let me ask ye something, Cait," he began. A flash of pain sliced through her as he used the name Douglas used when they made love. Cait.

"If I haid kept ye from him and refused him permission to be here, would it hiv stopped ye from being wi' him?"

Feeling a bit guilty in knowing that nothing would have kept her from Douglas, she hesitated.

"Weel? My stubborn lassie, I ken ye. Nothing would hiv

stood between ye and him. No amount of warnings or
threats would hiv worked. So why should I make this more
difficult than it already is?"

"Because yer my faither and that's what faithers do?"

He laughed again but only for a moment. Hugging her
tightly and then loosening his hold, he went on. "Do ye
regret what haes happened between ye and him?"

"No, Da."

"Would ye hiv regrets if ye haid slept through his leaving?"

"Aye, I would hiv."

"I've lived wi' regrets, Cait. Regret burns a hole in yer
heart and soul that never heals. 'Tis better to hiv loved him
when ye could than to regret no' doing so for the rest of
yer life."

Tears threatened again and she blinked to clear them
away. When had her father become so wise? She rested her
head on his chest and tried to control herself. She had no
regrets about loving Douglas but would the heartache of
not having him ever go away?

"Dinna fret, Cait. Yer heart will heal in time."

She looked at him. He must be picking up some of her
mother's skills at reading thoughts. Mayhap that happened
when two people lived together as long as her parents had?

"Ye canna be rested after the healing. Ye should go back
to sleep." He released her from his arms.

"I dinna think I could sleep right now."

"Weel, I am ready for it. I will see ye in the morning?"

"Will ye no' wait for Mam?"

"I learned long ago no' to worry when she is aboot in
the night. She'll return when 'tis time for her to do so and
no' a moment before. Good night, lass." He kissed her on
the cheek and walked into his chamber.

Sitting back down at her worktable, she waited to hear
his snoring begin. It didn't. Her father didn't sleep so
soundly as he'd have her believe until her mother was home
with him.

She sipped the tea, realizing that Douglas had made it for her while she slept. They could have had a life as simple and as content as her parents if he could have stayed with her. That thought struck her from out of nowhere.

Douglas had been there, tending to her supplies, preparing their tools for the next time they'd be needed, watching over her. She would have been happy to live that kind of life with him. But would he? He was from the future, when people did not ride horses, they *drove cars*. When doctors used *gadgets* and *tek-knoll-o-gee* to treat people in need. And when men stayed with women as they labored to give birth to their bairns.

Just thinking about Douglas being at her side as she birthed their babe sent shivers through her. How many things would be done differently if he was here to show the way of it? Could he be happy living in a time that was so primitive to the one he lived in?

Well, sitting around moping was not going to change her future. Douglas was on his way back to his time and, sooner or later, she would have to move on with her own life. But for tonight she would take her time to mourn all the things that would not be.

How would he live with this huge weight on his heart and soul? Douglas paused outside the cottage and listened to the muted sobs coming from inside. He'd thought she was awake but didn't want to see that look of sadness and longing in her eyes. He knew it was in his own eyes, but seeing it in hers would tear him apart.

He kicked several stones on the ground in front of him and took a deep breath. At least he'd been able to see and talk with her before he left for home. Douglas wasn't sure if making love again had been the right thing to do. He chuckled to himself—as if he could have refused her? And, did he want to?

The sobs subsided a bit, so he turned to leave. Pulling his jacket tighter around him and zippering it up, he lifted

the collar around his neck to block some of the frigid air.
The weather was taking a turn for the worse, as Caitlin told
him it did in the dark of winter, as she called it. Soon snow
would fall and pile in deep drifts throughout the village. If
it was deemed dangerous enough, the young and old of the
clan would gather in the castle for safety and companion-
ship.

The clan took care of its own.

Well, if he was going, he'd better leave. Douglas forced
one foot in front of the other again and again until Caitlin's
cottage was behind him. Walking had never been a con-
scious act before, but then he'd never left someone like her
before.

The wind howled through the trees and around him as
he made his way through the village. He passed the smithy
and heard Pol's deep voice from inside. He recognized the
other voice as Ramsey's and smiled. Further down the path
he paused in front of Aindreas and Beitris's small cottage.
Light flickered under the door and the whimpering of a
small baby drifted to him on the wind. Soon it was joined
by a soft, lilting voice that sang of sleeping and quiet.
Douglas smiled, so glad that he could be part of something
that ended in happiness and rejoicing.

Turning and taking a path away from the main gate,
Douglas decided to think about all the things he missed
from his own time. Surely it would help him look forward
to returning home.

Hot showers. Standing in the stall until the water ran
cold. Feeling the invigorating steam around him and feeling
so clean and refreshed.

Coffee. Brewing a pot so dark and rich that the smell
alone was satisfying. Savoring the strong flavor on his
tongue before swallowing it.

His family. His parents, his brother and sister. Separated
at times by continents or oceans, they were his link and
security. They kept his feet on the ground and the glitter

out of his eyes when his career made everything else disappear.

Medicine. Saving lives and making a difference in the quality of life of his patients. Money enough to do as he pleased in his free time. Prestige. . . .

No, that wasn't right. Thinking it over, he realized that the money and prestige were what made him lose touch with himself and why he'd originally entered medicine.

Douglas turned off the path and headed for the abandoned section of the keep wall. Even with the full moon, it was slow going through the thick trees and bushes. A few more minutes of creeping through the underbrush and he entered the clearing he'd found those weeks before.

The scene was surreal—bright beams of moonlight shone over the arch's curve, throwing shadows and light onto the ground around it. The wind ceased and an eerie quiet descended on him as he stared at the portal that would take him home. He tried to get his bearings; the archway in his time would be in an open field and not near the castle at all.

He stopped a short distance away from it and stared at it. It looked simply like a stone arch, not a gateway through time. If you didn't know any better, you'd assume that's all it was, an arch built of boulders, nothing more.

"The stonecutter should hiv kept a better watch on his son. The boy kenned no better and brought the sacred stones here. They'd been placed in the archway afore I could do anything aboot it." Moira's voice came to him from the darkness. Then he saw her, walking up to the arch from the one side.

"Where did they come from?" He remembered only bit and pieces of the old legends.

"There's a stone circle out in the forest. 'Twas made long, long ago by the Druids who worshipped here." She rested her hand on the stones. "Their power haesna been diminished by their place in this archway. Do ye feel it?"

He shook his head. He didn't feel anything.

"Come closer; touch them," she directed.

Douglas held back. A feeling of nervousness pervaded him.

"So much like yer maither, ye are! She kept her distance after her trip here, too."

"My mom?"

"She and yer da tried to return through the arch afore their task was complete. The power wi'in it made her ill. She kept her distance after that."

"You mean it doesn't always work?"

" 'Tis controlled by the Fates. Ye canna pass through until and unless they decide yer ready."

Just then a burst of light filled the sky above and Douglas looked up. A shooting star careened through the night and passed in front of the full moon. He shook from the inside out as he experienced that same terror as the night he'd traveled back. He tried to breathe; he struggled against the paralysis that immobilized him. Sweat trickled down his face and neck in spite of the freezing temperatures.

And then it was gone and he took in big gulps of air. Bending over, he held his head and waited for the panic to pass. A few minutes later, he stood up. Moira stood by the arch, her hand gliding lightly over the stones. Her eyes seemed to glow as she looked at him, or through him.

"The time is right and yer destiny is here, Douglas. Are ye ready?"

He stood where he was and looked at the arch. A buzzing noise grew around him and heat emanated from the arch itself. He'd waited for this time for months—surviving in this primitive time and place until the gateway through time was working again. Douglas forced his feet to take the steps toward the archway.

Standing before it, he hesitated. Finally he was going home. Douglas waited for the joy and relief to begin. He would see his family again, he could return to his life and his job. He would go back to everything that was familiar and live out his life as he'd intended. His success in medicine and his plans for his practice and his new house could proceed—he was going home.

"Weel?" Moira called to him. "Why do ye hesitate? The solstice has begun; the full moon has reached its pinnacle. The power is here. Now is the time to cross through."

The wind started blowing again, buffeting his back with its force as though it was trying to move him through the archway. He fought to stay in his place and not move toward the stone structure. He looked at Moira and suddenly realized why he hesitated.

"I don't want to go back."

The buzzing sound grew louder and blocked the words Moira spoke next. She stepped closer and called to him again.

"Now, Douglas. Ye maun go now."

He turned away from the arch and yelled again. "I don't want to go back."

Moira came and placed her hand on his arm. His skin tingled under her hand—the pulsations traveled right through the layers of clothes.

"I ken ye dinna want to leave Caitlin, but it is time."

He looked at her face—she did glow with some other paranormal energy that he could not explain. The power that controlled the arch now controlled her. She was the guardian.

He knew it was time to go and he pivoted around again to walk through the archway. Then he stopped. It was more than not wanting to go home. He couldn't go.

In spite of being born in the twentieth century, he had been conceived here in this time and place. His soul started here and this would be the only home for him. The love his parents had found in this time had created him. He would not be at home unless he was here, in this place, at this time.

Going back was not the answer. Every fiber of his being screamed at him not to step through the arch. He had to stay—that was his destiny. He knew it with such clarity that he laughed out loud.

"I am not going back, Moira. This is where and when I belong."

All the hesitations and doubts disappeared as he finally accepted what part of him had known all along. He was here because this is where he belonged. His life in the future was just preparation for this experience, for this existence. All that came before didn't matter—he was here and would stay here for the rest of his life.

"Yer parents and family await ye on the other side of the arch, Douglas. Go now." Moira pointed at the still-buzzing structure.

Pol's words came back to him. *Only love was stronger than fate.* That was the truth he sought and used now. His love for Caitlin would help him defy fate's plan to return him to the future.

"No!" he shouted as loud as he could into the wind and the roar of the arch. "I love her and I'm staying here with her."

Chapter 34

As if a switch had been thrown, the wind with its howling and the roaring buzz of the arch stopped. Douglas looked around and found only himself and Moira standing next to the archway.

"What happened?"

"Ye hiv defied the Fates. Love is the only power strong enough to defy them. By calling on your love for Caitlin, ye were able to resist their call back."

"I didn't think I had a choice about it." He was confused, but he felt strongly that he had done the right thing, made the right decision.

"We always hiv a choice, lad. Sometimes we dinna ken or dinna understand our choices, but they're always there for us."

"And now?" He thought he understood—he would stay here and live out his life; the one that began here with his parents.

"Ye are part of this time now, Douglas. Ye hiv rejected the other time and place, so it no longer exists for ye."

"My parents? Will they remember me? Remember that I existed?"

"Oh, aye. Ye will always live in their hearts."

He stepped away from the archway. One thing still didn't make sense to him. He had come back through the arch and Moira had said that if one came back, one would go forward. Douglas looked at her with a new awakened knowledge.

"If I stay here, someone has to go forward. I was right, wasn't I? You are *Mairi*?"

"I amna yet, but I will be called that in your time."

"Why? When?" Douglas couldn't imagine Moira leaving her family, her village, her clan and going forward to the future.

"When my time here is done, I will pass through the arch to your village of Dunnedin to finish my duty as guardian of the archway."

"What do you mean?" he asked. Rubbing his eyes, he noticed dawn was breaking. "When will your time be done?"

"I dinna ken the whole of it, only what I've seen in the wisdom, Douglas. There will come a time when ye and Caitlin care for the clan and my healing skills are no' needed."

"And Pol?"

"He will hiv passed on." She paused and a sad smile crossed her face. "We canna live forever."

"And your wisdom? Who will advise the MacKendimens of Dunnedin if you leave?"

"My daughter's daughter will stand in my place with the clan. Her visions will be the strongest of any of the women in my line—her wisdom will lead the clan through the dangerous times to come."

"Your daughter's daughter? That would be Caitlin's . . ." He knew but couldn't accept what he was hearing.

"Your blue-eyed, black-haired daughter. The one to be born nine months from this day. She will come forth on the full-mooned night of the autumnal equinox and be blessed by the Fates and by God with many gifts."

"Many gifts?"

"She will be granted my gift of sight and also my other gift." Her enigmatic smile teased him. He thought back to their many encounters, in this time and in the one before when he was growing up and knew her as Mairi.

"I knew it! You really can read minds!"

"I can hear and see some thoughts."

"It doesn't seem possible, any of this. I still feel like I'll wake from a dream and find myself back home in Chicago."

"That willna happen. Ye belong to us now. My Caitlin will be verra pleased to know that ye will faither her child, her children."

"Did you know that I'd stay?"

"Nay, Douglas. I only see what is granted to me. I saw us here on this night. I saw you standing as you did, under the arch with the full moon behind ye. I couldna see the rest of it."

"But, if I'd gone back, what would have happened to you? Could you still go forward?"

"We'll never ken, will we? Now, there's no reason to share what I hiv shared wi' ye. Many days and years are left to pass afore I will be called forward. I dinna want Pol and Caitlin to ken of this."

"I understand, Moira."

"Good. Weel, 'tis been an exhausting few days and I need some rest. Will ye come back wi' me to speak to Caitlin?"

"I don't think she'll be at the cottage. I think I know where she'll be as soon as the sun rises." He thought of Moira's words about what Caitlin did after a healing.

"After ye speak to Caitlin, there are others who need to be told of yer plans to stay wi' us."

Douglas groaned as he thought of Craig and his expectation of marrying Caitlin. He could see another battle in his future and he didn't need Moira's gift to see it. After he saw Caitlin, he didn't care what happened. Maybe she

would even heal him of any injuries Craig inflicted on him
in their upcoming fight.

Moira waved him off and he ran through the woods,
toward the lake and the shorter way to the cave. What
would her reaction be? Would she be glad he stayed? Or
would her temper get the best of her?

It didn't matter. He was here and he was staying and
now they would have a chance to live out all their dreams.
He would be the one to care for and love her. He would
watch over her after healings took their toll on her. He
would create children with her. They would be together—
he'd defied the Fates to stay with her.

Moira stayed behind as Douglas ran off through the woods.
She was tempted to use the sight but her other gift and her
mother's intuition served her just as well in times like this.
She'd heard the moans and breathless sighs in his thoughts
and she'd seen her daughter with him in the pools of the
cave. Only a fool would not know what was to happen
between them when he met Caitlin at that cave once more.
She was no fool.

Peering into the light of the rising sun, weak as it was
on this midwinter's day, she suddenly felt as tired as she'd
told Douglas she was. Wrapping her cloak more tightly
around her shoulders, she walked from the arch and toward
her home. Trudging over the cold-hardened mud, she kept
her glance on the roughened ground, not wanting to slip.

"Mam?"

"Caitlin, lass, I didna hear ye coming." She looked at her
daughter's tear-stained face and wanted to smile. She held
back, believing that Douglas's news should be his own.

"Is he . . . is it . . . ?" The poor lass couldn't even say the
words. Looking at her red, swollen eyes and blotchy skin,
Moira knew her daughter had not slept at all this night past.

" 'Tis done, Caitlin. He has accepted his destiny."

Her daughter didn't cry; she doubted if there were any
tears left for her to shed. Instead, she pulled her cloak

around her more snugly and turned to go back home.

"Hiv ye bathed since the healing?"

"Nay, Mam. I didna feel up to it last night after Douglas left."

Moira walked to her daughter's side and placed her arm around Caitlin's shoulders. "Weel, then, why no' go there now? A storm is coming, a bad one from the looks of it and ye may no' be able to get there for some time."

"Mayhap I will." They took a few steps together and Caitlin stopped. "I didna bring fresh clothes with me. I will come back to the cottage wi' ye and then go to the cave."

Fighting not to let the smile on her face show, Moira shook her head. "Dinna fret aboot that—I can send yer faither wi' those when he goes to the smithy."

"Would ye? That would be wonderful. The hot springs will feel so good this morn."

"He will be glad to. 'Tis been so difficult for ye and I can tell by looking at ye that ye hiv gotten little sleep. I will make a fresh pot of tea and hiv some food ready for ye, too, on yer return."

"Oh, Mam. Thank ye. I willna be long, I promise."

Moira kissed her daughter on the cheek and watched her trot off toward the lake and the hot springs. She held it in until Caitlin was out of sight. Then she erupted in laughter that echoed through the forest. She laughed until tears flowed and then she took several deep breaths to calm herself.

Love had triumphed once more in the MacKendimen clan. She offered up a quick prayer of thanks and went to tell her husband of the impending marriage. Well, she would tell him of Caitlin and Douglas at the cave together. A wedding would follow very soon after her husband found them there together and especially as he would find them. Mayhap after he chased them from the cave, she would join him there.

With a smile on her face, Moira, seer of the Clan MacKendimen and guardian of the archway through time, made her way home.

Chapter 35

SHE PICKED HER way carefully across the wet floor
of the first room in the cave. Steam billowed out of the next
room, overwhelming her and inviting her in. She loosened
her outer cloak to remove it as she walked through and into
the next room where the deeper pool was. Taking the cloak
off and lifting it so that it didn't get wet, Caitlin placed it
high up on one of the rock formations alongside of the pool.

The steam was so thick it was difficult to see the surface
of the heated water. She untied her hair and shook it loose.
A bath would feel wonderful even if it couldn't change a
thing. She walked over to one side of the pool and tugged
at the laces of her blouse.

Someone cleared their throat and she froze. It had come
from inside the pool itself. Someone had known about the
cave? Only her parents and she used the springs—they covered the entrance to the cave to keep its existence a secret.
She waved her hand in front of her face, trying to get a
glimpse of who had invaded her private place.

She saw him dip under the water and rise from it as in
her dream. Using his hands, he sluiced some of the water
from his hair and body before standing up in the water.

Nay, it could not be! She must be dreaming or hoping but he could not be here.

"I will turn into a prune if I stay in here much longer. But I wanted to wait for you."

"A prune?" was all she could say. It sounded real to her. His voice was the same, his body was the same one she had loved last night.

"A wrinkled but sweet piece of fruit."

She felt the tears begin to flow down her cheeks and onto her neck. He stood in the water and walked toward her with his hands extended. Without thinking she walked off the edge and into the pool, landing on her feet in front of him.

She wrapped a hand around that part of him that stood straight up in the water. "It doesna feel wrinkled to me."

"Ye wicked lass!" he whispered in that deep seductive voice and without warning, he pulled her close and kissed her. As she melted in his embrace, he kicked his feet from under him and took them both under the water.

A moment later he stood them back up, never releasing her lips from his. Still kissing wildly, he began peeling her soaking clothes from her until she was as naked as he. He lifted her up and she wrapped her legs around his waist, bringing him into contact with the place that already throbbed in anticipation of joining with him. Scant seconds later he eased himself inside of her to the sound of their passion-filled kisses.

She'd thought this would never happen again. She thought he was gone from her life forever, except in her dreams. And yet, he was here. She lifted her mouth from his and looked at him. Douglas walked them over to the side of the pool where she leaned back on the edge and felt him move within her.

"I thought ye were gone."

"I'm staying here, Caitlin. I'm not going back."

"But how? I didna think there was a choice in this."

He kissed her again before answering. "Your mother told me there's always a choice."

"She kens ye are here? That ye hiv stayed?" Her mother had never said a word, but she knew all along that he was here, in their time and in the cave.

"Yes. She told me you come here after healings to bathe."

"She is a devious woman, Douglas. Ye will learn that aboot her."

Douglas laughed and then looked at her with a serious expression. "I realized as I was about to step through that I couldn't leave you, Cait. I knew that my life would be nothing without you in it. I couldn't go back."

She began to cry at his words. He'd stayed for her.

"Dinna greet, my lass. I have other things in mind for us." He moved within her, slowly drawing out, then sliding in once more. She couldn't cry when he did that.

Soon his motions had her gasping and her moans echoed through the steamy rooms of the cave. They reached their peak together and loudly, with the water sloshing and steam swirling around them. He eased her back in the water and they separated. He walked to the side of the pool and reached for the small bowl of soap she always left there.

The next few minutes were wonderful as he washed her from head to toes and everywhere in between. It almost led to another joining but she knew about the interruption to come. She tried to warn him but he wouldn't listen. Her father's yell convinced him she was not joking.

"Caitlin!" her father bellowed. That was more like the father she knew. "Is he wi' ye in there?"

Douglas pulled her behind him and faced the doorway of the cave. She tried to move around him but he wouldn't let her.

"Aye, Da. Douglas is here."

"Now that yer staying I expect an offer to be made. Do ye hear?" She grimaced at the loudness of his voice. How could anyone in miles not hear him?

"I hear you, Pol." Douglas looked a bit peaked now. She slipped her arms under his and wrapped hers around his waist, sliding her body against his from behind.

"In the great hall, before the clan, Douglas. My daughter willna be shamed by ye or anyone else! Do ye hear?" His yelling bounced off the walls and echoed around them.

"I hear you. I'll be there." He turned his head and whispered to her, "Is that what ye want?"

"Ye daft mon, of course!" She bit him lightly on his back.

"Craig will wed you. You don't have to settle for me."

She pushed on the back of his knee, sending him tumbling into the water. How could men be so stupid at times? He sloshed around, trying to regain his footing and came up sputtering.

"Are ye weel, Caitlin?" Her father's voice was concerned, he probably heard the gasping and choking going on and wondered at it.

"Aye, Da. We will see you at the cottage in a wee bit."

"Yer clothes and his are here in this basket. Yer mam sent along some linens, too." Her father pushed the basket in front of the opening.

"Thank ye for bringing them." She waited for him to say more but he apparently was done with talking. She waited a minute or two and then turned to Douglas.

"Settle for ye? Are ye daft? I don't want Craig, I want you."

"Then you'll marry me?"

"Oh, aye, Douglas. I'll wed ye."

He strode through the water to her, pulled her close and kissed her until she couldn't breathe. She felt him hard against her belly again and laughed.

"Shall we try once more, Cait? Your mother tells me the baby girl with MacKendimen blue eyes and your black hair will be born in nine months' time. We would not want her vision to be wrong, would we?"

Caitlin smiled at him. He would be the father of her daughter, and all the rest of her children as well. The Fates had smiled on her at last. All of her dreams had come true.

Epilogue

"Y E HIV BOTH prepared him weel."

She put her arm around the crying woman's shoulder and drew her close, offering the support only a woman who'd lost a child of her own could offer. She looked at Alex—warrior, rightful heir to the clan, now desolate father. She took his hand and grasped it tightly.

"Did we, Mairi? Will he survive there? Then?"

The sobs were subsiding; Mairi could feel Maggie regaining the control and the inner power she'd been known for.

"We've all done our part and now he will do his. The Clan MacKendimen will be better for his presence."

"*Will be?* Don't you mean *was*?" Maggie stepped away but skirted around the stone structure as Mairi had always seen her do. Once bitten, twice shy.

"*Will be*, *was*—'tis all the same, Maggie. Time moves around and around us, ye must understand that by now."

"No," Maggie sighed, "I guess I really don't understand." Maggie looked to Alex whose face was etched with grief. "But will he? Did he live a long life?"

"Come, both of ye, give me yer hands." Mairi took hold

of them and moved to stand directly in front of the archway. "Now, look into the portal of the sacred stones."

Mairi closed her eyes and opened herself to the wisdom
for the last time. She felt it coming, the power coursing
one last time through her ancient body. She opened her
heart and soul even more and begged that the wisdom be
shared. Maggie gasped beside her and Mairi thanked the
Fates for allowing this kindness to grieving parents.

A young couple entangled in passion . . . a babe and another and yet again . . . a husband comforting his wife in
loss . . . two healers working side by side for their people . . .
an old couple surrounded by love and many children . . . a
long, prosperous, fulfilling life.

" 'Tis as 'twas meant to be. For ye and for yer son. Can
ye be at peace now?" Mairi slowly released their hands and
waited for her answer.

"I can't just let go, Mairi. It will take some time to accept
this," Maggie said. Alex, still unable to speak, just nodded
his head in agreement.

Mairi turned and led them away from the arch and toward her cottage. The tea was on to boil and she'd made
fresh oatcakes that morning. Now *was* the time to explain
her true role in the Clan MacKendimen and to let Douglas's
parents know what would come for him in the past. And
there was a letter to share with them, a letter written long,
long ago.

"Time? Why, Maggie, ye should know 'tis always a matter of time."

Author Bio

Wife to one, mother of three (all boys), dental hygienist to hundreds, and reader of thousands of romance novels, Terri Brisbin is now the author of two time travel romances. (Another Time Passages release is scheduled for Fall 2000.) Born and raised in southern New Jersey, Terri and her family live in a small town not far from Philadelphia, PA. When not writing or working as an RDH, she spends her time reading, playing on her computer, and driving her kids all over South Jersey.

If you would like to contact her, please send a SASE for a reply, bookmarks, or postcards to: Terri Brisbin, P.O. Box 41, Berlin, NJ 08009-0041.

You can visit her website at http://romance-central.com/TerriBrisbin or e-mail her at Tbrisbin@aol.com. She loves to hear from readers!

TIME PASSAGES